Rory le
different bo
was searching ... ... she found today's letter in a red-
bound book written about the ancient world. Rory wrote
with broad strokes and often smeared the ink because he
was left-handed, one more thing his father disapproved
of.

Joneta, Mo chridhe,

*Ye come to me every morning as soon as I open my
eyes. Ye fill my thoughts all day until I close my eyes, and
then my dreams are of ye. Even when ye are not with me,
I ken we are working together toward a better life. Not a
minute goes by that I dinna miss ye, kenning that when
we are together again, it will be all the sweeter.*

Rory

Joneta slipped her letters to Rory in and among
Lorna's pans, jars, and bowls on the shelves. Her
handwriting was small and the words tightly packed
together, often two letters on one page.

Rory, My Love,

*I never kenned what love meant until I met you. But
its power is greater than anything I could ever imagine.
I am waiting for the day when we can walk hand-in-
hand, with naught to keep us apart, and build our lives
as one. I love you in ways that words canna say. Only my
heart kens the truth.*

Yer love, Joneta.

Joneta read Rory's letters over and over until she
memorized them. At home in her bed, she repeated the
words softly, and they lulled her to sleep.

Susan Leigh Furlong (signature)

Forgiven
Never Forgotten

by

Susan Leigh Furlong

Forgiven Never Forgotten

Cover Art by *Lisa Dawn MacDonald*

The Wild Rose Press, Inc.
PO Box 708
Adams Basin, NY 14410-0708
Visit us at www.thewildrosepress.com

Publishing History
First Edition, 2023
Trade Paperback ISBN 978-1-5092-5295-4
Digital ISBN 978-1-5092-5296-1

Published in the United States of America

Dedication

This story is dedicated to
anyone who has survived violence in their life
or in the lives of people they love.
Survivors may forgive, but they can never forget.

Scottish Speech Patterns

coos - the hairy cows so common in the Highlands
bassa - bastard
bawbag - a Scottish insult
didna - didn't
dinna - don't
fash - worry
ken - know
kenned - knew
Mo chridhe - my heart
ne'er - never
no' - not
tattie - potato
verra - very
wasna - wasn't
willna - will not
ye - you
ye're - you are

Chapter One

Glencoe, Scotland—February 13, 1692

She expected betrayal from her enemies, but never from the man she had trusted to love her. At least not until tonight.

Deafening explosions and choking black smoke jolted her awake. Her lungs burned with each breath. Flames sizzled all around her, hissing like evil, consuming everything in their path. She called to her mother and father, but only a raspy gasp came out of her throat. Raging clumps of burning straw and wood fell from the collapsing thatched roof as she felt her way blindly through the smoke. She stumbled to her parents' bed and tripped over the body of her father, landing on her knees. As she moved her trembling hands across his lifeless chest, blood soon covered her fingers.

Strong hands grasped her shoulders. "Joneta, we have to get out of here! They shot him in the back and slit his throat! There's nothing we can do for him!"

"We canna leave him!" she cried to her oldest brother, John, hoping he could hear her over the roaring flames.

"We have to. He's dead!"

A loud crack sounded as the clay mortar between the two layers of stone wall of the house crumbled from the heat. She screamed.

"The soldiers betrayed us," John shouted as he swung her into his arms. "The whole of Glencoe is burning." He carried her toward the back of the small house, away from the worst of the fire.

Joneta struggled against her brother. "Where is Mum?"

"Alex has her. Hold tight to me."

"What about the animals?"

"We already let them out," he said in gasping breaths. "Our horses, cows, goats, and chickens are now scattered across the valley."

Turning her face to catch one last glimpse of her father, she saw someone in the doorway, a pistol in his hand and his dirk dripping with dark red blood.

"'Tis Rory," she whispered in John's ear. "He's here."

"He's one of the soldiers who killed our father," said John with a growl as he stepped over a burning timber and into the snow-covered yard to run toward the mountains surrounding the village and land of Glencoe. Tonight the survivors prayed to find shelter in the rocky hills. They had little choice.

"Rory betrayed us, brought King William's soldiers here," John said in a voice gravelly from the smoke. "Alex, Alex, over here!" he called to their brother, the second son of the Laird MacIain MacDonald of Glencoe. Alex carried the limp form of their mother while also herding three other women and four children ahead of him.

"We have to get to the caves," Alex shouted. "Some of the soldiers are following us. Rory Campbell is with them."

"Nay, it canna be," cried Joneta. "No' my Rory."

"What makes him *yer* Rory? Then, aye, *yer* Rory 'tis!" called Alex. "He convinced Da we'd be safe if we welcomed the king's soldiers to stay on our land, and now they're burning and killing us."

Alex leaned over and coughed out a thick glob of phlegm. It splattered in the snow, leaving a black stain. "Ye can ne'er trust a Campbell. They're our enemy and have been for all time. We always told ye to stay away from Campbells, and now ye ken why!"

Joneta loosened her grip on her brother's neck. She could barely breathe from the fear, panic, and regret. "I need to get down. I can walk now, John. Let me go. I can carry one of the children so we can move faster." John did as she asked, and she swept two-year-old Bryan into her arms. He struggled at first, but soon her soothing words calmed him, and he rested his head against her shoulder.

"Da didna come with us," said Bryan in his childish voice between coughs from the smoke of the burning houses blowing toward them. "Mum said he couldna come. I want him."

"Yer da wants us to go to the cave." Her heart tugged, knowing the lad's father would never be coming, having been burned or shot by the marauding enemy. Bryan snuggled closer against her despite her faltering steps over the snow and rocky terrain. She looked back, only to see acidic black smoke and orange flames reducing her beloved village to ashes.

Her words to Bryan may have calmed him, but Joneta would never be calm again, not until she knew the truth. The man she loved with everything she was, the man who had pledged his life to her with his whole heart and made secret promises that changed her life, could not possibly be the man who helped the king's soldiers murder her kin and neighbors as they slept. He could not!

But she had seen him inside the house. Rory's handsome face and his shirt smeared with black soot, his dirk dripping with blood, and his pistol dangling at his side, still smoking.

Chapter Two

The Highland Fair—Two years earlier, August 7, 1690

The annual Highland fair boasted over thirty booths selling everything from food to jewelry to weapons. It held the best in athletic contests, music, and entertainment, and Rory Campbell delighted in every bit of it. All year he waited and hungered for the sights, sounds, and smells of a field crowded with people and animals, and for the two weeks of the fair, he barely slept, not wanting to miss a minute.

And there she was, selling griddle scones in a booth at the very end of the row, the most beautiful lass he had ever seen. He'd thought a lot of lasses he'd met were beautiful, and sometimes he even told them so, but this one truly was the most beautiful, with long auburn hair braided across her head and down her back, and those eyes! He had to get closer to see those light brown eyes. She and the scones were just what he'd been looking for.

He slapped his hand lightly on her table. "Can ye hear me, lass? Can I have a griddle scone?"

Turning away from stirring the batter in the mixing bowl, she answered, "Would ye like it with currants or mayhap a tattie scone? Each is a penny."

Aye, those eyes, he thought, were well worth the walk through the muddy track between the rows of booths.

"They're only a halfpenny at the stall over there." He pointed across the path to another food booth.

"Ye're welcome to go over there if ye wish, but ye will most likely spit out that halfpenny scone after the first bite. My penny ones, on the other hand, are a treat for yer mouth. I promise ye that."

"Since ye promise, I'll take two of each, if ye dinna mind."

"I dinna mind." She took two puffy triangles of each kind of scone out of the warming pan on top of the iron stove and slid them onto a square of coarse cloth. Closing the edges of the cloth, she said, "Here ye are. 'Tis four pence. If ye'd like a cup of ale to go with them, that'll be two pence more. Have ye got yer own mug?"

"I usually like to carry the ale in me hands, but today, well, I think I'll use this instead," he said, patting the leather mug dangling from his belt. She barely acknowledged the jest.

Today he paid the price with a raging headache for having filled his mug with ale repeatedly last night, but he did enjoy watching this lass pour ale into his mug again. When the brown liquid spilled over the top and splattered on the table, he gave her his best smile, and this time she reacted exactly the way he wanted her to. She ducked her head in embarrassment, but raised her eyes briefly to meet his before sucking in her breath as she wiped up the ale with her apron. At the same time, he sucked in his own breath. He couldn't explain why she amazed him so, and he didn't want to know. He only needed to enjoy.

Rory opened the cloth and pushed one currant griddle scone into his mouth, washing it down with a swig of ale. Swallowing it after only three chews, he said, "Did ye make this tasty treat?"

"Up afore dawn to peel the potatoes for the tatties and mix the dough for both of them."

"I can hear the cow and chickens ye brought for milk and eggs out back, so I ken 'tis fresh. Others make the batches ahead of time, only heating them through once they get set up here at the fair."

"No' us. 'Tis why my griddle scones are the best ye'll get. Been busy today. The crowd is better than last year."

"'Twas a terrible winter and then a dry summer, so more people want to get away from the hard work and have some fun. I ken I do."

"I do wish I could see more of the games and wander through the other stalls, but we need to make money so we'll have some cash for the year. So if ye will pay me what ye owe, we'll be richer still."

After wiping the crumbs off his lips with the back of his hand, he took a stack of pennies out of his pouch and laid them on the table. "I'll gladly pay. No' only are yer griddle scones the verra best, ye're the most beautiful scone seller I have ever seen." His well-trimmed black beard curled up around another wide grin making crinkles around his ebony eyes.

A blush bloomed across the fair complexion of the auburn-haired lass, but she brazenly said, "Ye are a sassy one. Didna yer mum teach ye manners?"

"Me mum died when I was six years old, and Da doesna have it in him to teach manners to any but the horses we breed and train."

Her shoulders slumped. "I'm sorry. I didna ken. Forgive me."

The wind blew his thick coal black hair across his face, and he pushed it out of his eyes with his hand. "I'll forgive ye if ye have yer da look at the horses we brought for sale. We've got the finest stock around." Gathering up the rest of his scones and his mug of ale, he strode away before twisting his head back to wink at her and say, "Dinna worry, even if they dinna buy from our stock, I'll always forgive anyone who makes griddle scones as good as these. What is yer name?"

"Joneta MacDonald," she called after him. "Yers?"

"Rory." He walked beyond the stalls toward the meadow used for the contests, races, and the performances held every day. Looking back again, he saw Joneta following him with her eyes until he melded into the crowd. She smiled the whole time, and it made him glad he'd stop to buy a griddle scone.

He didn't tell her he was a Campbell, centuries old foe of her clan, the MacDonalds. The two clans, whose borders in the western Scottish Highlands touched, had been bitter enemies from the beginning of time. The MacDonalds lived in the glen of Glencoe, west of Campbell territory.

The glen, sometimes a blessing and sometimes a curse, was both a fortress and a trap. The vale, running east to west for about eight miles, was often referred to as "a deep scar left by the agony of Creation." Hard quartz and granite mountains surrounded it, and both narrow ends of the valley were often blocked by winter snows and summer storms. Even though Glencoe wasn't desirable land for farming, it was for raising cattle and sheep. The mountains and the river shielded their territory from attack, but, as Rory had been told for as long as he could remember, the Clan MacDonald always managed to sneak out and steal Campbell cattle, and whatever else they could get their hands on, telling notorious lies that they were only taking back what the Campbells had stolen first. Ha! The Campbells had enough of their own. They didn't need to steal!

Over the years, the Campbell clan claimed property and land in the Highlands and gained great influence, while the MacDonalds languished. This led to even greater jealousy and spite, but it had been a year since there'd been any real fighting between them.

He didn't hold much with feuding, but if she'd known he was a Campbell, she wouldn't have smiled so incredibly at him, and he wouldn't have felt the warmth of that smile for the rest of the day.

Chapter Three

The Highland Fair—August 1690

When she first saw him coming across the path toward her stall, the way he strode toward her—proudly, purposefully, as if he owned the world—made her heart nearly stop. A love for life sparkled around him, especially when he smiled. She fell into that smile. She couldn't help herself. He was like a splash of color in her gray world. He drew her in, and she went willingly.

After he left the booth, Joneta kept her eyes on Rory as he walked away until her older brother, John, came from behind the stall, rolling another keg of ale. "What are ye looking so happy about?"

She tried to force the smile off her face, but she couldn't do it. "Nothing special, just another customer."

"Did he tell ye a joke?"

"Nay, just a man, and he bought four scones and some ale. Biggest purchase of the morning. Six pennies." She gathered up his pennies. "Oh, look, he left nine. I'll have to find him and give him back the extra."

Her face fell when John said, "Ye'll do no such thing. I willna have ye wandering around the fair by yerself. Da would have me hide. 'Tis too dangerous for a lass. The crowd is full of pickpockets and outlaws, but if I find him, I'll give him the money, and if I canna, we count the extra as a gift."

John, a stocky, broad-shouldered man with short-cropped ginger-colored hair and a darker red beard, rolled the barrel of ale next to the nearly empty one. "I think I've seen that one afore, but he didna have a beard then. If I'm right, he and his father travel around the Highlands selling and trading horses and mules, and if that's him, he's a Campbell. They do fair and right horse business with us because our da willna let anyone cheat him, but business is business, and 'tis all a Campbell is good for. I dinna mind overcharging them."

"I think ye're wrong," said Joneta. "He was too friendly to be a Campbell."

John shrugged. "'Tis the way they are until they want to steal something from ye." The ale barrel dropped into place. "Ye always have to be on the lookout. Ye can ne'er trust a Campbell, ne'er."

"Ye always think the worst."

"There is naught worse than a Campbell."

He rolled the empty ale barrel behind the stall as Joneta fingered a small silver whistle on a chain she wore around her neck. She'd worn it every day since her great-grandfather gave it to her years ago on the day she learned to walk. Clutching the whistle and raising her eyes skyward, she prayed silently. "Lord, please, dinna let the man ye did some of yer best work on be a Campbell. Please, dinna make it true, no' a Campbell."

Suddenly a vision of her long-time neighbor, Zebulon Keene of Glencoe, popped into her head. She'd been pledged to him for nearly two years, but she hadn't accepted his proposal of marriage yet. Her brothers protested she should be wed by now, and combining Zeb's herd of cattle with theirs would make it the largest, and the most profitable, in Glencoe. They said she had a duty to her family, but her da, the Laird MacIain MacDonald, had promised her when she was seven years old the choice would be hers alone, and he kept his word.

Zeb would be a fine match, hardworking, kind, with curly chestnut hair and blue eyes, fair of face except for his left eye that drooped slightly ever since he'd been kicked by a mule when he was four years old. When she got home from the fair, she'd have to accept his offer. It was time. He would treat her well, and he'd make a good home for her and she wouldn't be unhappy. It wouldn't be a bad life, just an ordinary life, but she yearned for a life beyond the narrow glen of Glencoe, a life that wasn't ordinary, so until duty bound her to Zeb she'd enjoy every minute of the fair and the attentions of the good-looking charmer, Campbell or not, who bought griddle scones.

Early the next morning, Joneta turned over her first batch of currant griddle scones and sliced the first batch of dough for the potato ones while trying to remember a dream from last night, a dream about the dark-haired man who bought scones yesterday. The dream itself was foggy, but it felt so satisfying and enjoyable she didn't want it to end.

A familiar voice broke her reverie. "Looks like I'll be getting fresh scones. I'll take two of each again."

She startled, embarrassed at being caught daydreaming, but when she turned around, she couldn't help but grin at the man from yesterday. The air crackled around her. He stood taller than her brother, with a well-muscled build and broad shoulders. When he smiled back at her, a starburst of lines deepened around amazing ebony eyes and two semicircles appeared around his mouth and full lips. His skin had tanned to a honeyed perfection.

She scooped up the scones and laid them on a cloth in front of him. Again, he ate them in only a few bites.

Much to Joneta's delight, for the next five days Rory appeared every morning at the MacDonald stall and then again every evening for more scones. Joneta greeted him with a smile and a blush, and he always replied with a wink and a playful grin.

God did good work with this one! He is no' a Campbell. He couldn't be a creature with horns and a tail like all the Campbells.

"So that one's back again," grumbled John on the third day.

"He's a good customer," said Joneta. "Dinna scare him off. We can use the money."

"Aye, the tax man dinna care whose coin 'tis. Just watch yerself."

Each day when Rory came, they chatted while he ate, between her serving the other customers, sometimes talking for an hour until Rory's brother, Finn, stomped over and called for him to get back to work. They talked about simple things like their favorite foods or a favorite story told to them as children. They talked about their siblings, which ones treated them the best—for Joneta it was Alex and for Rory it was Finn—and who treated them the worst, usually the brother right above them in birth order. "I think 'tis jealousy," said Rory. "Mum and Da doted on Graham until I came along, but me being cuter and so much smarter, who could blame them for their favoritism?"

Joneta chuckled. This man made her laugh, and she loved to laugh, although the harsh realities of living in a poor clan in the rugged Glencoe valley left little time for laughter.

"Ye overpaid again," she said to him. "The last three days, ye've given me a penny or two too many, so today these will be on the house." She laid two currant griddle scones on a piece of cloth and flipped over the potato tatties in the pan to finish cooking them.

"I dinna overpay. I look forward to coming here afore I go to work and then again afore the sun goes down. Besides, I pay what the product is worth, and yer griddle scones are the best I e'er had in my mouth. My da is no' much of a cook. I was ten afore I kenned that porridge wasna supposed to be black or crunchy!"

He laughed from deep in his chest, and Joneta's heart skipped a beat. He made her mornings better and brightened her evenings. Here stood a man who enjoyed life, not like her father and brothers who were determined, uncompromising men who took hold of life with their fists and shook every bit of pleasure out of it. This Rory created his own happiness.

She kenned he flirted with her, but Rory didn't mean anything serious by it, not like he was courting her, not like the way Zeb did, but she did so enjoy it.

"Sorry ye dinna have anyone to cook properly for ye," Joneta said.

"Me sisters do the best they can, but it doesna match what ye can do with griddle scones. Are ye good at anything else?"

"I am good at a lot of things, but all ye'll get here are griddle scones. Mayhap my brother, John, can find some meat, and I can make meat pies for our last day here. Would ye buy a meat pie? The price would be dearer, mayhap four pennies."

"After I win the mountain race, I'll have two pounds

to spend, and I'll spend it all on meat pies, but only if ye're here to serve them. They wouldna taste the same if ye didna cook them up just right. Do ye ken the sunlight shines off yer hair?"

Biting her lip to keep from smiling, she said, "Aye, my hair is no' as ginger as most of my family, but there ye go being sassy again." Joneta swept her fingers through her auburn hair, sun-streaked with blonde, and tucked a loose strand behind her ear.

A slender man with a plump woman and three bairns came up to the stall and requested currant griddle scones for all. Joneta served up the five scones and waited patiently while the man slowly counted out the five pennies. "Thank ye," she called after him. "Come back again."

She pocketed the coins in her apron and watched Rory finish off two more of his scones.

"Are yer da and mum here with ye?" he asked before he swallowed. He leaned his elbow on the table and grinned at her. Her heart fluttered.

"Mum stayed home. She hates the noise and all the people, but that's what I like best. Glencoe is so quiet sometimes the only sounds are the coos mooing in the wind. John is the oldest son, so he's the one here with me."

"Will ye see me compete in some of the games? I won the sheaf toss two years in a row. Tossing hay into the mow for the horses gives me a lot of practice. And I'm going to run in the mountain race on the last day. The race began as a way for the king to choose the fastest messenger runners, but now 'tis just to see who's the best. I nearly won last year, but I'll do better this year. Does yer brother race?"

"Nay, he's more than ten years older than I am, so he leaves the racing to the lads."

He straightened his shoulders and his cheerful countenance vanished. "I'm no lad. I am partners with me da in the horse business. I dinna work for him. I'm his partner, and I'm good at what I do. I breed and train horses and mules for all the lairds in the Highlands. Ye can ask anyone." His voice tightened. "Does yer brother think me a restless lad with no ambition? I'll make something of myself. He'll see, and so will ye."

She didn't answer. Instead she took two tattie scones off the stove and laid them on the now empty cloth on the table. "My brother thinks ye might be a Campbell."

Rory answered quickly. "He'd be right."

Her eyes closed in disappointment for a moment. "I'm a MacDonald," she said flatly, pushing the cloth toward him, an ache growing in her chest. "That'll be four pennies. I dinna think ye should come back. John will take yer coin, but he willna take ye talking to me, since ye're a Campbell."

"The question is no' what *they* think, but what do *ye* think?"

Joneta looked at him from under long pale lashes, blinking away her regret that he belonged to a clan hated by her family. "I like having someone friendly to talk to, even as sassy as ye, but my brother would no' feel the same. He'd likely crack yer head or worse."

"I buy griddle scones whene'er I like, and I buy the ones I like the best. A Campbell talks to any fine young lass he wants." He tossed the pennies on the table and scooped up his scones. "Good day to ye, Miss Joneta MacDonald."

She watched him walk away again. This man dared

to cross the lines drawn so deeply by the longstanding feud. She admired his courage, but she doubted his wisdom, and she doubted her own wisdom for wanting to see him again.

The next morning, just after sunrise, Rory strode up to her stall. A fearful twinge sped into her stomach. "My brother wouldna like ye here. He's out back."

"I ken where he is. I looked afore I came. How are yer scones today?"

"As good as ever. Do ye have coin to buy some?"

He leaned over the table, putting his face right next to hers. He whispered, "I always have coin for the lass who has stolen my heart." His breath warmed her cheek.

Taking a quick glance to be certain her brother wasn't too close, she gently pushed his face away. His beard was soft, not like the rough frizzy beards of her father and brothers. "Do all Campbells spin a tale as good as ye?"

"Nay, only the most handsome. I'll have four potato tatties today. I need my strength. I'm competing in some of the games this afternoon. Do ye think ye might come and watch?"

"John would ne'er allow it. He'd be left to man the booth, and I'd have to go alone. I wish my other brother, Alex, had come. Then there'd be someone to go with me. 'Tis the going alone that bothers John the most."

"Even more than I'm a Campbell?"

"Naught bothers him more than that, but he still wouldna let me go."

"What if I found someone to escort ye?"

She wrapped the tattie scones in a cloth and slid them across the table. "Who would ye find? Another Campbell? Are ye daft in the head?"

"Nay, but I ken someone, several in fact, yer brother could no' object to. Be ready by three o'clock. That way ye can see me compete in the sheaf toss afore dark and then stay for the music and some of the dancing."

"Ye're awfully sure of yerself."

"That I am," he said as he darted away, three tattie scones in his hand and one in his mouth.

****

He already had a plan, a daring plan, to bring the lovely Joneta MacDonald close enough to kiss. On an impulse he'd even spent some of his hard-earned money on a gift he hoped someday to give to her. He was risking everything because, even though he wouldn't admit it, he'd already come too far from home to let his heart go back to the life he'd known without her.

Chapter Four

August 1690—Edinburgh, Scotland

John Dalrymple, Master of Stair and Secretary of State for Scotland, read the letter from King William again. Dalrymple had a plan, a plan to catapult him into King William's esteem and bring himself to a position of power more suited to his talents, and he wanted to make certain he understood the king's wishes accurately before responding.

The king's missive began. "I inherited from King James VII, now deposed and living in France, the unruly and barbaric Highlanders. They continue to be violent, brutal, and uncivilized with lingering Jacobite loyalties. The clans around the area of Lochaber are a thieving, cattle-raiding lot, resisting government control, with the worst said to be Clan MacDonald in Glencoe. MacDonalds are also Papist, and with Catholic James now deposed, they cannot be allowed to continue to spread those beliefs. If the MacDonalds are suppressed, others will follow and come into line. The recent defeat of a Jacobite attempt to reinstate James VII on the throne has given rise to the necessity that all Highlanders come fully under my command and control. If Scotland and England are ever to be united, this must be done.

"As Secretary of State, this falls under your purview. With government coffers being low because of the continuing need for military funding and for the building of a new military outpost, Fort William, in Lochaber, I can only offer a fund of £12,000 to be used at your discretion. I leave this task in your hands. Proceed as you see fit."

Signed King William of Scotland with the royal seal.

Dalrymple leaned back in his chair. "At last I have what I need, the king's permission to rid Scotland of the barbarians who dare to call themselves Scots. As an example to all the clans, I'll begin with the MacDonalds, a small clan, easy to deal with, and they will make a good start."

"Maxwell, Maxwell," he called to his secretary who dashed into the office.

"Aye, sir?"

"Take a letter to John Campbell of Breadlabane. As per the order of our King William and Queen Mary, your assistance is required. Our mission is to bring order and loyalty to the Highland clans by whatever means we choose. Negotiate with the lairds as you wish, but bringing them to compliance is an absolute necessity. Keep a keen eye on Clan MacDonald. Their laird, MacIain, is a sly fox and must be brought to heel. If he is, the other clan leaders will fall in line. Keep me informed as to your progress. The crown has offered £12,000 to be used at your discretion. You must not fail!"

Signed John Dalrymple, Secretary of State for Scotland.

Chapter Five

The Highland Fair—August 1690

Two hours later two older women approached Joneta's stall, arm in arm. Shocks of gray hair peeked out from under their colorful headscarves, and the arrays of wrinkles on their faces could only have come from years of demanding work and laughter. Joneta recognized their colors as from the Clan Cameron—red, bottle green, and yellow. One of the women leaned heavily on her cane while the other steadied her on each step as they made their way around the clumps of horse dung and muddy puddles left by the hundreds of people and animals crossing between the rows of stalls.

Eventually, they made their way to her table. "Have ye a stool?" asked the one with the cane. "Me leg could use a rest."

"Of course," said Joneta as she hurried to the back of the stall and carried out a worn wooden stool. The blue-eyed woman sat down with a sharp exhale of breath and propped her cane against the stall table.

"Thank ye, dearie," she said. "We've been hearing how ye have the best griddle scones of the entire fair, so we came for a taste."

"Here are our pennies," said the other as she reached into her sleeve, took out a small leather bag, and carefully placed two pennies on the table beside each other.

"Would ye like currant or tattie?" asked Joneta.

Both women tapped their fingers on their chin and looked upward in thought before saying in unison, "One of each."

She took one scone of each flavor out of the warming drawer and placed them on a small cloth. The women took one bite of each. Then they traded the scones back and forth until they were gone, all the while mumbling their delight. The standing woman said, "My name is Morag and this is my baby sister, Fenella. We're Camerons, born and bred, and we dinna have a thing against a MacDonald, and we hope a MacDonald doesna have a thing against us. Our mother's sister, Lorna, married a MacDonald more than fifty years ago. Now, what was his name?"

Fenella answered, "'Twas Clyde, but 'twas many years ago. I think they must be eighty years at least, mayhap older. We Camerons live a verra long time."

"I ken of Lorna and Clyde MacDonald," said Joneta. "They live on the far end of Glencoe in a house alone near the gap that leads out of the glen. I didna ken she was a Cameron."

"Aye, they're the ones, but 'tis yer brother we came to see. These griddle scones are as tasty as he said they were." She gave a lopsided smile to her sister who said, "I agree. Is yer brother around?"

"Aye, 'tis yer brother we want to talk with," said Morag.

"He's out back. I'll fetch him."

As soon as John appeared from the back of the stall, the sisters started talking, interrupting and finishing each other's sentences. His eyes darted from one to the other, trying to keep up with their rapid-fire speech.

"We're Fenella and Morag Cameron. I was marrit once," began Fenella.

"But he died," finished Morag, "and I, meself, ne'er wed. I'm the oldest and had too much to do to keep the family together. We have been watching yer lovely sister here serving scones for days now, and delicious they are."

"We sew the quilts ye can see at the booth across the way." She pointed to a large wooden stand with several colorful quilts draped over the slats.

"We noticed she has ne'er gone to see a single event in the field. So we were wishing—"

"She could accompany us," said Fenella.

"To the games this afternoon and stay for the music tonight. Tomorrow is the last day, and the only event is the mountain race, so today it must be. 'Twould be a boon to us, as ye can see I have trouble—"

"Getting around. We could use the help and the company."

John waited to see if they were done speaking. He started to open his mouth when Morag spoke up again. "Could she come with yer permission, John?" said Morag. "Ye could—"

"Sell the griddle scones, could ye no'?"

John waited again, and in the pause, he asked Joneta, "I dinna ken. Ye do all the selling."

"'Tis no' hard," said Joneta. "I could make a lot in advance, and ye'd just take them out of the warmer. Please, John?"

"The games seem like a place for lads and fools. Would ye really like to go?"

"Aye, more than anything. These ladies would take

good care of me, and I of them. Please, John?"

John interlocked both his hands behind his neck, a gesture Joneta had seen many times as he pondered a problem. "'Twill be all right for ye to go with these fine quilters. I've seen their stitching. 'Tis quite good."

Joneta beamed, but before she could thank her brother for his permission, Morag said, "Come to our booth by three o'clock so we can see some of the games—"

"Afore dark, when the bagpipes begin," said Fenella. "Mayhap ye could carry a quilt back to Lorna MacDonald for us from her cousins, and as ye are doing us this favor, we will bring everything we need—"

"For a comfortable viewing," said Morag, finishing the thought. "We look forward to spending time with ye."

Morag helped Fenella to her feet, and both women made their slow trek across the path to their booth.

"Thank ye, John," said Joneta, clapping her hands. "I wanted to see some of the contests. It seems senseless to come to the fair and not see anything but this booth."

"Ye must stay with the Cameron ladies, no wandering off on yer own," said John sternly. "I willna tolerate ye being alone. 'Tis for yer own good. No' everyone at the fair has yer best interests at heart." He patted her on the shoulder. "Ye see, I am no' the hard task master ye think I am."

"I ken. Ye're only in practice for when ye are laird."

"That will be a long time from now. Da will no' be turning over the title any time soon. Get me a supply of griddle scones ready, both flavors, so I'll have plenty to sell while ye enjoy yerself." He grinned. "I dinna think those two ladies need much looking after, but I'm glad they are going to chaperone ye. A bonny lass like ye could find herself in a great deal of trouble on her own."

"John, I'll be fine with the Cameron ladies," said Joneta, already imagining the sights she would see at the fair tonight.

After three o'clock, the three women, two older and one younger, slowly made their way to the field, where Morag said, "Let's sit over there." She pointed toward a spot next to a tall tree in front of a copse of more scrawny ones so typical of the Highlands.

They walked to the far side of the large tree, only to find someone waiting there for them.

"Let me help ye spread yer quilt," said Rory. He took the basket from Joneta, unfolded the quilt, and spread it out on the ground, making certain it was out of sight of the stalls, but within full view of the gaming field.

Morag dropped down two thick pillows, and Fenella nestled between them.

"'Twas all his idea," said Morag. "He kenned yer brother would ne'er let ye go with him, but with us, he might."

"And he did!" said Fenella.

Rory, his mouth and eyes drooping into an almost comical frown, asked in a nearly tearful voice, "Are ye angry at me for tricking ye and yer brother?"

Joneta shook her head. "Yer trickery amuses me, and I'd hoped to see ye again afore we leave the fair tomorrow. 'Twas quite clever of ye to include the sisters. John ne'er suspected a thing."

He took her hand in his and escorted her to the quilt next to the sisters. "I'll sit on this side of the tree, and we can talk without anyone seeing me. They'll only see three lovely lasses watching the games."

Morag and Fenella said in unison, with childish giggles, "Lad, ye flatter me."

Joneta giggled, too. "Ye sassy one. Dinna ye have to work with yer da and sell yer horses?"

"No' this afternoon. I'm upholding the good name of Campbell in the sheaf toss contest and have another surprise for ye later. Will ye cheer for me to win?"

"Aye, as loud as I can."

A soft breeze blew around them. Several long strands of Joneta's hair dangled down from her braids, and the wind fluttered them across her face. Rory combed his loose black hair back with his fingers, but it kept slipping out of the leather tie he used to hold it at the nape of his neck.

The long and short races went on in the field in front of them, but they paid them no mind, turning to look only when the crowd cheered. Morag and Fenella leaned their heads together and fell asleep, snoring softly, while Joneta and Rory's talk changed to things they wanted out of life.

"Someday," said Rory, spreading out his arms, "I want to be the biggest trader and trainer of horses in all of Scotland. I'll settle for just the Highlands, but a man should have dreams."

"I want a home to call my own," said Joneta. "'Twould be more than a blackhouse with stone walls and a thatched roof like those at Glencoe. A tall stone house to keep out the wind, one that doesna let the daub and mud holding it together blow in. My house will have a full second story for the bairns."

"How many bairns?" Rory interrupted.

"As many as the good Lord gives me, and I want a

vegetable garden out back and flowers along the front, so it has to be in a place with good soil, no' like Glencoe that has trouble growing even grass."

"Is that all ye dream about, just a fancy house and bairns?"

Her forehead wrinkled. She glared. "A home is what matters if 'tis managed right, if the family is clean, healthy, taught respect and, most importantly, how to laugh. Life doesna have to be all work and fried porridge. There should be something more. It takes a strong woman to make it so. Did ye ken I can make a stew out of hardly anything, and ye'd lick yer lips, it'd be so tasty. And I can back a wagon and a team of horses through the stable door. I can swing an axe and tan leather. I've sheared the hairy coos and woven the hair into coats. Aye, a woman can do all that and a lot more, and in the evenings she can laugh and sing and tell stories to her bairns, but only if she has a good man as her husband. Aye, she must choose that husband well, and no' settle for less than the best."

He waited for a moment, with his eyes half-closed, before he said, "Do ye think I might be a man like that for a lass like ye?"

She held her hazel eyes on him. "If ye were no' so sassy, and if ye prove yerself to be the best, then I'll see."

He leaned in, his face near hers. "I have said things like that afore to a lass, but to be honest, I meant it just for the night. But with ye I think I'd like to be that man for as long as ye'll have me."

She raised one eyebrow. "I'm certain ye've said that to a lass afore, too."

He paused. "I want to kiss ye."

"My brother would no' allow it." Then she slowly

added, "But he isna here."

Just then Fenella woke up. "We are here to chaperone, no' allow familiarity. Ye may take yer leave with other lasses, but no' with this one, no' while we are charged with keeping her out of harm's way."

He laughed and tried to look offended. "Are ye calling me 'harm'?"

"Nay, lad, no' harm by intention. 'Tis just yer daring way. The sheaf toss is starting. Dinna ye have to go?"

Still looking into Joneta's eyes, he said, "Aye, I do." With another wink, he leaned in and gave her a peck on the cheek before taking off running toward the center of the field.

She touched her cheek, caressing the spot of the kiss.

In the sheaf toss, a bundle of straw weighing about nine kilograms and covered in a burlap bag is tossed with a pitchfork over a high bar. The bar is raised bit by bit, and contestants are eliminated until a winner is determined.

The three women on the quilt watched as man after man pitched the straw over the bar, and man after man failed in the attempt. After nearly an hour, twenty-five men were eliminated. Only Rory and one other remained. Three times Rory and Ian MacGregor pitched their straw successfully over the increasingly higher bar until Ian's bundle flew into the air, bounced off the bar, and hit him in the face. The crowd laughed at the red-faced Ian, and then waited anxiously to see if Rory could pitch his bundle over the new height.

He stabbed his bale with the pitchfork and swung it upward. With ease, the hay flew over the bar, and the winner was declared!

"Rory won last year, too," said Morag, still clapping

her hands along with Fenella and Joneta. "He pitches a lot of hay to feed the horses and mules he and his father raise and train."

"How do ye ken Rory?" asked Joneta, settling back again on the quilt beside the sisters.

"His mother was a Cameron. His da a Campbell," began Morag.

"And every time his mother came to see her family Cameron, she brought little Rory with her," continued Fenella.

"After she died, his sisters brought him. He came to see us, first to get biscuits and funnel cakes that werena burned, but later, as he got bigger, he came to help us cut peat in the winter for heat or to help us bring in the vegetable produce."

"He even made Fenella a hoe with a special handle so she could reach the weeds from her stool or—"

"Dig the holes so we could plant some Scottish bluebells. We love them," finished Morag. "He's grown into a good man. He's full of spit and vinegar. No one will e'er tame his daring spirit. Lord kens his da tried, but the lad has a strong will. He'll no' be broken. Still, the woman who loves him with her whole heart will make him a changed man."

"I dinna want to change him," said Joneta.

"He's the kind who jumps in with both feet, and he doesna care how deep the water is," said Fenella.

"He believes he can conquer anything—"

"And he has shoulders strong enough to carry whatever comes his way, with a strong soul to match."

Fenella spoke with a set to her jaw. "One thing ye canna change is that he is a Campbell, and if ye're thinking ye can or ye should, ye'd be wrong. A Campbell is a fine thing to be."

Morag quickly added, "Just as 'tis a fine thing to be a MacDonald, and if ye let a century's old dustup come between the two of ye, ye dinna deserve him."

"I do want to ken him better," said Joneta. "He has a spirit I dinna see in many men, a real keenness for living." She sighed. "And that smile of his."

"That smile can make the angels sing, and that's a good place to start."

A commotion rose up at the far end of the field before Joneta saw Rory leading two prancing Clydesdale draft horses, huge beasts dwarfing Rory, who trotted beside them. Clydesdales, bred in Scotland, were the largest breed used on farms and in other trades. Right behind these Clydesdales trotted two Highland Ponies, a slightly smaller breed and used most often for carrying loads through the mountains of the Highlands.

Rory whistled and the Clydesdales continued to trot beside him while the ponies stayed where they were. The crowd oohed and cheered as Rory, using only a variety of whistle patterns, put the horses through intricate maneuvers, separately and in unison. After directing the Clydesdales to the side of the field, he made a pattern of clicking sounds with his tongue while the ponies trotted toward him in perfect unison. Different clicks put these animals through their paces in a routine that resembled dancing.

Rory clicked the ponies back to their stalls in the stable at the back of the field as he grabbed the mane of one of the Clydesdales and leaped astride it. Using only his heels and gentle tugs on the horse's mane, the horse trotted around the field until the two of them stood in front of Joneta and the Cameron sisters on their blanket.

Reaching into his vest, Rory pulled out an apple and tossed it to Joneta, who caught it handily.

"Give Adair his treat," Rory said. "Hold yer hand flat with the apple on it."

"I ken how to feed a horse," she said, reaching her hand under the horse's snout. The animal gobbled the apple up in one bite and then nickered his approval and gratitude.

Standing on the horse's back, Rory shouted to the crowd, "If I can train these enormous mounts to obey, I can teach yer animals to plow a field, walk quietly into the stall, and stand patiently while ye clean their hooves and wash them! My fees are reasonable and I guarantee success! Campbell and Son!"

With that he jumped down from the horse, whistled again, and both Clydesdales trotted back to their stalls, undisturbed by the men and children reaching out to pat their haunches. Only when a child picked up a stick did one of the horses turn his head and bare his teeth at the lad, who immediately dropped the stick and ran wailing back into the crowd.

Joneta clapped and cheered.

"How did ye like my horses?" Rory asked.

"They were magnificent!" said Joneta. "Yer skill with them is wonderful. Could ye teach me to do it?"

Touching the whistle around her neck, he tugged her closer by the chain, lifted the whistle to his lips, and blew gently into it. By moving his lips and using his fingers to cover the three holes in different ways, he made different sounds.

His scent of manly sweat and horse filled her head. She liked him close to her.

"Aye, I could," he said. "I could teach ye to use the

31

whistle, but we'd have to spend a great deal of time together." He gave her a sly smile.

She murmured, "I would enjoy that."

Rory held the whistle to his lips again and made two new sounds. "This whistle will work just fine. 'Tis made so fancy and beautiful. Where did ye get it?" He let go of the chain, but he stayed close to her.

"'Twas a gift from Ian Abrach MacDonald, the tenth laird of the MacDonald clan and my great-grandfather. He was very elderly when I was born, and he was so wonderfully pleased with the girl child at last, he had the whistle made and bestowed it to me on the day I learned to walk."

Rory put his hands on her arms, stepped even closer, and leaning in, kissed her on the mouth. The warmth and tenderness of his lips melted into hers as she wrapped her arms around his waist and purred a low hum of delight.

A man with ginger hair charged out of the crowd and ran across the field, bellowing, "Unhand her, ye filthy Campbell! Unhand my sister!"

Chapter Six

Joneta and Rory jerked apart as John MacDonald stormed toward them and swung his fist into Rory's face. Rory stumbled to the ground. Blood spurted from his nose and upper lip as John straddled him, his fists clenched. "Get up, ye Campbell bastard, so I can beat ye within an inch of yer useless life! Joneta, get back to the stall!"

Rory pushed out from under John with his feet, stood, and used the back of his hand to wipe the blood from his face. "I'll no' fight ye," he said.

"Then ye'll take yer beating." John swung out his fist again. Rory sidestepped it.

"Ye can beat me, but I willna fight ye. For Joneta's sake, I willna fight ye."

"Nay! Nay!" cried the Cameron sisters as they struggled to their feet. "Ye canna do this!"

John pulled his fist back, this time landing a blow in Rory's gut. Rory doubled over, but still made no move to fight back. John stuck out his foot, reaching behind Rory's knee, and wrenched him to the ground.

Morag picked up one of their pillows and swung it in John's face at the same time Joneta pushed against her brother's shoulder. "Stop it! Stop it!"

John seized her arm and shouted, "Get back to the stall!" He swung her off the quilt, and she fell on her back into the grass.

"Leave her be!" said Rory, charging toward her. "'Twas my fault. She didna ken I would be here." He lifted her to her feet and planted himself between her and her brother. "All she kenned was the sisters were bringing her to the games. I'll take my beating from ye, and I'll take one for her, too, but ye leave her be!"

John's face grew nearly as red as his hair and spittle shot out of his mouth. "I sent her with the ladies, no' ye, and she kenned that! I told her ye were a Campbell, and she kenned it. When she saw ye here, she had a duty to come back to the stall. Since she didna, she disobeyed. I'll see she ne'er comes near ye again!"

"If ye lay a hand on her," said Rory, his eyes narrow and his face dark, "I'll hunt ye down. Ye can take yer anger out on me, but no' on her."

"She kenned ye were a scabby bassa Campbell. She is pledged to Zebulon Keene of Glencoe."

"I ne'er said I'd marry him," she said, stepping from behind Rory with her hands on her hips. "And ye canna make me. I willna!"

"Ye will marry Zebulon to save ye from the disgrace of a Campbell." John hesitated before adding, "On yer lips!" Grabbing Rory by the collar, he tore his shirt and gave him another punch in the face. Rory staggered, but still didn't move to defend himself.

"I willna fight ye. I willna hurt her brother. I was wrong, and I deserve yer punishment, but I willna fight ye."

"Coward! Ye Campbell coward! Do ye all see that?" he shouted to the crowd now surrounding the quilt. "He willna defend her honor."

"He *is* defending my honor!" protested Joneta. "He chooses no' to fight with ye for my sake. Stay away, brother. Stay away." She took the edge of her apron and wiped the lingering blood off Rory's face. Rory moved her aside, keeping himself between her and her brother.

"I'll kill him!" shouted John, lunging again.

A stranger appeared beside John from out of the crowd. "Nay, ye willna," he said in a voice firm with authority. "I am the sheriff, and ye will both walk away or ye'll spend the night in the gaol. Make yer choice." Two more intimidatingly large men stepped out and stood alongside the sheriff. "These are my deputies commissioned for the fair. Do ye want to fight them?"

John's fiery scowl nearly burned the grass.

Rory faced John, his shoulders held back and his hands open at his sides. "I made a mistake in deceiving ye, John MacDonald, but I promise ne'er to lie to ye again about my intentions." Turning toward Joneta, he said, "Joneta, I promise ne'er to trick ye into seeing me." Then motioning toward Morag and Fenella with a hand dripping with his own blood, he said, "I promise ne'er to use ye in my schemes again."

Morag replied, "We were no' entirely innocent in this. We suspected something was afoot, but…"

"Ye are forgiven," said Fenella.

Rory wiped his hand on his shirt and extended it to Joneta. "Will ye accept my word? Ye're a fine woman, and I will court ye like a man from now on, no' a trickster."

"Ye'll no' court her!" shouted John, seizing him by the shoulder and turning him around before Joneta could put her hand in his. "I'll see ye dead afore ye come near her again!"

"John, I am no' foolish," said Joneta. "I kenned it might be like this, and I could have refused, but I came of my own free choice." She repeated, "My own free choice, John, and I accept his apology."

"His apology is no' worth the air it takes to say it. Ye canna believe anything from a Campbell! I will ne'er forget that I owe ye a beating, Rory Campbell. I'll see ye hanged. Someday, someday! Joneta, go back to the stall. Tomorrow we leave for Glencoe." He stormed away, calling his sister's name with each step until he was out of earshot. He turned back only once.

"Are ye aright?" the sheriff asked Joneta.

"I am."

"I willna let him punish ye," said Rory. "This 'twas my fault, and I accept responsibility, and I'll no' let ye take it."

"I'm no' afraid of him. He willna lay a hand on me," Joneta said. "Da would ne'er allow it. Ye dinna have to worry. He will scold me until the cows are old and tough, but I am no' afeared of him." She added, "I thank ye for a wonderful day at the fair. It felt good to talk and laugh and see the amazing sights. I ne'er spent a lovelier afternoon in my life."

Taking the hand of each Cameron sister, she said, "Thank ye, Morag and Fenella. I had a charming time with ye, too. I'll ne'er forget this day or this company."

"We'll leave the quilt for Lorna MacDonald at yer stall tonight. Ye can take it to her with our thanks."

Joneta nodded before lifting her palm to Rory's cheek. "I'll ne'er forget what a grand time I had at the fair, and I will think of ye every time I make griddle scones."

"I'll walk with ye back to yer brother."

"Nay, ye willna. If he sees ye again, 'twill only make things worse for ye and me."

She followed her brother back to the stall and braced herself for the reprimanding he was certain to give her, which she knew would continue all the way back to Glencoe, and it did.

****

Rory stood at the edge of the quilt watching her trudge behind her brother until his own father, Giles Campbell, a sturdy man like his son, came up beside him and barked, "Come with me, ye sorry excuse for a Campbell! To the barn, with the horses who ken what 'tis really like to be a Campbell! Ye've shamed me, and I willna have it!"

Barely hearing his father's words, and missing Joneta's touch, he said, "I have to help Fenella and Morag back to their stall. I'll come when I get done."

"Ye will come now!"

"Go ahead," said Fenella. "We will find a friendly face to carry our things. Dinna fash."

Rory caught up with his father at the stable door. "Inside!" his father ordered, grabbing him by the neck and hurling him to the ground. Rory stumbled into one of the stalls, landing on his back.

"Da, what's wrong?"

"I'll tell ye what is wrong! Ye stood there and took a beating from a MacDonald. A MacDonald! If he'd had a knife or ye'd been outnumbered, I could understand ye getting bloodied, but, nay, ye didna fight back, and ye shamed the clan, and ye shamed me!"

His voice filled the barn, and the horses reacted with stomping and snorting.

"I willna have a son who willna stand up for himself or his clan, especially no' in front of a MacDonald, no' in front of all the Highland Clans. The Campbells are cursing yer cowardness while the rest of them are laughing at a man as weak as a kitten. A kitten! Did ye no' hear what they said?"

"Da, I didna fight back because he's Joneta's brother. I couldna hurt him, no' in front of his sister."

"Joneta? Her name is Joneta? A MacDonald! Ye're carrying on with a MacDonald? Yer brother, Finn, said ye bought griddle scones nearly every day from a MacDonald! Ye've had yer share of lasses, but ye ne'er cursed this house with a MacDonald, and after today ye ne'er will. I canna bear the disgrace of ye taking a beating by a MacDonald for all to see. I tried to teach ye better, and now I will!" He grabbed the training whip draped over the side of the stall and swung it mightily at Rory. It cracked and struck him across the face, leaving a deep cut just under his eye. Rory threw his arms over his head and scooted into the corner.

"Da!"

"John MacDonald didna finish yer beating, but I will! I'll teach ye the lesson he started!"

The whip fell on Rory's arms, back, and legs over and over again, leaving bloody gashes wherever it landed. When the whip broke apart, Giles grabbed a harness from the end of the stall, and, with the buckle end, continued to flog his son.

The horses kicked and bucked against the sides of their stalls, some of them screeching and stomping in protest.

Over and over the harness fell, slashing into Rory's shirt and breeches until he grabbed the reins and held them firm. "'Tis enough, Da," he said.

Giles gasped for breath and released his grip on the harness. "No son of mine! Ye will be no son of mine! I ne'er want to see yer sorry arse again. Ye will have no part in our horse trade. Ye will leave with the clothes on yer back, and no Campbell will ever shake yer hand again." He stomped toward the door. "Ye can take yer horse, 'tis no good to me, only listens to ye, but no' yer saddle. Ye take anything else, and I'll have ye arrested for thieving and see ye hanged. Do ye believe me?"

"Aye, sir," came Rory's breathless reply.

"I ne'er want to see ye again. Ye are no son of mine."

"Ye dinna mean it, Da."

Giles rested his hand on the stable door. "Aye, I do. Ye've always been a burden to me, yer mind always on something besides yer work. I put up with ye because ye were good with the horses, and I thought, when ye were grown, ye'd amount to more of a man, but ye are no' good for anything. Yer mum spoiled ye, letting ye have yer head, telling stories and playing games. Ye got over on her with yer smile, and by the time she died, the damage was done. Yer charming ways are no good to me, and today was the last time I will call ye my son. Get out of my sight!"

The stable door clattered shut behind him.

The sun fell below the horizon before Rory stopped the worst of the bleeding from the cuts on his leg and the one on his face. He lifted himself to his feet and limped toward the Highland Pony he had raised from a colt and called Caraid, which meant "friend." Rory hadn't the energy to mount the dun-colored beast, especially bareback, so he led Caraid out the side door and into the darkness.

****

During the next two days, Joneta and John never

caught a glimpse of him as he followed behind their wagon back to the eastern edge of the glen of Glencoe. Caraid, a well-trained horse, let Rory rest over his neck and maintained a slow but steady pace so not to jostle his wounded rider, exhausted physically from the beating as well as emotionally shattered by his father's diatribe.

Rory stayed out of sight, hiding in small stands of trees or behind rock formations, but always listening. At night he watched the smoke rise from their fire, wishing he could be with her. He slept only a little, but always listening. He would never let her brother punish her for his deception.

His bloody cuts slowly stopped oozing, but the pain stayed with him, not only the pain of the flogging, but the pain in his heart, knowing his father never said a word he didn't mean. Rory had accepted early in his life that his knack for training horses was the only thing that mattered to his father, but he always hoped a bit of love might exist between them. There'd been none today. Mayhap there never had been. He had no family to call his own. A man without a clan was like a coo lost from the herd, alone and vulnerable.

He kept his mind on the woman traveling in the wagon ahead of him. He wanted more than to protect her. He wanted to glimpse the wind blowing her hair around her face and see the squinting of her eyes against the sun. He wanted to sit with her, to hear her voice while he ate another griddle scone. To see the sun sparkle off her hazelnut eyes, to watch her tuck her hair behind her ear. And a smile from her would complete his world.

Near the gap leading into the Glencoe valley, he rested on the far side of the mountain on Campbell land. He ate what he could pick or catch, and very little at that, and he snuggled against Caraid for warmth. He dreamed of seeing her face, her beautiful face, just one more time. He didn't care what happened to him, but no one would ever hurt her.

The next day he left for someplace where he could rest and heal. He let the horse lead the way, and when he fell onto the ground, friendly hands lifted him up.

Chapter Seven

One month after the Highland Fair—September 20, 1690

The end of summer came quickly in the Highlands, with all hands needed to work for the good of the clan. Joneta helped birth newborn coos, which had been bred in the spring. She worked to shear the sheep. Then came the carding and weaving of the wool, which often went long into the night. What crops came from the vegetable gardens and small fields of oats for animal feed were harvested and then prepared and preserved. As the days shortened, the task of herding coos and sheep to market fell to the young men, leaving behind a few animals to be slaughtered and the meat preserved for the winter. Exhausted, Joneta fell into her bed every night, only to be awakened before the sun the next day.

"Da," said Joneta to her father late one September morning as he mucked the straw inside the stable on the other side of their blackhouse cottage, "I've held this quilt for over a month for Clyde and Lorna MacDonald. The Cameron sisters from the Highland Fair made it and asked me to take it to them. I'm done with my chores for this morning and the rest can wait until I get back. 'Tis only about two miles, mayhap a bit more, to their house at the far east end of the glen, and I can walk there, visit a time, and be back afore nightfall."

"Do ye ken Clyde and Lorna?" asked Laird MacIain of Glencoe. "They're quite elderly and dinna leave their house verra often. They've kept to themselves for as long as I can remember. I doubt they have been here to our village since ye were a babe."

"The two sisters said the Camerons and MacDonalds were related through Lorna and Clyde. Lorna is their mother's youngest sister."

Talking about the Cameron sisters brought back memories to Joneta of the man God had done such good work on, Rory Campbell. Almost every night she'd seen his face in her dreams, and in these dreams, they always laughed. She had no idea what they were doing or where they went in the dream, but they kept laughing. She wished for more such laughter in Glencoe to ease the colorless life of work.

MacIain, a gruff man with everyone except his only daughter, said after a long thought, "I'll ask Zebulon Keene to walk with ye. Ye are pledged, and ye should spend some time together. I can trust him to protect ye."

"Nay, Da. Zeb is a fine man, and I ken he would make a fine husband, but I am no' ready to marry, mayhap soon, but ye promised me the time and the choice would be mine."

"Zeb is a proud man. He willna wait forever. There are lasses who would marry him tomorrow, no' make him wait. I have been looking at other clans to see if they have any eligible men for ye. I wouldna want to see ye leave Glencoe, but 'tis my duty to find ye a husband, especially after John told me about the man ye met at the fair, that Campbell."

Joneta hung her head. "The man at the fair was a mistake. I didna mean to disobey, but I wanted to see the games so badly. I didna ken he'd be there. It willna happen again, and Zeb is a good man. I will be ready for him soon, I promise, but today I'd like to have the time to myself, if 'tis aright with ye. 'Tis a lovely day for walking."

He sighed. "All right, no' this time, but I will have Zeb to the house for an evening visit verra soon. I canna see Clyde's house from here for the slope of the land, but I can watch ye most of the way. Ye tell Clyde to run a green flag up the pole when ye are ready to leave so we can be watching for ye."

"A flag?"

"Aye, 'tis a system we designed many years ago so we here in the village could make certain they were all right. Even though they chose to live at a distance, we wanted to take care of them, especially now they are up in years. The pole is quite tall, reaches high above their roof, and Clyde sends up different colored flags to tell us when they need something or when things are going well."

"I dinna ken why I ne'er noticed such a flag afore."

"Ye are no' so tall and probably couldna see it over the rise of the land. From here, it often looks like the flag is blowing on the ground, no' high in the sky, but 'tis my duty as clan chief to take care of and protect everyone in the clan, and that includes Clyde and Lorna. People in the village take a butchered cow and a pig to them every year, now that they canna raise the animals themselves. Sometimes they take extra foodstuffs or other gifts they can spare, too. We look out for each other. That is a clan."

Joneta gave him a hug around his waist.

"What is this for?" he asked, patting her on the back.

"I didna ken everything ye do for us. I ne'er paid attention, but I want to thank ye."

"For what?"

"For being our laird. I'll get the quilt and leave as soon as I can and be back afore dark."

The weather had been leaving hints of the coming colder winter, but the walk to Clyde and Lorna's house filled Joneta with the sweet smells of windblown grass and sunshine on her face. Walking across the verdant land, she kept the lone house directly in her sights. The sounds of the coos lowing farther up the mountain and the shouts of the men herding them to keep them from wandering to their deaths on the ledges and rocks all pleased her. The valley of her beloved Glencoe was a harsh but beautiful place. The five separate clusters of nearly 200 houses nestled along the valley floor acted as one heart in love and unison with the land.

If only Rory could bring his joy for life to this place. She only wished everyone in Glencoe could work together with the same delight that sparkled in Rory Campbell.

Smoke rose from the chimney of the two-story stone house built by Clyde MacDonald over fifty years ago. The house had been built close to the mountain just north of the opening to the glen so that anyone coming into Glencoe might not notice it as they passed by, but Clyde and Lorna could see all who came into or left the valley. A yellow flag flapped in the wind high above the house.

As Joneta came closer, a hunched white-haired woman stepped out the front door, waving her arm. The windows on both sides of the door let in the sunlight and the breeze while blue-flowered curtains fluttered in each.

"Ye came!" she said in a voice scratchy with age. "I

kenned ye'd come. Come in, dearie." She motioned for Joneta to follow her inside.

"I'm Joneta MacDonald, daughter of Laird MacIain MacDonald."

"I kenned ye'd come. Clyde, Clyde, she came!"

A white-haired man with a straight back and twinkling gray eyes came around the side of the house, carrying a rake. "I can see that. Welcome, lass. She looks just like he said she would. Come in for a biscuit and a cup of barley water made fresh this morning." He propped his rake against the outside wall and followed the two women inside.

A large fireplace along the side wall, burning small chunks of peat, made the room stifling hot today. On each side of the fireplace sat a comfortable chair. The walls held shelving crammed with crocks of vegetables, blankets and quilts, dishes, lamps, and one shelf filled with books looking worn and quite well used.

"I've ne'er been here," said Joneta. "This is a lovely home."

"Built it myself," said Clyde. "I built it for Lorna, who wouldna be my bride until she had a home to call her own. It took me near two years, with all my work in the village, and then to earn enough to buy cattle of my own to live on, but she waited, and we've been here ever since. We get by now with help from the village."

Lorna nodded her head. "I did want a house, but I would have waited forever for him, house or no'. I kenned from the start he was the man for me," adding with a snicker, "even if he were a MacDonald." She waved her hand toward a small room off to the side. "He had some help, but he added this bedroom after the ladder to the loft got to be too much for either of us."

"'Tis a wonderful home, but why do ye live so far from the village? Did the MacDonalds no' like the Camerons when ye were young?" asked Joneta.

"Clan loyalties change often. Camerons and MacDonalds did argue years ago, and when we first marrit 'twas safer for Lorna if we lived far away from the village, but things changed over the years. When yer grandfather was chief, he encouraged the others to accept us. We've been marrit over fifty years." He kissed Lorna on the cheek.

"Fifty-eight," said Lorna. "We are so glad to have a visitor to tell that story to, but enough about us. What do ye have in yer arms?"

"'Tis a quilt from Morag and Fenella Cameron. They gave it to me at the Highland Fair and asked me to bring it to ye." She opened and unfolded it over one of the chairs. "'Tis wonderful, intricate work."

A purple pattern known as "Thistle" adorned the quilt. A light beige-and-yellow background of patterned squares let the deep purple thistles and stems stand out, and the edges showed off delicate and intricate designs in the same deep purple.

"I told the sisters years ago that I wanted one of their quilts," said Lorna. "They are my cousins. My mother and their mother were sisters. Oh, Clyde, dinna ye love it?"

"'Tis perfect," said Clyde. "We can put it on the bed in the coldest nights, and 'twill keep us warm. Joneta, when we have passed on, this quilt will be yers. We have no bairns, so 'twill be yers."

Joneta shook her head. "I canna accept such a wonderful gift. 'Tis yers to keep."

"We insist ye have it later," said Lorna. "We will

love it for now, and ye will love it for the years after."

Joneta blushed. "I canna thank ye enough. 'Tis so beautiful. I could ne'er make anything so fine. I will treasure it."

Clyde and Lorna exchanged a glance before Lorna said, "We have something else for ye. Go out back to the garden and ye will see it."

"I dinna need another gift. I only wanted to bring the quilt and visit with ye a while."

"Ye will. Go see what it is, and be gentle with it."

Joneta looked curiously at both the MacDonalds before she left by the front door and walked around the side of the house. Flower beds with perfectly cultivated flowers, now drooping with the cooler weather, lined the stone walls. Turning the corner, she saw a well-kept vegetable garden with about half of it already harvested.

She nearly stumbled over the boots of the outstretched feet of someone sitting on a bench against the back wall of the house. "Rory, Rory, is that ye?"

He jumped to his feet. "Dinna be angry. Dinna be angry at Clyde or Lorna. 'Twas all my idea to meet ye here."

Her mouth turned down. "What happened to yer face?" She stepped closer and raised her hand toward the bandage over his left cheek.

He brought her hand down and ignored her question. "I dinna mean to cause ye trouble at the fair, and I dinna want to cause it now. Clyde's been telling me I started the trouble intentionally so I'd look like a hero in yer eyes. He says I always want to be the hero. He might be right."

"Tell me what happened to yer face? Were ye in a fight?"

"'Twas no' a fight, but all my trying to be a hero got out of hand, and I got the worst of it. Clyde showed me I canna always do whate'er I want, and how I have to take responsibility for what happened. 'Twas my fault, Joneta. Will ye forgive me?"

She crossed her arms and spoke in a voice she used on troublesome sheep. "What happened to yer face? Tell me. Did one of the horses trample ye?"

He rubbed the toe of his boot in the dirt, an uncharacteristic gesture for the outgoing man Joneta remembered. "Nay. 'Twas no' a horse." He hesitated before saying, "'Twas me da."

"Yer da? What? Why in the world?"

"I'm a grown man, and 'tis embarrassing to say me da beat me like this, but he didna like me no' fighting yer brother at the fair. He says I shamed him and everyone in the clan by no' standing up for meself. He beat me with a riding whip and then a harness." He pushed up his sleeves and showed her several cuts healing on his arms. "My legs and back look worse. I should no' have baited yer brother like I did. I kenned no' fighting him would only make him angrier. And that isna all."

"What else?"

He sucked in a deep breath and let it out slowly. "Da banished me. Said no Campbell would e'er shake my hand again. My horse brought me here." He stepped back away from her.

"'Tis a terrible thing he did to ye. I canna believe a father would beat his like this." Her eyes filled with tears. "And because of me. I am so sorry, Rory, so sorry. 'Twas my fault."

"Nay! Me and Da have been at odds all my life. He and I ne'er wanted the same things. I wanted to train the horses one way with my whistles and clicks, and he wanted to use a harsh voice and a whip."

She gasped.

"He didna want to harm the horses, only train them to respond to commands with what he called respect."

"I'd call it fear. Did he expect to train ye the same way?"

"He tried, but I fought him at every step. He called me hopeless but kept at me because I was good with the horses. I wanted to do things my way, no' just with the horses but with everything, but I'm on my own now, so I have to make better choices. Clyde made me see that."

"Are ye in pain?"

"I was, but Lorna and Clyde treated me well, and I'm healing. Some cuts were deeper than others. Lorna stitched this one on my face. She used delicate stitching, but too much smiling opens it up a bit. I need to frown more."

"Nay, ye dinna. I can frown enough for both of us."

He rubbed his finger on her cheek. "No frowning on that beautiful face."

"How did ye ken to come here to Clyde and Lorna to get help?"

"About five years ago I built a stable and corral and a small shack on the other side of the mountain on Campbell land so I could find wild ponies to tame and train and take them back to Da to sell. Sometimes following the ponies took me on this side of the mountain. About four years ago I saw the smoke from the cottage, so I came to see why the house was so far from the village. Clyde and Lorna fed me and let me spend the night in their shed, and I started coming back as often as I could to help with the work around here. I go with Clyde to cut peat from the bog for heat, and do other odd jobs. Sometimes I'd be here for a couple of days, sometimes more, but I have to be on the lookout for any MacDonalds who might come this way. I almost got caught a couple of times." His first grin of the day lit up his face. "A yellow flag means 'tis safe for me to come."

"Will ye live here now?"

He walked away from her again and turned his back. "I canna. Clyde doesna have enough to feed me. Besides, I need to start a life on my own. I thought I could live in the shack I built near the corrals, but I went last week and 'tis all torn down and burned."

She put her hand on his shoulder. "Yer da did that?"

Rory stared off in the distance. "He said I couldna be part of the horse business anymore, and he destroyed any chance I could do it on my own."

"I am so sorry this all started with me. What will ye do? How can I help?"

He faced her and put his arm around her shoulders. "I made my choice to trick ye into coming to the games at the fair so I could kiss ye, kenning yer brother forbid it. The choices were mine, and so now are the penalties." He touched the wound on his cheek. "Now I have no one to answer to. I can do what I want, when I want, and I have to do it right."

She said, "No' having to answer to anyone isna the same as no' having a family, no' having a clan. Everyone has to belong somewhere."

"Another thing I've been thinking about is where I want to be, what and who I want to have in my life."

She cocked her head in puzzlement.

"I've had plenty of time to think since I came here,

and Clyde has been a good teacher. I've needed a teacher to help me figure things out for myself, to find out what I really wanted.

"I see now that all my life I've been looking for the next adventure, trying to see what was beyond the next ridge, but now I've had time to think, and the one thing I want the most, and I ken it sounds foolish for a man like me, but I just want to be where ye are. We talked about so many things at the fair, things I wanted, things ye wanted, and everything felt right when I was with ye. Ye're like my firm ground to stand on. That's what I want, if ye'll have me."

"Rory," she whispered.

"Lorna and Clyde said ye'd come. They put up flags so people from the village would come, and they thought one day it might be ye. I prayed it would be ye."

"I only came to bring a quilt the Cameron sisters made for Lorna. I didna even ken about the flags until today, at least I ne'er paid any attention to them. I've passed the house whenever I left the glen, but I ne'er asked why someone lived out here alone. I am so sorry 'tis my fault."

"Joneta, ye canna blame yerself. I kenned what I was doing when I asked Morag and Fenella to bring ye to the fair. I wanted everything that happened to happen, except when yer brother showed up and later when my da did."

His eyes wandered and lingered in a sad place far away until Joneta asked with a bit of a smile, "Where is the happy-go-lucky rogue I met at the fair? The one whose words came out as smooth as honey on a spoon?"

That easy grin of his came back, setting crinkles around his eyes and delightful half-moon circles around his mouth. "He's still here, waiting for ye."

"Dinna think me too brazen, but do ye want to ken a secret?" she asked. "I ne'er told anyone. I didna dare."

He nodded his head.

"I remembered everything about ye from the fair, how ye looked, how ye laughed, but sometimes remembering all those sassy things ye said made me giggle at the wrong times, and I'd have to make up some tale about what I thought was so funny. Things are rarely funny in Glencoe, so people began to think I'd lost my mind."

She brushed the hair falling on his forehead out of his eyes with her fingers. When it fell back, she smoothed it away again and held it against the side of his head. "God did good work with ye, Rory Campbell."

He spoke softly. "Ye scolded me, calling me 'sassy,' so I worried mayhap I was a fool, and ye didna want me."

"Ye were ne'er a fool, Rory Campbell."

In a slow, easy motion, he encircled her waist with his arms. "I ne'er fell in love afore."

Her eyes opened wide. "Love?"

"It canna be anything else. Ye draw me in. Morag told ye I jump in without looking to how deep it is, and that first day at yer stall, that's what I did. I didna ken what I was getting into then, but every day afterward I realized exactly what I was doing and why. Ye're what I've been looking for. Ye make me feel things, and I canna explain the way of it. There's no reasoning to it, but I promise ye from now on my kisses will be only for ye, for as long as ye'll have me."

He lowered his lips to meet hers. At first touch, she didn't move, but she soon parted her lips and invited him in. As he tugged her closer, her breasts quivered against his chest and she stretched up on her toes. A soft, gentle moan left her throat.

He lifted his head to see her face before leaning in to kiss her again, but she straightened up before his lips could touch hers, shaking her head and blinking away sudden tears as she moved out of his embrace. "The truth is I've been looking for something, someone, like ye, too. 'Tis like I've lived my life in the shadows, but ye brought sunshine to me, and just thinking about ye, I see the sun like the first day of spring every day, full of possibilities.

"But there's one thing we can ne'er change, no matter how much we want to. I am a MacDonald, and ye a Campbell. My father and brothers would kill ye, and mayhap me as well, rather than see ye with me, and yer da beat ye raw because of me. I canna risk that. I couldna bear harm to come to ye."

Suddenly his unsinkable spirit burst out like a flash of lightning. He talked faster, and he jumped around like a boy who had just caught his first fish. "But I have it all figured out. We can meet here with Clyde and Lorna. Clyde will fly a yellow flag when I am here so ye can come. And if ye canna come, I will understand and come another time. No harm can come to love, no' to the love I have for ye. I promise ye!"

"But where will ye be? Where will ye live? There is no place in the Highlands safe from yer father or any of yer clan. And no place safe from my brother."

"Mo chridhe, my heart, I ken 'tis no' safe without the protection of a clan, and I dinna think ye will like to hear this, but 'twas my only choice."

She straightened up. "Tell me."

Taking her hand and stroking the back of it, he said, "There's no work in the Highlands, no' for me, and the winter will be hard. Clyde canna feed me, so I joined the army, and I'll live at the newly built Fort William. I rode to the fort and enlisted. They were glad to get a horse trainer. Lots of new and unbroken mounts, and untrained riders, so now I have work, food, and a bed."

Joneta stared at him with narrowed eyes. "Ye'll be a king's man? Why? Couldna ye find any other work, no other work?"

"I enlisted in the king's army, but only for one year. A year from now I can go anywhere I want. I have the captain's word. 'Tis a busy time for horse training at Fort William with the fort being so new. They need trained animals and riders, and I'm the best trainer around, and the colonel who is there to get the fort ready before he turns it over to Captain Campbell gives me extra pay and rank, so I'll stay. Sometimes I'll go on my own to scout for more mounts, wild ones, or sometimes to buy them from other lairds, so then I can come here. The fort is only sixteen miles away, so I had Clyde send the yellow flag up yesterday. I have to get back to the fort by tomorrow morn."

"I'm afeared for ye. Soldiering may no' be what ye expect it to be. Ye'd be doing what others tell ye to do whether ye like it or no'."

"They feed me and give me a place to sleep, and I've proven what I can do with the horses. I'll stay out of trouble. If the other lads be fighting, I'll walk away, no drinking or laying with the camp women. My hair is almost at the ten inches I have to have for the queue. All the soldiers have to wear one so they at least brush their hair once in a while. The captain is a Campbell, and he was glad to get someone to work with the horses. He doesna care what my da has to say. He just needs a good horse man. And 'tis only for a year."

Joneta tugged on his sleeve. "Ye'll look fine in yer uniform even if it will be the king's red, but I am worried it will no' be as easy as that. Ye could be trapped in the fort and ordered to march into battle. I dinna like that thought."

"Naught will happen. I promise ye!" He added with another boyish grin, "With my pay, 'tis two shillings a day, when I've saved enough I can build ye a fine house. I dinna ken how or when, but ye will have yer fine stone house. There is much to figure out, but we'll be close enough to see each other. Ye will come to see me?"

She nodded. "I'll find a way to come whenever Clyde flies the yellow flag."

"The captain lets me get away from the fort nearly as often as I want." Raising his eyebrows in a questioning slant, he said, "Mayhap in time we can wed. Do ye think mayhap?"

"Ye've been doing a lot of thinking and planning afore ye asked me what I wanted."

His brow crinkled. "Do ye think ye might someday want to wed me? If I turn out to be the man for ye? I'll do my best to be that man."

"I've already thought once or twice about ye being that man, but my Da has pledged me to Zebulon Keene and is set on me marrying him. So is Zeb. They both give me no peace, always asking me when I'll be ready. So naught is certain. Da promised I could choose my husband, but he might change his mind, and then I'd have no choice."

The wind blew his long hair around his face, catching it on the edges of the bandage on his cheek. "Anything worth having is ne'er easy."

"How can ye be so certain all will be well?"

"Because naught can stop me. It ne'er has, especially now that I ken ye care."

He kissed her cheek just as Clyde came around the corner and motioned for them to come inside for a slice of cake with barley tea.

Chapter Eight

Six months later, March 21, 1691

"I'll walk with ye today to Clyde and Lorna's," said Zeb. "I canna stay long to visit, but I can see ye there, and I'll come for ye afore sunset. Let me wash my hands first. I've been chasing after coos this morning. I saw the yellow flag, so they must be ready for some company."

Joneta had kept the secret for nearly six months that the yellow flag signaled Rory was at Clyde and Lorna's house. She'd gone every time she could, and the joy at seeing his face soon turned, slowly but surely, into love—deep, unshakable love.

When the flag fluttered along the horizon, she could hardly control her excitement, and she didn't want anything to spoil their precious time together, especially not Zeb, who still fancied they would wed.

"Ye dinna need to leave yer chores to come with me," said Joneta. "I'll be carrying some of Mum's dried fish and asparagus to them. 'Tis no' much, and I've been walking there in good weather, so I ken the way. Besides, I enjoy the peace and quiet."

"No need to be alone if I can come with ye." Zeb smiled his easy grin and squinted his blue eyes against the sun. "I would like a short visit with Clyde. Me da fashioned a tool for carving to give to him." He dried his hands with the length of his shirt. "I'm ready."

Ever since childhood, she and Zeb had spent their time together with easy talk, mostly about the coos or whether it would rain enough for the oats or how his chickens weren't laying like they used to and how he might have to eat some of the older birds. Today he talked about the house he would build for the two of them, and it troubled Joneta.

"I have the spot all picked out," said Zeb. "'Tis near a clump of trees so there'll be some shade from the sun and shelter from the wind. I'm carving ye a fancy wooden door, maybe no' as fancy as the ones at the king's house, but verra fancy for Glencoe. No one will have a door like it. 'Twill be special, just for ye. Then I'll build the house around it. Do ye think ye'd like a special door?"

"Aye, Zeb, I'd like a special door. But building a house will take ye away from yer other work. I dinna think ye should start one now, not with the summer chores coming on."

"Dinna ye mind about that. 'Twill be ready when ye are. Ye are the only woman I want, and I'll wait until ye want me. Ye'll see what a fine husband I will be and what a fine house ye will live in."

He reached over to take her hand, but as soon as his fingers touched hers, she shifted the basket to that arm, and he dropped his hand back to his side. A wounded look crossed his face, but he took in a slow breath and said, "I ken ye dinna love me, no' yet, but ye will, I ken ye will someday."

"Zeb," she began, but he interrupted her. "We're almost there. I can see Lorna in the window."

Lorna sat on a stool at the front window watching for Joneta. She sat there each day Clyde flew the yellow flag, watching and hoping, until past noon, knowing once the sun was high in the sky, Joneta would not be coming. Then she'd feed Rory a tasty meal and send him back to the fort to wait for another day. Today, engrossed in her stitching, she didn't see Joneta until she and Zeb were over the last rise, nearly to the house.

Hobbling out the door as fast as her stiff legs could move, she rounded the corner of the house only to see Rory in his loose white shirt, knee high black breeches, and the high red plaid socks of his uniform coming toward her carrying a sack of dried peat from the shed.

"He's with her!" Lorna cried out. "Go!"

Rory glanced around Lorna, and seeing his love and his enemy together, dropped the sack, and took off to hide in the shed at the back of the house.

Clyde knew what was wrong as soon as Rory dashed past him behind the house. Clyde moved quickly around the corner and started to pick up the sack of peat, but found it too heavy, dropping it, causing chunks of dried peat to scatter at his feet.

"Here, let me help," said Zeb, seeing the problem and running toward Clyde with Joneta close on his heels. She tugged on his shirt and called to him, "Wait, Zeb, wait for me." But he didn't slow his pace. When he reached Clyde, he stuffed the peat back in the sack and carried it to the front door.

"Good day, Mistress," he said to Lorna. "Where would ye like me to put this for ye?"

In a breathless voice, Lorna said, "Inside in the box beside the fireplace. I thank ye, Zebulon."

Rory's red uniform jacket swayed on a hook on the wall.

Joneta stepped around Zeb, hoping to block his view

of the jacket, before handing Lorna the dried fish and asparagus.

"Why, thank ye, dearie. Zebulon, would ye like some barley water afore ye head back to the villages? 'Tis fine of ye to walk Joneta here, but I'm certain ye have much to do this day."

"A mug to quench my thirst would be fine, Mistress," said Zeb. "Have the soldiers from Fort William been patrolling this end of the valley?"

The mug for Zeb slipped out of Lorna's hand, but Clyde caught it before it hit the floor and handed it to him. "I havena seen any soldiers today," he said. "They come near, but none stop here. I've waved to a few as they pass by, but they dinna wave back. Rude bunch."

"So far the king's men have left us be. Let's keep it that way," said Zeb. "Clyde, I brought ye a gift from me da, a carving tool so ye can keep making yer carved pictures." Along the walls hung several carved wooden scenes of Glencoe and one of Lorna as a young woman.

Clyde smiled. "It will get a lot of use. Thank yer da for me. Would yer da like me to work on something special for him?"

"Nay. 'Tis just his gift to ye. I'll be heading for the ridges to help with the cattle," continued Zeb, "but I'll be back later in the afternoon to walk ye home, Joneta. Have a good visit."

Joneta, Clyde, and Lorna stepped into the yard and watched Zeb until he was out of sight. They took a collective sigh of relief.

"I am so sorry," said Lorna, her lip quivering. "I let ye get too close afore I saw Zeb was with ye."

"Do ye think he noticed the jacket?" asked Joneta. "When we go home, I'll talk to him, and hope he doesna mention seeing a soldier to Da or John. They dinna ken Rory is a soldier, but I canna have anyone asking too many questions. They already wonder why I come to visit ye so often."

Lorna tugged the thistle quilt off the chair and handed it to Joneta, saying, "Take this and spend time with Rory behind the shed. No one will see ye there, and we promise we willna come around back unless trouble comes our way."

Joneta raced around the house and opened the shed door to find Rory pacing inside. She ran into his arms, and he lifted her off the ground, twirling her around. "I came as soon as I could get away. Zeb insisted he come with me, and Lorna didna see him in time. I hope we convinced him soldiers were no' about, that he made a mistake. I missed ye so much."

Setting her on her feet, he ran his fingers along her cheek and into her hair before kissing her firmly on the lips. Their lips knew each other now and understood just how to caress and deepen each touch. A simple kiss that meant everything.

Hand in hand, they went out the back door of the shed where Rory spread out the quilt on the grass and tugged her down beside him. "Ye being with me makes all the other days of waiting worth it." He kissed her again. "Ye taste like sunshine must taste."

Her tongue tingled as she licked his lips. "Ye taste like sweetness today."

"Lorna opened a jar of preserved sweet raspberries this morning. I had to taste the batch several times to make sure it wasna poison, and praise the Lord, it wasna. I'm certain she has some left."

"Nay, I'd rather lick it off ye." She rolled over on

top of him, her breasts pressing against his chest, warming his body and heating up one specific place he had to fight to keep under control whenever she was near.

She whispered in his ear, "When I saw the yellow flag this morning, I got so excited, I could barely eat my porridge. Da and my brothers took some coos to Fort William to sell yesterday and will be gone a few days more."

"Then 'tis a good thing they're at the fort and I am no'. Has yer da been suspicious of yer visits here?"

"He kens I made a friendship with Lorna, and he's glad because it means he doesna have to take the time to check on them as often. My only trouble is finding an excuse no' to have Zeb come with me."

"Zebulon Keene," muttered Rory. "Do ye think Zeb has any idea ye come to see me? Is he still wanting ye to wed soon?"

"He is carving a door for the house he will build for me, but Da has promised the choice of a husband will be mine. Still, he thinks my excuses are feeble. He also talked to three other lairds about eligible men for me. So far, no one has come forward, because I have no dowry."

He kissed her and the sweet sensations lingered long after he said, "A kiss will be yer dowry for me. We only have to wait until next autumn when I can leave the army. 'Tis no' as long as it sounds, especially when we can be together, even if 'tis in secret. I've been saving my pay, letting Clyde hold it for me."

He put his hands on either side of her face and lifted her head to kiss her again. "Being close to ye makes me feel that at last I belong in the world. Ye fill in all the empty spots of my life." She sucked in her breath at the feel of his lips and eagerly responded with caresses of her own.

Between kisses, she murmured, "I love ye. I ne'er looked for love. I ne'er thought I'd ever find it. After the fair, I thought I'd live the rest of my life without ye, but now I ken my soul would collapse if I couldna be here."

Shaking his fist in the air, he shouted, "I choose ye, and it matters no' what tries to keep us apart. I will fight the devil himself to stay with ye, even the bloody MacDonalds if I have to!"

He watched her face to see if he'd gone too far, said too much against her clan, but he grinned when she raised her fist and bumped it into his. "I will fight them, too, and ye can throw in the bloody Campbells." Her voice softened. "'Tis us together. We'll find a way to make it so. Like the stars in the sky, even when we're separated, we're together."

They lay back on the quilt and rested in each other's arms until Joneta gently tugged up his shirt, and reaching under it, ran her palm over his chest. Her hand moved to his back and a low moan of satisfaction oozed out his lips as she rubbed her fingers over the faded scars. She pulled his shirt farther out of his breeches, and he leaned into her, splaying his hand across her back over her clothing, moving it slowly down to her bottom, and pressing her into him. She kissed him on the neck.

"Make me yers," she murmured.

With a jerk, he scooted away. "I love ye more than I can say, and to have ye touch me like this pleases me so verra much, but I will no' dishonor ye by making ye fully mine afore we are wed."

Joneta's face fell. "My brothers say 'tis harder for a man to wait, but for me, my body aches for yer touch so much. Sometimes I canna think for wanting ye so. 'Tis shameless of me, I ken, but there is no shame about anything when I am with ye."

"'Tis my shame I bring ye to this. Ye are worth more than a secret love. I want us to be together forever."

He stood and walked away from her as he willed his body to ease the urgency to be with her in every sense. He released long deep breaths until he faced her again, saying, "I ken ye want a house of yer own, and I want to build it, a house better than any Zeb could build. We should plan exactly how we want it to be. It should start small, mayhap only two rooms. A large room with space for two soft chairs for sitting, mayhap even one big chair so we can sit together, with a fireplace for cooking, and a table for eating." He took a stick and etched his idea in the dirt. "Then the next room will be just large enough for a bed, but I'll be able to add on when we have bairns."

"Bairns?" She paused thoughtfully. "I want bairns with yer dark looks, but no' with yer talent for getting into mischief. I want bairns with yer smile, but no' yer sassy talk."

He grimaced. "Ye dinna love me mischief? Or me sassy talk?"

"I can laugh at yer mischief, but others dinna laugh so much, and I hate to see ye in trouble. So where is this house ye are building?"

"I have an idea, but I want to see if ye agree."

Her eyes lit up. "Where?"

"I went to Glasgow a couple of times with Da, and 'tis a fine city and large enough for us to get lost in, at least lost from kin who could do us harm. I could build a house and start a horse trading business." Excitement raced through his voice as he spoke faster. "People in the city need horses for their buggies and wagons and some will need a place to board their animals. They have races every year and will want their beasts to be properly trained to win. 'Twill be a big change from the country life here, but I could find a lot of work. Do ye think it will be right for us?"

Joneta stood and paced around the quilt, her eyebrows furrowed, and her thoughts weighed her down. After six times around, she knelt and said, "No one can ken where we go. If anyone finds out, my family will kill ye. Please, Rory, tell me we can be safe in Glasgow."

He pulled her into his embrace. "I'll make it so."

"Will the army let ye leave? Ye canna desert. They will hunt ye down and hang ye."

"Captain Campbell gave me his word I could leave when the fort had enough trained horses at the end of my year enlistment. Now that 'tis peaceful in Scotland, it may be sooner. I'll train yet another man so there will be three to do what I do with the horses. Then they'll have no need of me, and I could leave sooner. But before then there's one way we can ne'er be parted, no' in this life or the next." He took her hand in his and knelt on one knee. "Will ye marry me? Will ye be mine to protect and care for?"

She gazed into his handsome face, amazed by how much love she saw in the softness of his eyes. The love she felt was deeper and richer than any she had even imagined. "Our clans will ne'er be happy about it, but it has been over a year since there have been any bad doings between MacDonalds and Campbells. Mayhap the feud will be forgotten."

"Ye didna answer me. Will ye marry me and make me yer husband?"

As she rubbed her hand over his neatly trimmed black beard, she said, "Ye silly man, how could ye no' ken the answer? Aye, I will marry ye." She bent down to him and their kiss lingered, growing deeper each passing moment. Her knees trembled.

Finally, Rory broke the spell. "I already talked to Lorna and Clyde, and they're willing to help us."

She bit her lip and pressed her hands against his chest. "When? I have dreamed of being wed to ye for so long. Every time we're together, I have to force myself to walk away without loving ye completely the way I want. 'Tis wicked how many nights I dreamed of ye touching me and kissing me in all the places that make me a woman." That urgency rose up in her again.

"'Tis no' wicked or shameful. Dinna ye ever think as much."

"It makes for restless nights," said Joneta.

"For me, too, but ye are worth the wait."

"What I feel, what I want, is real, and 'tis only for ye. I want more than to be with ye, I want to build a life so we can work together, live together, and I dinna care where or how that might be."

"Joneta, I, too, want to make a life with ye as a man does with his woman, his wife." His breath quickened. "Sometimes I think I'll break into pieces with all the thoughts and feelings jumping around inside me." He stepped closer, and she felt his body craving her. "But each of those pieces, even if scattered across the winds, each piece will be for only ye. I promise myself to ye alone for as long as there is life in me."

He kissed her and gave a growl from the back of his throat. She dug her fingers into his hair and refused to let him leave her lips. Pressing her hips into his, he gave another soft growl and moved his leg between hers.

He pressed his mouth to hers with even more fervor than he had before. Her lips parted and let his tongue slip inside so he could give her mouth soft caresses. He felt her breath against his cheek as he splayed his fingers over her back and slid them down to her hips. She leaned into him. Time stood still. There was only him and only her, and he wanted it to stay that way forever.

He bent his knees and carried her down with him until they lay on the quilt together.

She whispered, "Make the wedding day soon. I'm begging ye."

He lifted his head, his lips swollen and red. "I will."

Giving her one more kiss, he stood up and said, "Go for a walk with me. I saw some wildflowers for yer hair."

She smiled and nodded.

****

Joneta struggled to keep up with Zeb's long strides on the walk home. "What's the hurry?" said a panting Joneta. "We've got plenty of time before sunset."

Zeb abruptly turned back to face her. "I saw the man run into the back yard, and I saw the red jacket. A king's soldier was there. What was he doing?" Before she could answer, he spit out the words, "Who are ye meeting at Clyde's behind my back?"

She said as calmly as she could despite her sputtering heart, "No one."

"Liar!" He turned and started to stride away.

"Please, Zeb, ye have to listen to me. Please."

He stopped walking and faced her again. "I've been mulling it over all day. Ye go there so often, and ye dinna want me to go with ye, and ye willna marry me even though ye have no other offers. Ye've turned me away so many times, it must be another man. And I saw him today. Well?"

The lie she was about to tell stuck in her throat. How could she lie about the man she loved—the man who loved her—but she had no choice. "'Tis no' another man, no' one I come to see. Please, Zeb, ye canna tell. 'Tis Clyde and Lorna's secret I am sworn to keep, so I canna explain, but 'tis Lorna's kin, and none can ken he comes there. The reasons are long, and I canna tell ye all the truth. 'Twill only bring trouble to those who dinna deserve it. Ye have to believe me. Please, dinna say a word about what ye saw to anyone. 'Twill only hurt Lorna more than she deserves."

He didn't answer.

"Please, Zeb, if ye love me like ye say, ye will no' tell anyone about the man or the jacket. For Clyde and Lorna's sake."

The strong wind blew his hair straight out behind him, and he squinted against the sun. "Aye," he said softly before turning and walking back to the village without saying another word.

Chapter Nine

August 1691

John Dalrymple, Secretary of State for Scotland, grimaced at the man he had summoned to his office, the sloppy, overweight captain named Robert Campbell of Glenlyon and now the captain at King William's newly rebuilt Fort William in the Highlands. It completely escaped Dalrymple how this drunken, chronic gambler ever rose to the rank of captain, and then was placed in charge of a fort, but here he was.

"May I sit?" asked the captain, slurring his words. His eyes watered. He belched.

Dalrymple looked down his aristocratic nose upon everyone, but especially on this poor excuse for a man, and scowled. He had no sympathy for a man with a hangover. "Nay," he said, "ye may tell me what ye ken of this meeting of the Highland lairds at Achallader Castle two months ago in June."

The captain belched again and tried to cover the sound with his fist to his mouth. "I only have secondhand knowledge from my kin, John Campbell of Breadalbane, who is on the Privy Council, ye ken. He ordered the lairds to a meeting at King William's demand to get the clans to submit to a loyalty oath."

Dalrymple sniffed and nodded his head. "Of course, I ken that. Get on with it."

"He invited all the clans to send representatives to Achallader Castle to convince them to support King William over the now deposed King James who's hiding in France."

"Get to the point and quickly," he said through gritted teeth.

"Ye ken many of the clans support the return of the Catholic James to the throne, but Protestant King William needs the Highlands if he's e'er to bring Scotland and England together as a united country."

Dalrymple pounded his hand on the desk, making the brass handles on the drawers rattle. "I ken the reasons for the meeting, ye fool! 'Twas my idea! Tell me the result!"

Swallowing hard, Robert Campbell, sweat bursting on his forehead, said, "As was told to me, there was discussion about King William's order for all the clans to sign a loyalty oath. Some were willing to sign, but then they would go on as they pleased because they said the oath was a mere piece of paper. They'd sign to keep the king out of their business. Others refused to sign, saying an oath should be taken in truth, and since their loyalty had been to King James, it should stay with James. Eventually, my kin, Breadalbane, came up with a compromise."

The captain wobbled on his legs and started looking for a chair. Spying one in the corner, he stumbled his way over to it and flopped down hard on the leather seat. As he did, he farted loudly. The noise and the odor were foul.

"Are ye all right, Captain?" asked Dalrymple. *If Campbell throws up on the carpet, I'll rub the man's nose in it.*

71

"A bit under the weather. Do ye have some strong drink that might settle my stomach?"

"Nay," said Dalrymple, curling his lip in disgust. "What was this compromise?"

Wiping an already soggy handkerchief across his forehead, Captain Campbell said, "Breadalbane would draft a secret letter to the exiled King James in France asking permission for the clans to sign King William's oath. If James gathered funds and troops enough to return to Scotland afore the deadline of December 31 of this year and reclaim the throne, no harm done, and the clans would continue to support him, but if he couldna get France's backing and return to Scotland, signing William's oath would prevent reprisals against the clans." Campbell put his hand to the side of his mouth and said quietly as if to keep anyone else from hearing it, "He also offered a signing bonus in coin, which I ken was no' enough for all the lairds, and even if it were, 'twould ne'er be paid."

Dalrymple leaned back in his chair, steepled his fingers, and tapped his chin. "Good, we shouldna be paying these Highland savages to do what they should do in the first place. Now who gave the most opposition to signing the loyalty oath? Who should we watch for signs of rebellion? We need someone to take the blame if this signing business falls through. How did the Laird MacDonald take it?"

"Most of the chiefs grumbled, but the most vocal against signing was Alasdair MacDonald, called MacIain, of Glencoe. He heads a small clan near the west coast with nothing to distinguish it except a reputation for cattle theft."

"I ken it. 'Tis the reason I asked."

"And even with the bounty Breadalbane offered for signing, 'twas no' enough to pay what MacDonald owes the king in taxes. He agreed to sign only if James gave his approval. Several others mean to do the same." Campbell wiped his sweating brow with the sleeve of his jacket.

Dalrymple stood and walked over to the window, pulling the curtain back. The sunny weather of late August did little to raise his mood. "The clans are naught but barbarians and must be brought to heel. 'Tis well kenned that Highlanders are no' more than animals in plaids. King William ordered the signing of a loyalty oath for the sake of a modern united Britain, but it could also be a way to get rid of the worst of them. Keep me informed on this matter, and especially the actions of MacIain of Glencoe. If the deadline for signing by the end of this year is missed, there will be reprisals for all disloyal clans. Deadly reprisals. You are dismissed."

Captain Campbell wobbled to his feet and lurched toward the door. He went out, leaving the door open to swing in the wind.

Dalrymple sat back at his desk to draft a letter telling King William about these circumstances. He pondered his words carefully. Crafting a plan to sacrifice an insignificant clan like the MacDonalds, one the king already knew was rebellious, would go a long way in proving his own loyalty and advancing his standing in King William's good graces.

He urged the king to stand firm in requiring the Highland clans to sign an oath and to enforce the edict with the strictest of punishments. He wrote the only way to establish law and order in Scotland was to make an example of any disobedient clans by calling for "an exemplary punitive expedition," and the time of year to do such a thing must be carefully chosen. "The wintertime is the only season in which we are sure the Highlanders cannot escape and carry their wives, bairns, and cattle to the hills. This is the proper time to maul them in the long dark nights.

"I urge ye that we focus our attention on the Clan MacDonald of Glencoe as to their signing of the oath, as it would be an act of great charity to be exact in routing out that damnable sept, the worst in all the Highlands."

He closed the letter with his own wax seal and couldn't suppress his smile as he handed it to his aide to be posted. After the king's certain approval, he would be on his way up in the world at the same time the MacDonalds would be on their way down.

Chapter Ten

Early in the summer of 1691

Three days after Zeb had seen Rory's jacket, Joneta returned from the river with a bucket of fresh water and saw Zebulon Keene talking with her brother, John, just outside their stable. She couldn't hear what they were saying, but suddenly John stormed toward her and grabbed her arm. She dropped the bucket.

"What have ye done?" he shouted. "Zeb says he'll no longer pledge for yer hand! Ye have ruined yer best, and mayhap only, chance to wed! What have ye done?"

She sputtered, "What did he say?" If Zeb exposed Rory's visits to Clyde and Lorna's, and he suffered at the hands of her brother, she'd never forgive herself or him. *Please, Lord, protect Rory from my brother's wrath.*

"He said he canna wait for ye any longer and will marry another. He'll ask for Eileen MacDonald, daughter of Seebon. Ye foolish lass, what have ye done?"

"Did he say anything else?"

"What else is there to say? How long did ye expect him to wait for a selfish lass like ye? I'm surprised he waited this long! Now ye will be a burden to me for the rest of yer life. Da was wrong to let ye choose yer husband, and now Mum will ne'er see ye wear the wedding dress she made for ye. Ye foolish, senseless lass." He shook her arm, and she stumbled back. He stormed off.

Leaving the bucket and what was left of the water beside the door of the house, she ran toward Zeb's cottage. He stood next to a pile of ashes with chunks of wood still burning on top. "'Tis yer door," he said. "I'll ne'er make another carved door."

"I am so sorry, Zeb. I didna mean to hurt ye so much. Did ye say anything else, anything about…"

He gave her a fierce look. "I didna mention yer secret, if that's what ye mean. I told ye I wouldna, but do ye think me a fool? I ken 'tis yer secret, no' Clyde and Lorna's. I ken ye have found another man."

"Please, Zeb."

"I'll no' be yer fool any longer. Marry me by the end of summer or I will find another."

She hung her head. "I canna, Zeb. Please forgive me."

He stirred the hot ashes and the flame burst up, consuming the rest of the fancy, carved door.

****

Zeb kept his word to stay silent about seeing a man at Clyde and Lorna's, but he did not come to visit her. Even though he didn't marry Eileen as he told John he would, Joneta had lost a friend. This pained her, but the fear he might spill her secret pained her even more.

Through the rest of the summer of 1691, Rory and Joneta met as often as they could. Rory had much work to do at the fort and Joneta had her own share at Glencoe, and the yellow flag only flew once or twice a month. So they started a new tradition. Any time they could not be together, they would each leave a letter for the other.

Rory left his letters tucked inside Clyde's books. A

different book every time, and part of the fun for Joneta was searching for it. She found today's letter in a red-bound book written about the ancient world. Rory wrote with broad strokes and often smeared the ink because he was left-handed, one more thing his father disapproved of.

Joneta, Mo chridhe,

Ye come to me every morning as soon as I open my eyes. Ye fill my thoughts all day until I close my eyes, and then my dreams are of ye. Even when ye are not with me, I ken we are working together toward a better life. Not a minute goes by that I dinna miss ye, kenning that when we are together again, it will be all the sweeter.

Rory

Joneta slipped her letters to Rory in and among Lorna's pans, jars, and bowls on the shelves. Her handwriting was small and the words tightly packed together, often two letters on one page.

Rory, My Love,

I never kenned what love meant until I met you. But its power is greater than anything I could ever imagine. I am waiting for the day when we can walk hand-in-hand, with naught to keep us apart, and build our lives as one. I love you in ways that words canna say. Only my heart kens the truth.

Yer love, Joneta.

Joneta read Rory's letters over and over until she memorized them. At home in her bed, she repeated the words softly, and they lulled her to sleep.

Lorna, knowing neither of them could carry the letters with them, saved each one in colorfully painted boxes she stored on a shelf beside her chair. Clyde made the boxes out of scraps of wood and Lorna painted them,

Joneta's with yellow flowers and birds and Rory's in blue stripes.

On days when they were together, they read the letters aloud to each other. "I want to hear yer voice say the words," said Joneta. "That way I remember them better, and I ne'er want to forget even one of them." He often read them aloud in funny voices, sometimes high and squeaky, other times deep and scary. Her laughter only encouraged him to come up with new accents.

One day in July, Joneta sat alone with Lorna as she finished reading Rory's most recent letter. "I canna say the words as lovely as he can."

"Yer words come from yer heart, and he cherishes every one of them," said Lorna. "I see it on his face as he reads them."

Joneta dropped Rory's latest letter into her lap. "The lairds of the Highlands were called to Achallander Castle to talk about signing a loyalty oath to King William. Da is no' in favor but says he will wait until our deposed King James in France releases us from our allegiance to him. He doesna want his loyalties divided."

"When must he sign this oath to King William?" asked Clyde.

"All the clans have until December 31 this year."

Chapter Eleven

The autumn 1691

Rory took over more chores for Lorna and Clyde. The older couple did what they could, working diligently at less strenuous tasks, but Rory did the lion's share of the heavy work. He dug out and stacked peat for the winter and washed the wooden floor inside the house. He repacked the daubing between the stones of the walls to keep out the coming winter winds, prepared the vegetable garden for winter, and brought in enough food from the fort for Clyde's aging horse.

On the days when Joneta ran into his arms, they did these chores together and many more. Although they were worn out by the end of the day, these were the best days either of them could imagine. They were together. Rory walked her home as far as he dared and gave her kisses to last until the next time.

During the third week of October of 1691, a heavy rain kept them inside doing small household tasks, such as sharpening knives and tools, and mending torn sleeves and hems on their clothing. As midday approached, Joneta and Rory sat around the table with Lorna and Clyde, enjoying a simple meal of fried bread and eggs.

"I canna believe we have three whole days together," said Joneta. "'Twas like Heaven when Rory said he could get a three-day leave, and 'twas Heaven again when Mum agreed to take over my jobs at home so I could come here to help Lorna get her house ready for the winter."

"We are as glad as ye," said Lorna. "We can dip candles this afternoon, and with the peat and kindling stacked in the shed and the chicken butchering done, we will have a delightful winter."

"And we've had a delightful two days here with one more to go," said Rory, taking Joneta's hand and gently flicking her fingers with his. He handed her the silver whistle, saying, "She's getting better at playing on it every day. Today she learned to blow a tune. Want to hear it?"

"We heard ye practicing," said Lorna. She began to hum the tune Rory had taught Joneta, asking, "Does it go like this?"

Joneta put the whistle to her lips and joined Lorna's singing.

"It has words, ye ken," said Rory. "Mum used to sing it to me. 'Tis a tale about a man named Tam Lin who is captured by the Queen of the Fairies when he falls off his horse, but then he's rescued by the lovely Joneta."

"Was her name truly Joneta?" said Joneta.

"Nay, but it should have been. 'Twas Janet. She's beautiful and brave and she saves her love from a terrible fate. Just like ye and me."

"And what fate did I save ye from?"

"The fate of being alone." He grinned. "Keep playing. There's a dance that goes with it, too."

"It has some naughty bits in the story, as I recall," said Clyde. "Seems this Tam Lin had a knack for getting all the maidens, shall we say, with child."

"Oh, dear," said Lorna.

"That made the Fairy Queen angry, but the lovely Janet rescued him despite her unexpected condition. Still, 'tis lovely music. Rory, ye call the horses with it, while Joneta calls the angels."

The music ended as Rory said, "The rain is keeping us indoors today so we can talk about our plans to be off to Glasgow and our life together."

"Aye, but ye canna simply go around the Highlands asking for someone to marry ye," said Clyde. "Too much danger yer families would find out, and traveling to Glasgow without the benefit of marriage is also risky. If ye were discovered, Joneta could be sent back to Glencoe or mayhap to a nunnery, and ye, Rory, who kens what might happen to ye. It could be flogging or prison, mayhap both."

"When can ye leave the army officially?" asked Lorna. "A charge of desertion would be even more disastrous. Ye would be branded or hanged or both."

"Captain Campbell," said Rory, "assured me when I signed up I could end my enlistment anytime I wanted after a year, and it has been over that now. He has more than enough trained horses and three men skilled enough to work with them. I'm just staying on until we are wed so I can save more money before we leave for Glasgow."

"Will he keep his word?"

"He's been generous with me so far. He may be too often in the whisky, but I trust him. Joneta wants to be wed Catholic, and so we have to find a priest to marry us in secret. We need a man who will ne'er reveal our names. In other words, a priest who is willing to break a commandment and lie, a priest willing to compromise his soul for us."

A knock at the door startled all of them. Rory and

Clyde stood up while Lorna and Joneta took each other's hands. Could it be a MacDonald come for Joneta? Or a soldier from the fort looking for Rory?

Rory moved in front of Lorna and Joneta, shielding them, ready for anything, as Clyde very slowly opened the door. A man stood just outside drenched to the skin. "May I come in and get out of the rain for a bit?" asked the man, his dull-colored green-and-black plaid pulled tight over his head and around his neck. He held up his water-logged cowhide slippers. "My shoes and feet are soaked through. I didna want to get trench foot from water lingering in my shoes, but my bare feet are freezing. I would be grateful for a chance to dry out."

Swinging the door open wide, Clyde said, "We always have room for an outsider in need. In the Highlands we ne'er turn a stranger away as ye may someday be that stranger. We always practice aid in trust. We are reminded of a man who welcomed a stranger into his house only to find out that the man had killed the host's own brother. Still, he aided the man in his escape as is the ancient custom. Ye havena killed my brother, have ye?"

The man laughed. "Nay, I havena."

"Then come in. Stand over here until we can dry ye out, and ye can warm yerself by the fire."

The man stepped inside, laid his soggy shoes on the floor beside the door, and lifted off his rain-soaked plaid, revealing his cassock and his heavy gold crucifix around his neck. "I am most grateful. I am told there is a Catholic clan nearby, one of the few remaining in Scotland, the MacDonalds. King William may have banished our religion, but I havena." He took the towel from Lorna and dried his hair and his feet. "Ye are kind folk, and I am blessed to have found ye in this storm."

"We are the ones who are blessed!" said Rory. "Will ye perform a marriage for us?"

"A marriage?" said the priest, squeezing rain from his plaid onto the mat on the floor before he let Rory drape it over the chair by the fire to dry out.

Rory tugged Joneta into his arms. "We wish to marry, and there is no one to do it. Ye see, Joneta, I told ye all will be well. We found our priest!"

"Have ye been waiting long to wed?" asked the priest.

"Too long! We need to talk."

Before Father Josiah MacHenry could protest, Rory and Clyde led him toward the back of the house while Lorna ushered Joneta into their bedroom.

"While they are sorting out things with the priest," said Lorna, "we must find ye a wedding dress."

"Are ye certain Father Josiah will marry us secretly?" asked Joneta.

Lorna nodded as strands of her stark white hair fell out of the twisted knot at her nape. "A priest who risks his own life to find the remaining Catholics in the Highlands would defy the strict order of things for the two of ye and no' speak of it. Now let me see what I have we might turn into yer wedding dress."

Together Lorna and Joneta hauled a heavy painted chest from the corner of the room and opened it. "This was my wedding chest," said Lorna. "Now let me see what I still have in here." After lifting out several neatly folded blankets and quilts, she found what she was looking for. "Here it is."

She held up a gown with a gold-colored satin bodice covered with delicate lace and embroidery. The skirt was made of the same embroidered material, white with a swash of gold satin draping down the middle.

"'Tis beautiful," said Joneta.

"I wore it when I married Clyde. I stitched every piece. I had to do it at night after I was supposed to be asleep and hide it under my pallet so my Mum wouldna find out. She kenned, but she ne'er said a word. Try it on. Then we can air it out and make alterations if need be."

Joneta slipped the gown over her head, coughing at the musty smell, but the dress fit well. All it needed was some tucking in at the waist and two buttons replaced on the bodice.

"I love it," said Joneta. "I ne'er thought I'd have something so pretty. Ye must have been a beautiful bride." She coughed again.

"In my younger years I was almost as lovely as ye, if I do say so. Now slip it off so we can hang it by a window and let the breeze air it out. We canna have a smelly bride." The lilt in her voice encouraged Joneta that they could indeed marry today and she would wear this lovely dress. "Rory can wear Lloyd's best jacket and trews. I'm certain we'll have to take them in a little as well."

"We're going to be wed!" said Rory, dashing into the bedroom and hugging Joneta. He held her away from him. "That gown is lovely. Is it the one ye will marry me in?"

She nodded.

"I dinna mean to insult ye, but it has a strange odor. I told ye it would all work out for the best. Father MacHenry says he'd be glad to do the ceremony." Rory's grin set his face nearly aglow.

"Now, lad, I didna say I'd be glad," said the priest, standing in the doorway. "I said I'd be willing because I disagree with clan pettiness. Ye may think the fighting is grounded in truth, but I dinna. 'Blessed be the peacemakers, saith the Lord.' I believe that a marriage between conflicting clans could be the beginning of a lasting peace, so I will do my part. Keeping yer names secret is also my part. Ye two will have to do the rest."

"I dinna care why ye do it, only that ye do."

As if on cue, the storm cleared and the sun shone bright, matching the joy inside the stone house.

Lorna and Joneta set the dress aside and readied a meal of cold meat and raspberry jam on thick slices of bread.

Together Joneta, Rory, Clyde, and Lorna talked of their plans for the ceremony. They would exchange vows the next morning, the last day of Rory's leave from the fort, and spend the night together here. The next morning Rory would ride to Fort William to resign his commission. After he returned, the married couple would leave for Glasgow, and all could be done before Joneta was due back at the village. After they had gone, Clyde would fly a green flag for two days and then a yellow one, this code telling the people in Glencoe that all was well, but Joneta would be staying a few more days. Three days of travel would put the couple far enough out of reach of her brothers to be safe.

"What if John and Alex want to harm ye for letting us go?" asked Joneta.

"There are advantages to being old," said Clyde with a confidence that helped ease Joneta's worries. "No one will try to hurt us, and an old face can seem so honest, or then so sorry, if need be. We'll be fine. Dinna fash about us. Ye two let Caraid carry ye as far and fast as he can."

Father MacHenry added, "I will delay anyone who comes after ye. I can pray for forgiveness for two or three lies as well as I can for one."

"I've wanted this for so long," said Joneta, "to be with Rory. I dinna look forward to leaving Glencoe and my family, but staying will bring naught but trouble into everyone's life. I canna imagine a life without Rory in it. I dinna care for the consequences to me, only that the man I love and my two precious friends will be safe. Clyde, if ye canna convince my brothers to leave ye be, tell them the truth. I willna see ye harmed in any way."

"'Twill no' come to that," said Clyde. "I promise ye."

Chapter Twelve

The next morning, October 19, 1691, marked Rory Campbell and Joneta MacDonald's wedding day.

"Ye are so beautiful," said Rory when Joneta emerged from the bedroom dressed in Lorna's wedding dress, which had been brushed with lavender to make it smell sweet.

Rory took her hand. "Will the most beautiful woman I ken, please, marry me?"

"I can think of nothing I'd rather do than be yer wife."

Outside the rain fell in heavy sheets, and the sun couldn't find even a slit in the clouds to peek through, but inside the house, it was a perfect bright day to join two hearts.

Father MacHenry stood in front of the fireplace and said, "Usually the exchanging of the vows is done outside on the church steps." He motioned to the window and the renewed deluge outside. "As the weather will no' permit it, we are gathered together here in the sight of God and His bounty of angels to join together this man, Rory Campbell, and this woman, Joneta MacDonald, in a binding of life. 'Tis an honorable estate, ordained in Paradise, and into which holy estate these two persons present come now to be bound.

"If any man do allege and declare any impediment, why they may no' be coupled together in matrimony, by

God's Law, or the laws of the realm, will be bound to prove his allegation. Then the solemnization must be deferred, until such time as the truth be tried."

Clyde shouted out, "'Tis all well with us, let them marry!"

The priest smiled and rubbed his fingers over his crucifix. "The Lord is pleased." Continuing to read from his small book of liturgies, he said, "Rory, will thou have this woman to be thy wedded wife, to live together after God's ordinance in the holy estate of matrimony? Wilt thou love her, comfort her, honor, and keep her, in sickness and in health, and forsaking all other, keep thee only unto her, so long as ye both shall live?"

"I will! I will for as long as I live!" said Rory, his grin broad.

"Joneta, will thou have this man to be thy wedded husband, to live together after God's ordinance in the holy estate of matrimony? Wilt thou obey him, and serve him, love, honor, and keep him in sickness and in health, and, forsaking all other, keep thee only unto him, so long as ye both shall live?"

Joneta looked at Rory from under her eyelashes, her eyes wet with tears of joy, and said quietly, "I will."

"Who gives this woman to be married to this man?"

Clyde again spoke up. "These two people give each other to be wed. They have their own free will and are certain in their own minds. We have seen the love and caring they have for each other, so 'tis with our blessing they are joined."

"Then so be it." Father MacHenry took Joneta's right hand and placed it in Rory's right hand. "Repeat these vows after me. I, Rory Campbell, take Joneta MacDonald to my wedded wife, to have and to hold from this day forward, for better for worse, for richer, for poorer, for fairer or fouler, in sickness and in health, to love and to cherish, till death us depart, according to God's holy ordinance; and thereunto I plight thee my troth." Rory repeated the words with a strong voice.

The priest then laid Rory's right hand in Joneta's. "Repeat after me. I, Joneta MacDonald, take Rory Campbell to my wedded husband, to have and to hold from this day forward, for better, for worse, for richer or poorer, in sickness and in health, to be bonny and buxom at bed and at board, to love and to cherish, till death us depart, according to God's holy ordinance, and thereunto I plight thee my troth." She repeated her vows in a voice confident and sure of her love.

"Do ye have rings to give one another?" asked Father MacHenry.

"Nay," said Rory. "I have something else." He drew out of his pouch a small brooch, made of silver, featuring two intertwining hearts with a crown joining the two on top. He handed it to Joneta, who turned it over in her hand and rubbed its smooth edges with her finger.

"'Tis so lovely," she said.

"'Tis a Luckenbach brooch. I bought it at the fair, just waiting for a day like this. Joneta, I promise ye are the only woman I will ever love, and the only woman who will wear this brooch for the rest of my life."

Joneta wiped her tears on her sleeve until Lorna handed her a lace handkerchief with blue embroidery along the edge, and Joneta dabbed at her cheeks. "Ye kept the brooch all this time?" she asked.

He nodded. "At first I didna ken why I had to have it, but I saw it and I wanted it. Later, I kenned it was for ye. I will love ye for all my life, and even when we canna be together, this brooch will always be yers, and knowing that will keep me smiling."

Kissing the brooch, she held it out to Rory, who also kissed it. "We are the two hearts tangled together, always to be only one heart. I will wear it always. Put it on me."

As Rory pinned the brooch to her gown, he said, "Two bodies, two minds, but one heart for always and forever."

"I dinna have anything to give ye," she said with a wounded look in her eyes, but after a moment's hesitation, she unclasped the chain around her neck and handed it to Rory. "If ever ye need me, this whistle will bring me."

He clutched the whistle in his palm. "I'll wear it always." He untwisted the hook and eye on the silver chain and put it around his neck, but it was too small to reclasp.

"Wait," said Lorna. "I have another chain, a bigger one." When she returned from the bedroom, she held a narrow copper chain woven in a wheat pattern. "'Twill be my wedding gift to ye." She handed it to Rory, who slipped the whistle on it and then clasped it around his neck. It hung below his collarbone.

"Silver and copper," said Clyde. "Just like the two of ye. Different, but perfect together."

"'Tis a lovely thing ye do for these two," said Father MacHenry to Lorna. "The ceremony is done, and I will put yer names in the church book I carry and 'twill be official, ne'er to be put asunder. I will also write it on a page torn from this same book for ye to carry as proof of yer marriage, since no banns were read, and yer names will be kept secret."

The newlyweds kissed as if they would never stop

until Father MacHenry cleared his throat. The pair stood to one side, but still holding hands.

"We thank ye, Father," said Rory. "Now no one can keep us apart. We will leave tomorrow after I give my resignation from the army in the morning. I can be back here by midafternoon. We canna thank ye enough, Clyde and Lorna. Yer names will be on our hearts for all time."

He embraced Father MacHenry. "Ye have done us the greatest of all boons. I will light a candle at every Catholic church I come to in yer honor."

"Make it in the honor of God, and I will be satisfied."

Clyde put his hand on Rory's shoulder and pointed to the ladder leaning against the back wall leading to the loft. "That room was our first as man and wife, and we are pleased 'twill be yers. Be in each other's arms, and ye will see that the love is stronger than anything ye might face. Tonight is all yers."

"'Tis ready for ye," said Lorna. "Ye'll see. Go on. We will be down here until 'tis time for us to go to bed, and we will no' bother ye."

"Ye will have complete privacy, so take as long as ye want," said Clyde with a wink. "I was once a young man, and I remember our first night well."

Lorna ducked her head, saying, "Clyde, will ye let them be?"

Chapter Thirteen

To Joneta and Rory's delight, Clyde and Lorna had turned the enclosed loft into a cozy room, complete with a plump soft mattress on the bed, a small brazier in the corner already lit and glowing, curtains on the windows, and a thick warm rug on the floor.

Joneta looked up at him with her arms around his waist. "I want our first night to be a symbol of how our life will be, the two of us together safe and warm, but I'm trembling." He nestled her under his arm, and she laid her head on his chest. "I want to stay here forever. If we leave, there is only secrecy and anger waiting for us."

"Aye, we have many struggles to face, but for tonight there is nothing, and no one, but us. Can ye see the rain outside?"

She nodded.

"'Tis on the outside, but in here is exactly where we're meant to be. Ye and me, we are the whole world right now." He combed his fingers through her hair. "Want to hear a story? 'Twill put our troubles out of yer mind," he said with a roguish grin. "'Tis a true one! I swear!"

She laughed. "All right, tell me one of yer true stories."

They lay down on the bed close to each other, and Rory began. "In the beginning of time, God was discussing the creation of the world with the Angel

Gabriel while leaning back against His golden throne."

"Really, just sitting there on his throne?"

"'Tis truly made of solid gold and shines like the noonday sun."

"How do you ken what the throne looks like?"

"I was there, of course," he answered. "Otherwise, how could I swear this tale is true?"

"Now I believe every word."

"Anyway," Rory went on, "leaning back against His golden throne, and, before I was interrupted, our Lord said to Gabriel, 'I have great plans for Scotland. I am going to give Scotland towering mountains and magnificent glens resplendent with purple heather. Red deer will roam the countryside, golden eagles will circle in the skies, salmon will leap in the clear rivers and lochs, and the surrounding seas will teem with fish. Agriculture will flourish, and there will be a glorious coming together of water with barley to be known as whisky.' "

Joneta came up on her elbow to look directly into his face. "I might have kenned a man would think of whisky!"

"Hush," said Rory. "I'm no' done yet. 'The Scots will be intelligent, innovative, industrious and…' " He paused.

"And what?"

"That's when Gabriel interrupted Him. He said, 'Are ye no' being just a wee bit too generous to these Scots? Willna the rest of the world be jealous?' But the Almighty replied, 'No' really. I havena told ye yet who their neighbors are going to be!' "

Giggles overtook Joneta, and her high tinkling laugh caught Rory with her glee, and he giggled, too. "Feel better now? Feel safer now?"

"Aye," she said. "The fire in the brazier is dying out."

"I ken how to keep us warm, my wife." He leaned over and kissed her lips, slowly and tenderly, until she eased her head back, letting the sensations of him touching her wash over her like the sea on the shore. Her body responded, climbing to heights only imagined in her dreams. Her breath quickened, her heart raced, and a tingling awareness sparkled from her lips to her toes.

His hands roamed over her wedding dress, and the fabric slid over her skin, increasing her body's sensations until she pushed him onto his back and lifted the thin material of the dress over her head and off, dropping it to the floor.

"Ye are no' wearing anything under it," he said as his breath caught in his throat.

"I didna want to waste time."

His lips curled up happily. "Ye ne'er cease to surprise me. From that first scone, everything about ye has surprised me, and I love it." He stripped off his shirt and his wedding clothes. "I didna think I should wear Clyde's MacDonald colors and plaid, even though 'tis yer clan, and I willna until we are welcomed home here in Glencoe. After we are settled in Glasgow, we will decide on our own name, one that is ours alone, one that tells the world I will ne'er let ye go."

"I do no' marry a name. I marry a man. So stop talking," she said as she tugged him over on top of her. "I ken how this lovemaking is done, but it already feels like so much more than I ever dreamed of. Show me even more."

He willingly and eagerly smothered her body with his hands and his mouth, letting both wander wherever he could reach. With each new touch, she sucked in a welcomed breath and let the awareness of her body deepen and grow. She moved her own hands in rhythm across his back and buttocks. Yet every time her fingers touched one of his scars, he twitched.

"Is it aright if I touch them?" she asked in a voice thick with emotion.

"'Tis aright. In fact, I like it. Yer touch releases the memory until there is only ye."

He lowered his head, letting his kisses begin at her throat. Each one left her gasping as he moved to her shoulders and then to her breasts. She purred like a cat being scratched behind the ears in front of the fire, total joy mixed with eagerness to know what would come next.

"Hurry," she whispered.

"Nay, yer pleasure is my pleasure."

His head moved to her stomach and finally to the sensitive skin of her inner thighs. He found her core with his lips and tongue until she tugged on his hair, lifting his head, saying, "I will burst into pieces."

"No' yet," he answered from deep in his throat. Moving up her body, he held himself up on his elbows and entered her moist core. He gave her slow thrusts, feeling her move with him. He gained speed and power until she cried out, "Rory!" That was all he needed to hear before he gave one final long plunge and collapsed on top of her.

Pulling the quilt up over them, they let each other's body heat surround them in their own private cocoon. When their breathing returned to normal and the raging sensations under their skin eased, Joneta said, "Teach me. Teach me to do for ye what ye did for me."

And he taught her where to touch, kiss, and caress every inch of his body until he begged to become part of her again. Afterward, they slept with her nestled under his arm until morning when it was time to leave the security and bliss of this upper room.

The rain ended, and the sun scattered through the window across their bed as Joneta eased herself out of Rory's arms and slipped on her kirtle and overdress, tying it at the waist. His eyes opened.

"I'm going to see if Lorna needs help with the morning meal," she said.

"I have a better idea. Come back to bed with me."

Her face brightened as she stripped off her clothing and snuggled under the covers close to him. "I canna resist ye," she said, and they made love again.

"I could stay here all day," she murmured.

"Nay, we canna. I must go to the fort and resign from the army. We must leave by this afternoon, afore yer brothers come looking for ye. They will search for us, so we must be far away."

He slipped into his army uniform. As he buckled his belt, he said, "Stay here with Clyde and Lorna until I'm back. I should be here long afore dark. 'Tis only sixteen miles to the fort, a lively jaunt for Caraid. Will ye wait for me?"

Leaping across the bed and into his arms, she cried, "How can ye doubt it? Even afore we wed, I could ne'er separate my heart from yers. I'll wait for ye for as long as it takes! I love ye, Rory Campbell."

He kissed her firmly on the lips, and set her on her feet, but didn't break his hold on her. "I'll ride like the wind and be back afore ye ken it. Naught will stop us now from being together for always. Dinna fash. I promise ye. I ne'er break my word, especially no' to the most beautiful griddle scone maker I ken!"

She laughed, and he gave her one last enduring kiss.

Downstairs, Clyde said to Father MacHenry, "Will ye help me raise the green flag? 'Twill tell those in Glencoe that all is well here, so they dinna come looking for Joneta."

By the time the men came back to the house from the flag raising, the sky had clouded over again.

****

Rory reined his horse to a stop inside the walls of Fort William, leapt out of the saddle, and dashed into the captain's office in the corner near the back wall of the fort. Captain Campbell sprawled across his desk, a half-empty bottle of whisky in his hand. His drool dripped over the papers under his head.

"Captain, Captain," said Rory. "I must speak to ye." Reaching across the desk, he shook his captain's shoulder. "Captain."

Captain Robert Campbell of Glenlyon raised his head and opened his bleary eyes. "What is it?"

"I have come to resign my enlistment in yer service as of today."

"Dinna be a fool. Ye canna resign." He burped and again dropped his head to his desk.

"Sir, ye assured me I could leave the company any time after one year. Ye gave yer word. Has been over a year, and today I have come to resign."

"Ye canna resign."

"But, sir—"

The captain's head popped up. "Ye canna resign because of orders from Master of the Stair Dalrymple." He shook the papers on his desk and some of them fell to the floor. "He orders all companies to be at the ready if any of the clans refuse to sign the loyalty oath." He tried to stand but flopped on his shaky legs back in his chair. "The lairds must sign the loyalty oath before December 31, and we are ordered to be on alert in case they dinna comply."

"Sir, ye gave yer word. Ye willna need me. I have trained three other men to do my work, and 'tis two months before the deadline for signing the oath. I am going to leave the fort this afternoon."

Captain Campbell staggered to the door, flung it open and shouted, "Put this man in irons! He is threatening to desert!"

Two soldiers ran into the office, one of them carrying a pair of iron leg shackles. When he saw the man was Rory, he said, "'Tis Rory Campbell, sir. He willna desert."

"Do as ye're ordered!" shouted the captain just before he fell on his backside into the corner. "Shackle him, and dinna let him out of yer sight or ye'll be in shackles yerself!" His head fell to one side.

"Nay!" shouted Rory as he lurched toward the door. Two more soldiers blocked the way and pushed Rory back inside and then to the floor. They held down his flailing legs and arms as a soldier locked the shackles around Rory's ankles. "I'm sorry, Mr. Campbell."

Rory's fury burned from the inside out. He screamed his rage and tossed two of the soldiers to the floor on their backs. He blackened the eye of another. More soldiers, hearing the ruckus, came and swarmed over Rory and the other struggling men. Soon Rory hung limp and exhausted, gripped tightly by these men he had counted as friends. They dragged him into the yard and pushed him to the ground.

"Dinna make us put ye in the stocks," said one of them. "Please, Mr. Campbell, stay still."

He screamed in frustration. He had to get back to Joneta! She would think he only married her just to leave her on her own to face her clan. And what if he'd left her with child? She trusted him, and now she would think he had abandoned her.

****

For the next three days, he hobbled around the fort's open yard doing the best he could with the horses, but the shackles were never removed, not even when he was ordered to work inside the stable. He was constantly guarded. He searched for a friendly face among the troops, but even the men he had trained and thought were his friends stayed silent.

"The captain gave ye special privilege," said another with a sneer. "Ye came and went as ye pleased. Now those chains will show ye what 'tis like for the rest of us."

"We have to obey orders, so why no' ye? Yer no better than us," said another, giving Rory a strong push and sending him to his knees. Rory didn't respond, but his anger ate him from the inside out.

Every night Rory rubbed a broken piece of a horse mouth bit he kept hidden in his bedding over the chains between his feet. After five nights he spread his legs apart and the chain broke. Grabbing the loose ends dangling on each leg, he hobbled out of the barracks toward the side gate and waited in the shadows until the posted guard turned toward the other side of the wall on his tedious marching watch.

Rory needed only a minute to open the lock on the

door with the key he kept hidden in his jacket pocket, the one he'd been trusted with for the times he wanted to leave with his horses. The lock clattered open. He froze.

A light from a torch showered his face.

"Hey, there!" shouted a voice.

Rory darted through the gate, but after only six strides, he stumbled over the chains still dangling from his ankles, landing on his face. Seconds later, the rough hands of three soldiers dragged him to his feet and back inside the walls, where the captain ordered him thrown into a prison cell on an underground level.

Day after day he paced along the walls in the cold dank space. The only light came from a small, barred window at the ground level of the yard above. Once, trying to have contact with someone, anyone, he reached out to touch a passing soldier's boot, only to have his hand stomped on. The rats found his rations better tasting than he did, and by the second week in January 1692 Rory was unrecognizable. His weight had plummeted, and his beard had grown long and tangled. The uniform he'd worn since coming back to the fort was in near shreds, and he couldn't stand his own filthy smell.

But worst of all, desperation overflowed in him. Not even a thought of his beloved Joneta consoled him now. Every morning he started the day with the hope that he might be set free and get back to her, only to see any optimism he had slowly drift away with the setting sun.

He prayed every night, "Dear Lord, If I lose her, I'll be nothing. Please make her understand. Ye canna have led me this far to lose it all. When I lost my clan, it left me on my own to build my world as I see fit, but losing Joneta will leave me a ghost to wander this world, no longer a man but a wraith with no home and no peace.

That canna be Your plan."

He buried his face in his blankets.

****

Joneta paced the floor. Rory did not return by nightfall nor by the next morning. He was still not back by the afternoon of the second day.

Lorna said, "Rory is strong and capable. If trouble has happened, and I am no' saying it has, he will overcome it. He will be here. We just have to wait."

"Mayhap he has to fulfill some duties at the fort afore he can be released," said Father MacHenry. "Ye ken how slow an army's paperwork can be. He will come. I dinna ken the man well, but I am certain for ye he will come no matter what. He will ne'er let ye go, ne'er."

"I need to go to the fort," said Joneta. "Mayhap the horse threw him on the way. He could be lying in the grass, hurt."

"Ye canna go alone," said Clyde.

"I will go with ye," said Father MacHenry. "I feel an obligation to see this through until ye are together."

Early on the third day, Joneta and Father MacHenry rode in Clyde's small carriage with Clyde's only horse in front. They hardly spoke while Joneta scanned every inch of the road and beyond. They found nothing.

At the fort, Captain Campbell greeted them cheerfully. He had not yet fallen completely into his cups. "Ye are looking for Rory Campbell?"

"Aye, he is a soldier in yer regiment," said Joneta.

"Aye, he is, but he left with three of his horses some time ago. He did mention he was interested in some mounts to be found near the coast, but I dinna ken where. He goes on these buying and trading journeys quite often, and I ne'er ken when he will be back."

"'Tis no' true," protested Joneta. "He came to resign his enlistment."

"He didna mention anything about leaving the army to me." The man licked his lips. "Mayhap he was no' being honest with ye. I dinna mean to be indelicate, lass, but mayhap he is done with ye and made promises he didna intend to keep. Has happened with many a lass and a soldier afore."

Joneta, too stunned to speak, turned her back on the captain while Father MacHenry said, "We thank ye for yer time, Captain. Will ye send word if Rory Campbell returns?"

"I will. I am sorry, lass. 'Tis a life lesson."

"Ye are lying," said Joneta as she left the office and climbed into the carriage.

Once back at Clyde and Lorna's, Joneta paced in the yard behind the house, scanning the gap between the ridges for any sign of Rory. Every twig cracking or bird whistling set her on her feet and calling his name. And still he did not come.

The morning of the fourth day, Joneta rested her head on the table beside the bowl of mush Lorna set before her. "I had a bit of sweet raspberries left over. I thought ye might like yer mush sweeter today."

"He's not coming," whispered Joneta. "Something has happened. If he's hurt, Caraid would return here, and the horse hasna. The captain lied about Rory leaving to get more horses, but where could he be? We will ne'er ken what happened to him." She swallowed a sob. "Mayhap he can no longer marry a MacDonald."

Lorna wrapped her arms around the younger woman. "That is no' the case, and ye ken it. We have to wait. He will come."

Joneta bolted from her chair. "Then where is he? Where is he?"

Father MacHenry said, "I have kenned many young men, but verra few were as bound to their women as Rory Campbell is. Ne'er has one pleaded so fervently for me to wed the two of ye as did Rory. Whate'er has kept him away, is something he canna help, but he will find ye no matter how long it takes."

"Are ye certain, Father?"

"I will pray, and God will provide."

The next morning, Joneta looked through the window to see her brothers, John and Alex MacDonald with Zebulon Keene, walking toward the house. Quickly wiping her eyes with her sleeve and combing her fingers through her hair, she went to the door and opened it.

"Is all aright here?" asked John. "When ye stayed so long, we worried something was amiss. Zeb told us he saw a king's soldier here. We came prepared for anything." He touched the dirk hanging from his belt.

"John, Alex, I am glad ye came. I was just getting ready to come home. We got all the chores for winter done," Joneta said.

"We?" asked Zeb in a sharp voice. "Is he here? The king's man?"

"There's no one here besides us three," said Clyde. "And a traveling priest who left at dawn this morning."

"We passed the priest, but I saw another man here afore," insisted Zeb. "Where is he?"

"How dare ye call me a liar?" said Clyde, giving the younger man a withering stare.

"'Tis enough," said John, putting his hand on Zeb's shoulder. "My sister would no' betray us that way. She gave her word. Didna ye, Joneta?"

Joneta hung her head so he couldn't see the stricken look in her eyes. "Aye, John, I gave my word to ye." She looked up at Zeb. "And I gave my promise to Clyde and Lorna. Why, Zebulon, did ye forget yers to me?"

Zeb frowned and nodded before storming out the door.

"Joneta has been a great help to me," said Lorna, "and I am glad ye let her stay for these past days." Laying a woven shawl over Joneta's shoulders, she whispered in the young woman's ear, "We will send a yellow flag as soon as we see him."

With a dull ache in her soul, Joneta left for home in Glencoe.

****

She scanned the sky every day for the next two months, but the yellow flag did not fly over Clyde and Lorna's home. By the first week in January, misery engulfed her. She gave up hope, not the hope that he loved her or that she loved him, but the hope they would ever find each other again. Whatever had happened to him, none of it mattered. He was gone, and she was alone.

The only time she found him was when she was alone in her bed. No distance could separate her heart from his, and when she closed her eyes, soon he lay beside her. She reached for him, and she felt his touch. Her skin tingled as fingertips quietly moved along her arms, then down her stomach and over her legs. She shivered and tugged him closer. His body heat warmed her. His breathing matched hers, softly in and out, then faster and deeper. For one brief second, she saw his eyes sparkle in the fading firelight, and they became one soul, one heart, and one body. Together even though apart. She sighed, and she slept.

Zebulon Keene visited her every day, but she never stopped looking for the yellow flag.

Chapter Fourteen

December 28, 1691

Three days after Christmas, a winter storm howled outside the MacDonald clan chief's blackhouse in Glencoe. The icy wind blew snow under the door and through the cracks in the stone walls. Joneta stuffed a quilt under the door and pushed some rags into the gaps in a vain attempt to keep the cold out.

Laird MacIain MacDonald held a copy of a letter in his hand from John Dalrymple, Master of Stair and Secretary of State for Scotland. He read aloud, "The clans will be punished with the upmost extremity of the law for failure to sign the loyalty oath by January 1, 1692."

"That only leaves three days for us to meet the deadline," said John MacDonald to his father and brother. "The deposed King James released us on December 12 from our loyalty oath to him, but the messenger didn't arrive in Glencoe with that news until yesterday. That leaves us only three days to make King William's deadline."

"Do ye think we can make it in time?" asked Alex. He scratched his cheek, wishing his beard grew in as thick as his brother's so he wouldn't have itchy dry patches on his face.

"We have no choice," said MacIain, looking at his

sons from under unruly gray eyebrows. "We agreed to sign if James couldna return, and I willna risk the safety of our clan. Get ready to travel to Fort William at dawn tomorrow and hope to reach the fort afore the winter darkness sets in."

The worst of the Highland winter swept through Glencoe and the surrounding area as MacIain, John, and Alex MacDonald trekked toward Fort William sixteen miles away in Lochaber. The horses needed frequent rest from struggling through the snow and wind, so it was midafternoon on December 30 when they arrived wet and very cold. Colonel John Hill, in command while Captain Campbell was in Edinburgh getting final commission from the king, gave them the warmth of a fire and a hot meal. "But I regret to tell ye," he said. "Ye have come to the wrong place. I canna accept your signature on the loyalty oath. I am no' authorized. Ye have to go to Inveraray and see the sheriff. 'Twill be the only way it can be legal."

"'Tis forty miles!" protested John, his fists clenched. "We can sign here."

"Ye have to go to Inveraray and see the sheriff there. His name is Sir Colin Campbell."

"Campbell? Ye must be joking. Do ye think a Campbell will let a MacDonald sign if we canna make it in time? Will he hold us away out of spite? We came to sign here and now."

"Sheriff Campbell has to let ye sign," said the colonel. "The law requires he take all legal signatures. I will give ye a letter of safe passage, explaining yer situation in coming here by mistake. I'll give ye fresh mounts and some dry blankets."

John turned to his father with a sneer. "Do ye think

this winter weather will honor the letter and make our trip easier?"

Maclain gave his oldest son a hard push. "Get on yer horse! Now!"

Maclain and his two sons left immediately despite approaching darkness, hoping to get a head start on the forty-mile journey to Inveraray. Travel was hard, but the next afternoon, on December 31, they were only halfway to their destination. Appearing out of the continuing storm came a patrol of soldiers from Argyll's regiment and surrounded them. This regiment, organized and led by men from Clan Campbell, was originally sent to suppress Jacobite opposition to the king. They now roamed the Highlands seeking rebels among the clans with orders to detain and arrest as needed, thus asserting their authority at will.

Maclain identified himself as a MacDonald, and the Campbell captain immediately ordered swords and pistols drawn. "What are ye doing here in this weather?" demanded the man.

"We are heading to Inveraray to sign the loyalty oath," said Alex with the point of a sword at his neck. "We canna be delayed."

"We will miss the deadline if ye dinna let us go," said John, staring at the pistol aimed directly at his chest. "We have a letter from Colonel John Hill explaining how we went to the fort in error but are on our way to sign." The paper he held out fluttered in the wind.

"All the clans have already signed the loyalty oath to King William," said the captain, snatching the letter out of John's hand. "If ye havena done it by now, ye ne'er intend to." After only a brief glance at the paper, he added, "Only fools would be out in this weather with such a claim, and I see 'tis MacDonald fools." The rest of the company chuckled.

"We're telling ye true," said John, gritting his teeth against the insult. "We only want to get to the sheriff at Inveraray and sign. We havena much time."

"We will see about that. I have more questions for ye. Dismount."

It was not until the following day, on January 1, that the Campbell captain announced he was finally satisfied with MacIain's answers. He handed John the now crumpled letter and let the MacDonalds continue their journey. "I'd say 'beannachd leat' to ye, but ye're going to need more than good luck."

After another grueling day of travel, at sunrise on January 3, 1692, the MacDonalds led their horses to the nearest stable, where the animals could rest and be fed, before hurrying to the sheriff's office. After warming their hands by the iron stove in the center of the room, MacIain asked to see the sheriff.

"He isna here," said the man who'd been sleeping in a chair in the corner. When he sat up, the legs of his chair clapped on the floor. "'Tis Hogmanay, the new year's celebration, and he is visiting with relatives. He willna be back for three days. Can I help ye? I am the deputy."

"Can ye witness our signing of the loyalty oath to King William? I ken 'tis beyond the deadline, but we have been delayed by no fault of our own," said MacIain, holding out the tattered letter from Colonel Hill.

The deputy wiped the sleep out of the corners of his eyes and shrugged. "I canna help ye. I canna take yer oath. Ye'll have to wait for the High Sheriff."

The MacDonalds spent a tense three days at a nearby tavern surrounded by drunken Campbells until the date of January 6, 1692, glared back at MacIain MacDonald on the pledge he had just signed. His stomach twisted. "Are ye certain our signatures will reach Edinburgh? That the king will ken we have signed the oath?"

"I will do everything I can to deliver this quickly, despite my deputies who have no' returned from the holiday," said the sheriff. "I also canna guarantee that Dalrymple will accept it, but the pledge is signed. That is all that can be done, so if there are to be consequences, there is naught ye can do except go home and wait."

"'Twill be an uneasy wait at best," muttered John.

****

Edinburgh, a week later

Dalrymple swept his papers off his desk and stormed to the door, his expression hardening into a stony gaze. "Who let me down this time?" he shouted at his clerk as he waved the letter in the air. "The MacDonalds signed the loyalty oath? Damnation!"

An hour later he dictated a letter ordering the clerks of the Privy Council in Edinburgh to do a thorough inspection as to the authenticity of MacIain's signature. "I would put nothing past that sly fox," he wrote.

The not-surprising report came back to him that the examiners found it to be a forgery.

Dalrymple's next letter informed the Privy Council in Edinburgh of Laird MacIain's failure to sign and for them to stay ready to enforce punishment at an appropriate time.

Chapter Fifteen

January 1692

Rory vanished into himself. He had no thoughts, only emptiness. He struggled to keep Joneta in his imaginings, but she never faded from his heart. Then Captain Campbell summoned him to his office.

"What do ye have to say for yerself, Rory Campbell?" asked the officer after a much-weakened Rory staggered in, held up on the arms by two guards. He sucked in the first breath of fresh air he'd had in nearly two months.

"We caught ye trying to escape yer duty."

"Ye promised me I could resign my commission, and I expect ye to keep yer word."

Captain Campbell's narrow eyes became slits. "My word is whate'er I say. I have orders to march to Glencoe and quietly investigate why the MacDonalds didna sign the loyalty oath. The council in Edinburgh has no' gotten a legal signature from Laird MacIain."

"The laird kens his duty," said Rory. "I am certain he signed. He wouldna put his clan at risk."

"'Tis of no matter to me whether, or when, or even if he signed. We will be riding to Glencoe next week, and I have need of a good horseman to manage the mounts. I also believe ye ken John MacDonald, son of Laird MacIain."

No need to remind the captain of the feud between the clans or tell him how the hostility escalated after John saw him kissing Joneta at the fair. Even before that time, Rory had met Laird MacIain and his sons, John and Alex, when he and his da worked the horses for them, selling, buying, and training the animals. Both sides were wary of the other, and tense situations existed, but none got in the way of their business dealings. Also no need to tell the captain he would lie, cheat, and steal to see Joneta again. Anything for the chance to hold her in his arms.

"I do. I ken them."

"I need ye to smooth the waters, so to speak," continued the captain, "to be a familiar face so we may stay in Glencoe until I receive additional orders. Do ye think ye can persuade the laird and his sons to cooperate and no' give us trouble?"

Rory's mind raced. How could he make this come out the way the captain wanted, thus giving him a chance to escape? "The laird has traded horses with me afore. They were favorable dealings. He always got a fair exchange, so I think this one might be again."

"I ken ye can charm the birds out of the trees," said the captain with a dubious expression. "I've seen the way ye train the horses, and how ye can get yer men to obey without threats, but I need ye to make it work with men who already dislike the king's soldiers. As soon as we ride up, there could be trouble. I want ye to see that there is none."

"I'll do whatever I can, sir, but I have one request," said Rory. "Release me from service when this assignment is over."

"Ye are no' in a position to make requests of me. I can throw ye back in the cell and forget ye exist."

"Aye, sir, and as long as I am in these shackles, ye can do what ye want, but ye asked for my help with the MacDonalds. Can anyone else do what I can? Does anyone else offer a friendly face to Laird MacIain?"

Captain Campbell opened his desk drawer and took out a half-filled bottle of Scottish whisky. He set it on the desk and faced Rory with bleary eyes. "Only if I have yer word ye will cooperate, and no' get the regiment into a fracas. I will release ye from service then."

"I had yer word afore," Rory said slowly.

"This time ye have it in writing." Captain Campbell scribbled on a small piece of paper and handed it to Rory. Written on it was: *Upon successful completion of his duty, Rory Campbell is released from the king's service without restriction or penalty.*

"Do we have an agreement?"

Rory nodded. "Ye have my word. Take off these chains."

The captain tossed him a heavy key.

Rory sat on the floor and unlocked the manacles, exposing his raw and bleeding ankles. "I also want a bath, in a real tub with hot water and soap for as long as I like."

Captain Campbell sniffed. "Granted. Now get out of my sight."

Rory walked out of the office, smiling, not only because of the paper he held in his hand or the thought of a bath, but because he would see Joneta again.

****

In the third week of January 1692, a regiment from Fort William marched into the glen of Glencoe, passed the house belonging to Clyde and Lorna, and continued straight to the western villages of Glencoe. Leading the troops sat Captain Campbell astride a tall black stallion, and right behind him sat Rory Campbell on Caraid.

MacDonald men, spotting the troops from the ridges, ran from the hills to warn Laird MacIain of the unexpected visitors. MacIain strode from his house toward the regiment and waited on the path just below the fence on the south side of the villages.

"We have business here!" shouted Captain Campbell.

"And what may that be?" returned Laird MacDonald. His two sons caught up with him and stood on either side of their father. The rest of the clan stood farther back on the ridge.

"Yer tax due King William. Will ye pay in coin or in aid?"

John nudged his father. "Do ye see Rory Campbell in the ranks? He's the one who gave unwanted attention to Joneta at the fair. I didna ken he was a king's man." His face darkened. "Mayhap 'twas his red jacket Zeb Keene saw at Clyde's house."

MacIain whispered as softly as his deep voice allowed, "'Tis of no matter now. They are all king's men. Campbells the lot of them." To the captain he shouted, "We havena coin. Come back in the spring when we have cattle to sell."

"Nay," answered Captain Campbell. "Yer tax is due now." A strong wind threatened his regimental hat, and he tugged it onto his head.

Scowling, MacIain said, "We dinna want unruly soldiers on our land. Our bairns and lasses willna be safe."

"I will guarantee the safety of all yer clan folk."

MacIain didn't answer.

Captain Campbell hadn't had any whisky since he left the fort that morning, and he swallowed back the excessive saliva in his mouth. He wanted to spit on the ground but needed to maintain his dignity, at least for the time being. "Ye ken Rory Campbell. He has traded horses and mules with ye. He will speak with ye. Rory Campbell, front and center!"

Rory, free of his leg irons, felt his raw ankles rubbing against the inside of his boots with each movement of his horse. He wanted to get down and rewrap his legs, but it wouldn't be anytime soon. Already having convinced Captain Campbell he knew the laird well, and that the two were friendly, he now had to convince MacIain.

He took a cleansing breath and forced a smile. He had told lies before, but this would be the biggest one ever! The soldiers were to billet with the MacDonalds for the next two weeks, and it was up to him to make it happen.

He rode to the front of the regiment, where he saw John look in his direction and then whisper something to his father. It could only be John reminding his father of the trouble at the fair.

Rory sucked in another deep breath and announced, "Laird MacIain, our captain has given direct orders to all the troops about proper behavior here. I assure ye that this regiment will behave with the utmost respect and consideration during our tenure with ye. Captain Campbell has ordered harsh punishment for any who disobey. Mention any offense or threat of an offense to the captain and it will be dealt with immediately and that man expelled from yer presence."

MacIain stayed silent as Alex and John said almost

in unison and loud enough for Captain Campbell to hear, "I dinna trust him."

MacIain said under his breath, "We have no choice."

"But he made advances to Joneta at the fair!"

MacIain looked directly at John and then at Rory. "Do ye ken my daughter, Joneta? Ye met her at the Highland fair more than a year ago."

"I met many lasses at the Highland fair. I canna remember them all."

John barked as his hands balled into fists, "Do ye remember the beating I gave ye? The one I promised to finish?"

"I do, but I've forgotten the reason, and it doesna matter after this long time."

"We heard how ye shamed the Campbell clan and they disowned ye. Ye shamed them by taking a beating from a MacDonald. How can ye show yer face anywhere in Scotland?"

"I have found my place at Fort William, and I am content." The lies settled in his throat, and he gulped to swallow them down.

John took a step toward Rory and the horse soldiers, but his father put a calming hand on his arm, saying, "We will protect her. We have no choice. 'Tis the law. If we show them Highland hospitality, they willna bother us. 'Twill give us time to gather what money we can."

"'Twill no' be much," said Alex. MacIain nodded in agreement. "Aye, coin is hard to come by, and the clan faces hardship getting through the rest of the winter as it is. But we will do the best we can to keep the peace. We signed the loyalty oath, so the soldiers are bound to protect us."

To Captain Campbell, MacIain said, "We will pay

in aid. How many of yer men will we have to lodge and feed? For how long?"

"We have one hundred and five men, and we will need lodging and food for two weeks, mayhap three, and officers will no' be boarded with the enlisted," answered the captain. "'Tis by order of King William."

MacIain MacDonald sighed. "I understand. Give us time to alert our people and make plans for yer lodging and their food. We are a poor clan and most canna spare more than a small morning meal and one in the evening. Dinna expect more."

"We will tell the king of yer meager offerings."

John sneered. "Meager offerings? We'll all be hungry by the time they leave." He and his brother and father turned their backs on the soldiers and headed up the slope toward the dozen MacDonald men and their families waiting there.

The men of Glencoe murmured as their leaders approached. "They are here to harass us because we signed the oath late. The king is digging his claws into our backs because of it."

"That may be," said MacIain to them, "but we have no choice. The tax was in place long afore the oath needed to be signed. We havena paid but a pittance in tax in three years. I kenned the king would come looking for more, and now he has. John, Alex, talk to the men and divide up the soldiers as best ye can. The poorest families will house only one, but the stronger families will take more according to their ability. Be as fair as ye can."

As John and Alex entered the crowd and began assigning duties, the questions and the protests continued.

Chapter Sixteen

Rory Campbell sat uneasy in the saddle. His eyes scanned the village and the people, but he didn't dare move his head. He missed Joneta so much he ached, and he had to tell her, to explain, but he couldn't appear to be looking for her. He had so many plans in his head, so many hopes, and all of them included the auburn-haired woman. If she could forgive him. If she still loved the man who deserted her. If.

Behind the cluster of MacDonalds, Joneta stepped out of a shed and into the light, putting her arm up to block the sun blinding her to the mass of soldiers.

Rory had to bite his lip to keep from grinning. So beautiful, so loving, and he prayed she was still his.

"Campbell, move your men forward!" shouted the captain.

Rory jolted back to reality, raised his arm, and signaled for the six men in his squad to move forward and up the slope where John MacDonald pointed to housing at the far end of the valley, the opposite end of the village from the laird's dwelling and Joneta. Rory gave John a stiff tip of his head as he passed, and John returned with a menacing scowl.

Rory stayed busy for the rest of the day, seeing that all the company's mounts were sheltered, warm, and fed, which would be no small job in this cold, bleak valley. When could he go to see Joneta and tell her the truth?

Rory's six men found shelter in three small blackhouses on the west side of the valley. Rory gave strict instructions for the men to sleep against the walls of the houses as far away from the family as they could manage, and that they roll up their blankets every morning and store them in the corner out of the way. He also ordered them to carry in water, stoke the fire, and tend to the animals in the stables before dawn. They would eat after the family was fed, and they would not make any more work for the woman of the house with their untidiness. He also stressed that any coarse remarks or leering directed at any woman or lass would be dealt with rigorously, and Rory would deal out punishment himself long before Captain Campbell had a chance.

He spent the first week in Glencoe working with the men and the company's horses in the open fields behind the houses, making certain the animals maintained their training. He also insisted his animals be housed in clean warm stables at night no matter what the temperature, even if it meant additional blankets and food from the villagers. He caught the occasional glimpse of Joneta going about her chores, but he had no chance to approach her.

Once she looked in his direction while hauling in the water buckets, before her mother smacked her on the arm. "Dinna be friendly with these soldiers. They will only treat ye badly."

"Aye, Mum," she answered.

On the eighth day, Rory called to Gordon and Michael, staying in the house with him, and then to Jack, Thomas, and Cade in the cottage next door. "We're going to check on all the mounts."

"Tonight?" protested Thomas.

"Aye, tonight. Get yer boots on. We must make certain they are well fed and comfortable. A storm is brewing. Get extra blankets and more feed from the houses if need be. We'll divide up into three sections, and I'll check the farthest ones away, so when ye're done ye can have a shorter walk back to bed."

The men grumbled but tugged on their boots and followed Rory.

"Ye go here, Jack and Thomas, the closest houses and sheds. Ye other three are assigned the middle ones. I'll go this way to the far end." He pointed toward Laird MacDonald's house on the far east side of Glencoe. "Dinna miss a stable. Check every horse."

The stars in the cloudless night sky twinkled as Rory moved quickly from shed to stable. He patted down his horses, adjusted their blankets, and refilled their feed bins as needed. The last animal shed on the east end of the glen was attached to the house belonging to Laird MacIain. After checking on the three mounts stabled there, he crept along the outside wall to a small window in the sleeping quarters in the back portion of the house. Cautiously peering into a corner of the window, he spotted Joneta asleep on her bed. *She is so beautiful*.

Her eyes flew open. She gasped and clamped her hand over her mouth, her eyes wide. Tossing back her quilt, she wrapped it around her shoulders, slipped into her boots, came to the window, and pointed toward the door. The three soldiers sleeping on pallets on the floor didn't stir. Nor did her parents sleeping on the opposite side of the house.

The next time Rory saw her, she was in his arms.

"I thought ye were dead!" she whispered. She kissed him, warming him to his toes. "Ye ne'er came back. I thought ye were dead!" She kissed him again and again.

"I wasna dead," he said as soon as his lips were his own once more. "I only wished I were. I couldna come back to take ye to Glasgow. The captain put me in chains." Then he asked the most important question of all. "Do ye still love me?"

"Follow me. I dinna want anyone to see us." She led him behind a large boulder on a rocky ridge and kissed him again. Neither of them felt the cold. Together they made all the heat they needed.

"I thought ye were gone forever. My heart broke in two."

She reached up for him, but he held her away. "I have to tell ye what happened. I ne'er stopped trying to come back to ye." He sat on a flat rock on the ground and pulled her into his lap.

Tears ran down her cheeks as he told her how Captain Campbell had refused to release him, had put him in shackles and locked him in a prison cell. "Do ye still love me? Will ye keep me as yer husband?"

She buried her face in his chest to muffle the sounds of her sobs that came harder now. She gasped for air.

"Am I too late?" he asked.

Chapter Seventeen

She wiped her dripping nose with the edge of her quilt as she sputtered, "All the things I thought, and none of them were true. Forgive me for doubting ye even for a moment." She buried her face against his shoulder. "Ye pledged yerself to me forever, and forever it will be. I have my brooch." She lifted the corner of her nightshirt, showing him the token pinned to her woolen undershirt. "I ne'er took it off even when I believed ye would ne'er return. My heart wouldna let me."

Rory hugged her tighter. He could not get her close enough. "I am so sorry ye suffered because of me. Does anyone suspect we are wed?"

She gave a long sniff as she wiped her face again. "Zeb saw ye, saw yer jacket, but he doesna ken who ye are, just a king's soldier. He was so angry with me for no' wedding him that he broke his promise and told Da and John he saw a jacket, but he didna ken whose it was. Clyde said no soldiers had been there, and Da trusted Clyde's word. All I care about is that ye are here now."

She straddled his legs and rubbed against him. "I prayed every day that ye were still alive, and ye are! I need ye. How many nights I dreamed of being with ye again. I relived our wedding night o'er and o'er."

He struggled to catch his breath. She was so close. He wanted her so. "I want ye here by this rock, but it willna be the way I want to love ye."

"I dinna care where we are, only that we are together, absolutely together."

She pulled her quilt around both of them, lifted her nightdress, and tugged at his breeks until they fell open. He moved her until she sheathed him. In movements that came faster and faster, they satisfied their need for each other. He covered her mouth to keep her from crying out as she quavered in his arms.

When both had regained their breath, he said, "I can ne'er love ye enough. Even here in the cold and dark, ye warm me to my verra core. There, ye are shivering again. Get under my jacket." They clung together, and neither felt the cold, only each other.

"Captain promised he'd release me from service as soon as the mission here is over. I have his written word." He patted his jacket pocket. "But it dinna say anything about me having to stay in Glencoe, only that I'm free of enlistment. If no one looks too closely, with his letter we can leave any time we want. When can ye be ready?"

"Joneta! Where are ye?"

"'Tis my da," she whispered, straightening her clothes. "I will leave anytime ye say. I'll have a pack ready in the morning."

He nodded and tugged her head down to kiss her again on the lips. She clung to him, and he had to slowly push her away so she could answer her father.

When she stood, her head barely peeked over the rock. "I am here, Da. I came to use the outhouse, but the stars are so bright, I wanted to watch for a while." After rubbing her hand over Rory's head, she walked out toward her father. "I am sorry ye were worried. Mayhap I can sleep better now."

"'Tis no' safe outside for a lass alone with all the soldiers about. Next time ask me to come with ye." He pulled her into his embrace. "I'd ne'er sleep again if anything happened to ye."

He walked with her to the door, but before going inside, he asked, "Have ye seen that Rory Campbell is here in Glencoe? He is one of the soldiers."

She cleared her throat. "I saw him, but it has been a long time since the fair. The soldiers will be gone soon, and so will Rory. Ye dinna have to worry."

"Ye're pledged to Zebulon Keene, and I'd feel better if ye were wed to him. Mayhap ye can fix a date as soon as the soldiers leave."

"As soon as the soldiers leave, Da."

Slipping through the door, she rushed to her bed and buried herself in its quilts and closed her eyes, but instead of sleeping, she relived Rory's touch. She thanked God for his safe return to her. She dreamed of leaving with him so she could love him every day.

****

The unexpected snow came just before dawn the next day, leaving eight inches of snow on the ground and another six inches the following day. Blustering winds whipped around the villages, keeping everyone inside, and the soldiers with them. Rory braved the weather to check on his animals, but he and Joneta couldn't risk leaving as long as the storm continued. Not only would it be easy to track them in the snow, but a horse with two riders would have a tough time in the blustery weather.

The weather eased somewhat on February 12, 1692, windy but still with snow flurries. On the excuse of checking on the horses again that night, he made his way to Joneta by walking in windblown spots where the snow was nearly gone and walking in other men's footprints to hide his own. He tugged his jacket collar around his neck and tapped lightly on Joneta's window.

She came out, and they huddled against the wall of the house where the wind was not so strong. She had her pack in her hand.

"I'm sorry, but I couldna bring the horse, still too much wind and snow tonight," he whispered in her ear. "The weather is clearing, so we will leave afore dawn tomorrow. I'll be behind that boulder there with Caraid. I canna risk stealing another horse. We can be out of sight afore the sun rises enough for anyone to miss us and be a full day away afore anyone starts looking for us."

"I already have a sack packed, here it is. I willna sleep until we are away, just ye and me." She pulled her shawl over both their heads and kissed him without the urgency of before, but tenderly and softly.

"Ye are on my mind every minute I'm awake," he whispered. "And all my dreams are of ye. Ye are more than I deserve, and I will spend every day for the rest of my life making certain ye dinna regret marrying me."

She snuggled closer.

"The minute I saw ye making those griddle scones, I kenned that all my life I've been looking for something, something to ease the itch in my soul, something to fill my heart, and I found it in ye." He kissed her forehead. "I am empty without ye and full with ye. We will be together tomorrow." Wrapping the shawl more tightly around her, he said, "We will be away tomorrow."

She raised her head. "My words will ne'er be as sweet as yers, but when ye are near I cry less, I smile more, I am better than I ever hoped to be. Even when we are apart, please, dinna ever doubt that my heart is yers, that my everything is yers, body and soul."

A trumpet sounded from the other side of the glen.

"'Tis a call to order," said Rory, turning his head in that direction. "I have to go. Until the morning." He kissed her again and quietly closed the door behind her after she slipped inside.

"Joneta, is that ye?" asked her mother.

"Aye, Mum. I got up to stoke the fire."

"Leave the fire be. The coals will last until morning. Get in bed under the quilts and ye'll be warm enough."

Rory made it back to find the regiment assembled at the far end of the settlement behind a cluster of houses known as Inverrigan. Taking his place among the soldiers, he listened in horror as Captain Campbell spoke.

"These orders arrived from Major Duncanson of the Earl of Argyll's regiment." Captain Campbell read, "You are hereby ordered to fall upon the rebels, the MacDonalds of Glencoe, and to put all to the sword under seventy. You are to have a special care that the old fox and his sons upon no account escape your hands. This you are to put in execution at five of the clock precisely."

Rory's stomach rolled over. *Kill the MacDonalds? I canna let that happen.*

"We will muster here until the given time," said Campbell. "Prepare yer weapons, loaded guns and sharpened swords and dirks. No one is to leave this area until the command is given. No talking in the ranks. Rory Campbell, front and forward to me."

"Rory," said Captain Campbell. "I need ye to tell me where we might find the most resistance among the clan, and where there will be the least. Which homes should we target first, leaving the weaker ones for later?"

"I canna tell ye," said Rory. "I ken only a few of the clan personally. But, sir, we shouldna be doing this to innocent people. 'Tis a violation of Highland trust. We canna murder innocents."

Captain waved the letter in Rory's face. "These are my orders and they will be carried out. Get back to yer patrol and prepare to move out or find yerself in irons again. Dismissed!"

Rory paced nervously. No chance to get out of the mass of soldiers without being noticed. No one talked, but Rory saw their faces, some troubled, some eager.

At the appointed hour, Captain Campbell of Glenlyon spoke to the troops again. "Groups of twenty men will be dispatched to the other clusters of houses to enter and kill without hesitation." Sorting out one group of twenty that included Rory, he ordered, "Go to Polveig at the far east end of the glen to dispatch MacIain and his sons. Yer task is most important! See that MacIain and his sons do not escape! They must not survive!"

The attack began at five o'clock in the morning, before the sunrise.

****

In the dismissal confusion, Rory ignored his assigned group and ran toward MacIain and Joneta, rapping on the doors of as many cottages as he could, calling out a warning. "Escape! Quickly! Soldiers are coming!" Several families heeded his alarms and vanished into the darkness to the mountains or across the river.

The charging cries of the rampaging soldiers behind him mixed with the screams of innocent victims and the crackles of the fires spreading from house to house.

He ran faster.

But when he had MacIain's house in sight, three soldiers from the regiment caught up to him.

"Halt, Campbell," shouted one of them. "We've seen ye giving warnings to houses on the way. Ye've disobeyed orders, and ye'll hang for it!"

A house not far away burst into hot flames with a loud crack.

Rory planted his feet and held out his sword. "'Tis an unjust and vile thing ye do. I canna let ye kill innocent people."

"Then ye'll die along with them!" The three attacked.

Weapons clashed and pistols fired. Before it was over, one of the other men clutched at a belly wound and the other had a deep slash across his chest from Rory's dirk. They crawled away. The last man raised his arm, putting Rory in his pistol sights, but Rory fired faster and his bullet hit the man's neck. He left the body where it lay to slog his way through the falling snow to Laird MacDonald's blackhouse. He had to warn Joneta!

Deadly flames racing through the laird's house told him he was too late.

Chapter Eighteen

Glencoe, Scotland—February 13, 1692

Deafening explosions and choking black smoke jolted her awake. Her lungs burned with each breath as flames sizzled all around her, hissing like evil, consuming everything in their path. She called out to her mother and father, but only a raspy gasp came out of her throat. She felt her way blindly through the smoke as raging clumps of burning straw and wood fell from the collapsing thatched roof. She stumbled over to her parents' bed and tripped over the body of her father. Moving her trembling hands across his lifeless chest, blood soon covered her fingers.

Strong hands grasped her shoulders, lifting her up. "Joneta, we have to get out of here! They shot him in the back and slit his throat! There's nothing we can do for him!"

"We canna leave him!" she cried to John, hoping he could hear her over the roaring flames.

"We have to. He's dead!"

A loud report sounded as the mortar of clay between the two layers of the stone wall of the house crumbled from the heat. She screamed and buried her face in John's chest.

"The soldiers betrayed us," John shouted. "The whole of Glencoe is burning." He swung her into his arms and carried her toward the back of the house.

Joneta struggled against her brother. "Where is Mum?"

"Alex has her. Hold tight to me."

"What about the animals?"

"We already let them out," he said in gasping breaths. "But the soldiers slaughtered them anyway."

Turning her face to catch one last glimpse of her father, she saw someone in the doorway, a pistol in his hand and his dirk dripping with dark red blood.

"'Tis Rory," she said into John's ear. "He's here."

"He's one of the soldiers, one of them who killed our father," said John as he stepped over a burning timber and into the snow-covered yard. Tonight, the survivors of King William's soldiers' massacre had little choice but to climb the rocky ridges surrounding the glen and pray they could find shelter in the hills.

"Rory betrayed us. Brought the soldiers here," John said in a voice gravelly from the smoke. "Alex, Alex, over here!" he called to their brother, carrying the limp form of their mother while herding three women and four children ahead of him.

"We have to get to the caves," Alex shouted. "Some of the soldiers followed us. Rory Campbell is with them."

"Nay, it canna be," cried Joneta. "No' my Rory."

"What makes him *yer* Rory?" called Alex. "He convinced Da we'd be safe if we welcomed the king's soldiers on our land, and now they're burning and killing us." He leaned over and coughed out a thick clog of phlegm. It splattered in the snow, leaving a black stain. "Ye can ne'er trust a Campbell. They're our enemy and always will be. We told ye to stay away from Campbells, and now ye ken why!"

Joneta loosened her grip on John's neck. She could barely breathe from fear, panic, and regret. "I can walk now. Let me go. I can carry one of the children so we can move faster." John let her down, and she swept two-year-old Bryan into her arms. He struggled at first, but soothing words calmed him until he rested his head against her shoulder.

"Da didna come with us," said Bryan in his childish voice. "Mum said he couldna come. I want him."

"Yer da wants us to go to the cave." Her heart tugged knowing the lad's father would never be coming to them, having either been burned or shot in the dark by the marauding enemy. Bryan clutched her neck. She looked back, only to see acidic black smoke and orange flames reducing her beloved village to ashes.

Her words may have calmed wee Bryan, but Joneta would never be calm again, not until she knew the truth. The man she loved with everything she was, the man who pledged his life to her with his whole heart and made secret promises that changed her life, that man could not possibly be the man who helped the king's soldiers murder her kin and neighbors as they slept. He could not!

But she had seen him inside the house. Rory's handsome face and his shirt smeared with black soot, his dirk dripping with blood, and his pistol dangling at his side, still smoking.

She expected betrayal from her enemies, but never from the man she had trusted to love her. At least not until tonight.

Chapter Nineteen

February 13, 1692—the afternoon after the massacre

The rocky, damp floor of the small cave where John MacDonald led his kin sent shivers up the legs of the survivors, most of them wearing only thin, wet stockings after running through the snow in their night clothes. Few of them wore coats, and none carried blankets, food stuffs or other provisions. Their only thoughts had been to save their lives from the fire, smoke, and pistols.

Joneta kept her arms around her mother, helping the shivering woman limp toward the back of the cave. The older woman wept quietly, muttering incoherent words as if not fully understanding what had happened. "Where is he?" she pleaded with Joneta. "Where is my MacIain?"

"Dinna fash, Mum. Ye're safe here," said Joneta as she used strips torn from the hem of her nightshirt to bind her mother's injured hand where a soldier had ripped off her ring. Now was not the time to tell Mum that her husband of so many years was gone forever.

Joneta fingered the brooch pinned to her shift. She hoped it might comfort her. It did not.

"Mum," she said, "Alex, John, and I are here and safe along with some others. All will be well."

Her mother nodded and closed her eyes.

The seven surviving men closed in around John and

Alex MacDonald near the opening to the cave, but they were anything but quiet or comforted.

"Is yer da, our laird, dead?" said one of them.

"Aye," answered John in a voice that couldn't hide his grief or his anger. "He took a bullet in his back, and his throat was slit."

"How could our laird have let this happen?" called out an older man. "He welcomed those king's soldiers and asked us to show them Highland hospitality for nearly two weeks. They ate our food and slept in our houses. And they slaughtered us in our sleep! He had to ken they meant us harm!"

Shouts of anger echoed against the walls of the narrow cave.

John waved his hands in the air, calling out, "Listen, listen! Ye canna blame our da. As the Laird of Glencoe he had no choice but to let the soldiers stay on our land. Feeding and housing them is part of our tax owed to the crown. We had already signed the loyalty oath to King William, so the soldiers were sworn to protect us. They broke their warranty."

"They were mostly Campbells, our enemies for generations. The captain was Robert Campbell, a drunken scoundrel. 'Twas a trap from the start!" said another man. "To punish us because yer da came late to the signing of the oath! The king punished all of us!"

"Aye, if yer da hadna been so stubborn, he would have left here in time to sign afore the end of the year. He could have avoided the snowstorm that held him up."

"And if he hadna gone to Fort William first, but to the sheriff in Inveraray like he was supposed to. That made him near six days late. He snubbed his nose at the king, and now look what happened!"

Another called out, "And a regiment of Campbells stopped him on the way. Part of their plot to murder us!"

"How many of us were killed because of MacIain's stubbornness and Campbell treachery? How many?" The men crowded around Alex and John, shaking their fists.

Alex climbed up on a protruding rock and shouted over the din. "We canna change the past. We can only take care of what is afore us. We have to survive. We have no food or warm clothing, and we have to make plans to save as many as we can. John as eldest son is yer new Laird MacDonald of Glencoe. 'Tis the way it must be! Listen to him!"

The men's voices lowered to a dull murmur, and the crying and moaning of the women and children eased as well.

"Huddle together," said John. "That way we can warm ourselves. Alex and Tom, scout outside to see if the soldiers have followed us, but be careful. Not all our foot tracks have been covered by the falling snow. We dinna want to lead more soldiers here. Who has a weapon?"

Two men raised their hands. "I have a pistol," said one.

"I brought my sword and my cutting knife," said another.

"We'll have to make do," said John.

"What if we find more of our kinfolk out there?" asked Tom.

"If ye come on any others, bring only the ones who have no' found shelter. 'Twill be too easy to finish us off if we are all in one place, but make certain the rest are doing the best they can to stay warm. We have to make plans. We will survive!"

"This way," said Joneta to the women and children. "There is an alcove in the wall in the back, a smaller space that will keep us warmer. Stay close and feel yer way along the wall. This way." She helped her mother stagger along as the women put their hands on each other's shoulders and followed Joneta toward the small area deeper in the darkness. Once there, two women took her mother from Joneta as the others lifted their children into their arms. They dared not sit on the cold cave floor for fear of freezing more than their feet, so they stood and rocked the littlest ones, who soon dozed off. The others became quiet despite their shivering.

When Joneta thought all the women and children were as warm as possible, she moved toward the front of the cave to be near the men. She shuddered from the freezing wind blowing in from the entrance.

"How many are there of us?" she asked.

John said, "Four more found their way here just now. Take the woman and child to the back with the others. The two men said every house and stable in Glencoe has been fired. Half the soldiers left with the rest of the animals, and those who stayed behind are searching for survivors, killing any who couldn't find their way to the mountains or down the river, stabbing or shooting or even burning them as they escape."

"I dinna understand," pleaded Joneta. "Why kill everyone and burn everything? We took them into our houses and fed them. It doesna make sense to slaughter and burn without cause."

Will Henderson hovered over her with his fists clenched. "Those filthy Campbells dishonored our Highland hospitality. 'Twas murder under trust, the worst betrayal. King William wanted us to die!" He screeched, "Die!" as he lifted his hand to strike Joneta. She covered her head, but Alex grabbed his swinging arm and hurled him away. "Leave her be!"

"We've all heard the story of how ye and Rory Campbell were caught together at the fair, of how ye lied to yer brother to be with him. Rory sold us horses and mules, and even some cattle. Probably stole some of our own coos to do it. He kens the land and the best way to destroy us. Captain Campbell ordered Rory forward so he could convince MacIain that the soldiers offered no threat. Rory Campbell lied!"

"Rory would have no part in murder," said Joneta.

"The verra name 'Campbell' means 'twisted mouth,' ye foolish lass! They all lie every chance they get."

Alex dragged her toward the far wall of the cave. Speaking into her ear, he said, "Rory Campbell is part of this. If he didna kill Da himself, he helped those who did. Accept it and keep yer mouth shut afore ye get us all killed by our own, here in this cave."

Joneta felt a rock in the pit of her stomach, but she said, "Aye, I will no' speak, but ye canna convince me of any evil done by Rory."

Movement caught her eye, and she leaned around her brother to see someone just outside the cave opening.

She gasped. "'Tis Rory."

He stood in the snow, his pistol dangling at his side.

As Alex turned to look, Rory darted down the hill and out of sight.

Chapter Twenty

February 14, 1692

Morning came slowly, on the day after the massacre, for the MacDonald clan huddling in the stony cave. The breach between the mountains didn't allow bright, warm sunlight into the opening until almost noon, when the survivors inched their way out of the dank cavern to embrace the sunlight on their faces. At the same time, the light exposed a godsend of life-saving supplies stacked up just outside the opening.

Alex, Joneta, and William carried in twelve blankets with burned edges, a half-eaten beef roast, nine chicken eggs, and three pots filled with fresh water. Also against the stone wall sat a small pile of singed wood, along with chunks of peat, obviously taken from the burned houses in the glen.

"We're saved!" called out Claire Anne MacDonald.

"Not yet," said the new Laird, John MacDonald. "'Tis only enough for one meager meal. We might be a little warmer, but still not fed. I sent two men out to hunt for game, but 'twill be hard to find. MacConnor only has six pistol balls. Alex has his knife, but it'll just be by luck if he can find a lazy squirrel or rabbit."

As the women wrapped the children, two or three to a blanket, the men carried in the burnt wood and a pile of peat and lit a small fire. Over and over the fierce wind blew it out, but the men kept at it until the wood smoldered and caught flame. After adding peat, the warmth spread.

"Rory brought this," Joneta whispered to John as she carried two pots and one frying pan inside.

John whirled around on her, nearly knocking her down with his armload of peat. "Ye canna make him a hero just by saying it. I dinna ken where this came from and neither do ye!"

Joneta started to defend herself, but John silenced her with his words. "Yer heart might say 'tis Rory, but my head says he's a traitor, and I'll kill him if I ever see him again. I should have done it at the Highland Fair two summers ago." He leaned in closer. "And ye better keep yer mouth shut with that nonsense about Campbell's innocence, or someone here is likely to kill ye. Many have lost loved ones, and that Campbell man is the cause."

Realizing the danger she put herself and her brothers in with her talk, Joneta nodded. "I understand. I willna speak of him again."

But in her heart, she knew it was Rory who brought the supplies. Only the Rory she had cherished from the first moment he bought her griddle scones at the Highland Fair would have the heart and the courage to help the survivors against the army's orders. If they had left a day earlier, both of them might have escaped this slaughter, but in some strange and unexplained way, she was glad she was here. She could help keep the others alive, just as Rory was doing outside the cave.

After sharing her egg and her allocation of water with two of the children, she curled up by the fire and tried to sleep.

"Joneta, Joneta," said Mary MacDonald in a low voice, shaking her by the shoulder. "Come here." She beckoned her friend back into the alcove.

"Look." Mary pointed to the longtime wife of the now dead chieftain of Glencoe and mother to his seven children, six grown sons and one daughter. She sat propped against the wall of a cave in the hills above Glencoe, her eyes shut.

"I think she's…" began Mary. "I think…"

Joneta knelt beside her mother and brushed her hand across her mother's forehead. It felt cold and dry. She pressed her hand against her mother's chest and, feeling no movement, looked back up at Mary. Barely above a whisper, she said, "Is she dead?"

"I'm so sorry, Joneta."

Joneta fell across her mother's body, sobbing and wailing. In her anguish over the devastation and death of many in her clan, and now her mother, her anger burst out from a deep place inside until it smothered whatever love she had in her heart. She'd seen her father dead and now her mother! She'd seen how the others suffered from the loss of their loved ones and how they struggled with the cold and hunger of this cave. The pain she'd buried in order to survive flooded her in a wild furious rush. What had once made her strong now collapsed and died out.

Could John be right? Had Rory been part of this? Could he really have been forced to stay a soldier instead of coming back to her, or had everything he'd said to her been a lie? Had he planned their escape to take her away from here so she wouldn't find out about his guilt? Was there an explanation for her village now being a pile of ashes? For her mother and father being slaughtered so savagely?

Grief swallowed her in darkness, and even her memory of Rory's bright smile couldn't penetrate it.

****

Through the night, Rory slogged up and down the mountain in the snow, over rocks and the rough terrain, carrying what he could salvage, things like blankets, some food, pieces of wood and squares of peat for fires, all the while avoiding the still-raiding king's soldiers. If they caught him, they'd run him through or hang him on the spot, maybe even burn him alive like they had two MacDonald men whose corpses still lay smoldering on the ground.

After he'd done all he could to help the survivors that first night, he buried himself deep into the straw of the only stable left standing in Glencoe and listened to the noisy chaos outside. The bodies of nearly a thousand cattle and more than five hundred horses lay rotting on the ground, while the rest had been driven out of Glencoe and back to Fort William. A lone chicken squawked in the corner of the stable.

Even if some of the MacDonald clan could return to Glencoe, there'd be nothing to come back to, but Joneta had to survive. She had to survive. He couldn't live without her.

Chapter Twenty-One

The days after the massacre—February 15-20, 1692

Six adult survivors trudged into the cave, trailed by four children.

"We've been outside all night," said one of the men through chattering teeth. "There were two more of us, but we couldna get them to stir this morning. Frozen. The only shelter we had was an overhang." Laird John MacDonald greeted each by name and offered a share of their meager provisions.

John organized all the survivors into groups with specific tasks. The women were charged with organizing and distributing edible foodstuffs as fairly as they could, the elderly and the sick getting the first servings. He sent out the men hunting in groups of two, but with only a few bullets and knives, they had to devise their own traps for squirrels and ptarmigans. Edgar MacDonald carved a crude bow and a sharpened stick for an arrow and with it brought down a deer. The deer was only staggered from the shot, and the beast gave Edgar a deep cut on his chest with one of its hoofs before his knife finished it off. The women dressed Edgar's wound as best they could and then prepared the animal. Everyone in the cave ate well that night.

A major problem remained water. They melted snow, but there was nothing to store it in until on the third day a metal tub and a wooden bucket appeared outside the cave entrance.

Then the supplies stopped coming.

The next morning a MacDonald hunting party found a red soldier's jacket in tatters, ripped to shreds, halfway up the mountain.

More people hiding in the hills died each day.

A scouting team of three men returned to the cave late that afternoon. "The redcoats are gone, but all our houses and stables are destroyed along with the cattle, chickens, horses, and any other livestock. Nothing left to feed us through the winter," reported one man.

"The weather today," said another, "is cold and windy, but thankfully the snow has stopped and there are bare patches of ground. 'Tis little consolation, but does give us hope for an early spring."

The next day John sent another man and a teenage boy down the hill to the burned village to see if anything at all could be salvaged. They came back to the cave with empty arms.

Two nights later, two more men with three young lads and a lass appeared at the cave entrance. One of the men carried a wounded man on his back. "We began as a cluster of eleven," said the man, "but the others died, so yesterday we started out to find help. We survived on the few rabbits we could trap and a hen that miraculously kept laying eggs. Praise the Lord, we saw the smoke from yer fire. Help me put Callum Gillis down so someone can tend to him."

"Zeb?" said Joneta. She hadn't recognized him until he brushed the snow and ice particles off his face and beard. "Zebulon Keene, let me get ye a blanket for Callum."

Zeb laid Callum across the blanket, exposing a bleeding, pus-filled belly wound. Joneta gagged at the smell. "Ye'll get used to it," said Zeb. "Have ye anything that might ease his suffering? He took a dirk to the gut trying to protect his bairns. All of them escaped, but his wife perished in the snow last night. Check the wee one of the bairns. His toes are frostbitten."

Another of the women led Callum's bairns to the back of the cave while Joneta tore a remnant of cloth and pressed it into the wounded man's stomach. Callum cried out in agony.

"Callum," said Zebulon, "we're safe here. 'Tis warm, and they have a bit of food."

Callum's hands balled into tight fists as he choked out the words. "I canna eat. Feed the bairns. Ye have to save them." He rolled to one side and infection squirted out of his wound.

"I give ye my word, my friend. I will care for yer bairns just as ye would until ye are better. I swear. Now lie quiet. Let Joneta tend to ye."

Callum moaned.

"We'll do the best we can for him," said Joneta quietly, "but we have naught."

"He begged me to leave him in the snow to die," said Zebulon, "but Callum's been my closest friend for all my life. He saved me from my own foolishness more times than I can say, and I willna leave him. I'll do anything I can for him just as he would for me." Zeb leaned over his friend to talk into his ear. "I'll take care of yer bairns, Callum. I give ye my pledge."

Callum groaned again and mercifully fell unconscious.

After Zeb wrapped Callum in a blanket, he said to

Joneta through chattering teeth, "I watched the others die, frozen or starved. I thought I'd ne'er see ye again. There's naught left for us. The air is barely breathable with the smell of rotting dead animals and the smoke, and I dinna ken how much longer we can stay in these mountains. Where are Callum's bairns? I have to take care of them."

"Dinna worry, Zeb. The other women are doing a good job of keeping the bairns warm and calm. We are all afeared, but John shows us courage. I'm glad ye're safe." She tugged another scrap of a blanket around him and rubbed his arms to get the blood flowing again.

His voice cracked with pain as his limbs defrosted. "My sisters died in the fire, and my mum was shot. I couldna save them."

Joneta blinked back tears that came every time she heard of another death, but the grief wasn't hers alone. Everyone had lost loved ones. If only she kenned why.

"My da and mum both died, Da in the house, and..." Her voice choked up. "And Mum died here. I canna understand the reason the king wanted to kill us. I dinna ken why we were betrayed."

Zeb spat out the words. "He's no king of mine when he murders my kin in their sleep. The Campbells did the deed for him. I'll kill every Campbell I find!"

Zebulon Keene, two years older than Joneta and usually soft spoken, had a square face, a prominent chin and soulful blue eyes. His too-large teeth overwhelmed his smile, but that smile spoke of his kind heart, his generosity, and his steadiness in every situation. Tonight he talked in a way she had never heard from him before.

"Please, Zeb, 'tis pointless to talk that way. We need calm heads to stay alive. John is leading us as best he

144

can. Someone brought us a bit of supplies, food, burned wood, these blankets, and such, but we havena had any more for two days now."

Zeb took a long deep breath and held out his frostbitten hands as close to the flames of the central fire as he dared. "I thought about a lot of things in the cold, and how all can be lost so fast. A knife to Callum and my best friend will die in agony. I pledged for ye to marry two years ago, but ye said ye wanted to wait, so I waited, but now I see how quickly things can change. I canna wait anymore. I ask ye again to be my wife." He blew across his numb fingers.

Joneta admired him and cherished his friendship, but she did not love him, not in the way a wife should, not in the way she loved Rory.

"Zeb, now isna the time," she said while gently rubbing his fingers, "to even think about such things. I'll see what I can get ye to eat."

He held her arm and stopped her from leaving. "But Joneta, 'twas decided a long time ago, at least I decided a long time ago. Ye're the only woman I'll ever want. I love ye. I always have even when we were just bairns and played together. I love ye, I do. I'm asking ye to marry me. I'll see we both survive this. I promise ye."

"But, Zeb, in this disaster, I canna consider marrying anyone."

The man from the fair still owned her heart, even though her love for him felt shattered into a thousand pieces like a fallen icicle. Had the dark-haired man who had pledged his life to her led the soldiers to their land and spoken lying words to her da? How could she still love a man who watched from the door as her father died, a man whose deeds caused her mother's death and the deaths of so many others? She felt hollow inside, yet desperate to feel whole again. She just had no idea how to do it.

"I dinna ask for a wedding tomorrow or even next month," Zeb went on. "'Twill take time to rebuild, time to build up our herds again, time for me to build us a house."

His words "build us a house" stabbed her, and she clutched her stomach. Rory had promised her a house, but if what the others said was true, she could never live in a house of his. How long did it take to abandon a marriage? Declare a man dead? Father MacHenry, Lorna and Clyde—if they all still lived—knew she had wed him, but could she honor a marriage after losing so many people dear to her? She was married only in the legal sense, not in substance, the way a man and a woman should be.

Zeb reached out for her, but she stepped away. "Zeb," she said, "come over here and get a bit to eat. We dinna have much, but we will share." She led him to the meager supply of food set against the wall.

Zeb chewed slowly on the small piece of remaining deer meat. Taking her hand, he said, "Sit with me."

Folding up the blanket, she stuffed it under the two of them so they didn't have to sit against the cold stone wall.

Zeb said, "We've been betrothed for over two years." Raising his hand to keep her from protesting, he said, "I ken, ye havena agreed to wed me, at least ye havena said it aloud, but I am counting on it when ye're ready. I started to build a house for us a few months ago, but 'tis destroyed now. Dinna ye worry, I'll start again and build ye an even finer one."

"Zeb," she began, so unsure of her feelings. Her grief and her fear engulfed her heart. She couldn't think straight.

"Dinna say anything now. I ken I am no' the richest or the handsomest man in Glencoe, but none will treat ye better than I will. Ye'll ne'er want for anything, and we'll have bairns who'll be as beautiful as ye. Please, Joneta, this slaughter has made me see that we canna wait any longer. Ye have to say 'aye' and soon."

She rubbed her fingers over his still near frozen hand and let her thoughts wander aimlessly across her mind.

Could she go back to Rory? The man who played a part in bringing murdering soldiers to their village and caused the deaths of so many? But how could she move ahead in her life with Zeb? How long would it take her to forget the pain? Would she ever?

She tucked Zeb's hand under the edge of the blanket and did not answer him.

****

That night she tugged a fitful young Bryan into her lap and rocked him, saying soothing words. Eventually, he dozed off with his head tucked under her chin. She leaned back against the cave wall and tried to sleep.

Bryan kicked out his leg, waking her from a dream filled with flashing visions of the fires, her father's body, the shivering of the children, and the agony of Callum Gillis. Rory appeared in each of them holding his dirk and pistol, both dripping with blood. Voices shouted at her. "He let them die! He abandoned ye! He betrayed yer clan! His heart is false!" She awoke with a start, in a sweat.

She wrapped Bryan in the blanket and laid him on the floor. He tossed for a minute and then fell back to sleep. "Ye deserve better than this, wee one," she whispered.

Moving quietly and quickly out of the cave, she shivered in the chilly wind. Her toes throbbed on the frozen ground. Reaching under the torn blanket draped over her shoulders, she unpinned her wedding brooch and held it up to the moonlight. It glittered. It had meant hope and love and a future. Now all of that was gone.

"I promised I'd ne'er take this off, Rory Campbell, but I'm breaking my promise. My clan needs me, and I choose them. If they survive, then so will I, so I am breaking my promise."

Drawing her arm back, she flung the brooch as far as she could. It disappeared in the darkness and sank in the snow and mud.

Chapter Twenty-Two

May 1692

John Dalrymple, Master of the Stair, stomped his foot and furiously shook the letter in his hand.

"Get in here!" he screeched at his aide sitting just outside his office door. The young man dashed in. "Aye, sir?"

"This letter says that two of MacIain MacDonald's sons survived! Two of the old fox's sons were not killed as per the orders! Why?"

The young man's hands shook. "I dinna ken, sir."

"Take a letter to everyone on the Privy Council, to Captain Robert Campbell of Glenlyon at Fort William, and to Major Duncanson, with a copy to our King William."

The words sputtered out of his mouth as the young man struggled to take down each one.

"I am furious that MacIain and the rest of his family were not dispatched as planned on February 13. The orders were specific, and each man responsible is in dereliction of his duty. King William depended on me to exercise control of the savages in the Highlands, but ye incompetents have disobeyed me. I demand immediate reply and action. I order that all survivors of the MacDonald clan be hunted down and sent to the plantations as slaves in the West Indies or be killed."

"West Indies or killed," repeated the young man.

Dalrymple continued dictating. "Britain cannot be united without control of the Highland barbarians! Do ye have all that?"

"Aye, sir."

"Prepare the letters, and when you are done come back for my signature and seal."

Three weeks later Dalrymple received word back from King William. "Ye obviously misinterpreted my orders," wrote the king. "The horror of this mass murder falls on yer shoulders and those of John Campbell of Breadalbane for conspiring with the lairds to send a letter to the exiled King James to ask his permission before signing their oath to me as their rightful king. Charge Breadalbane with treason and have him imprisoned.

"Many here in court, including my wife, Queen Mary, are demanding monetary compensation to the MacDonalds. Since the treasury cannot afford such payment, I will demand that a person or persons be publicly punished to express our regret for the clan's losses. Tell Captain Campbell of Glenlyon to choose someone who will appease MacDonald, someone they will see as recompense for the disaster carried out without my knowledge.

"Ye, Dalrymple, are dismissed from all positions of authority."

King William—signed and sealed.

Chapter Twenty-Three

June 1692

The indomitable clan of MacDonalds came down the mountain to rebuild their lives out of the ashes of Glencoe. Thirty-eight people died in the fires and over one hundred more died from exposure in the hills, so the clan's first task was to bury the bodies. Out of respect, they buried Laird MacIain and his wife in the traditional cemetery of Eileen Munde on the island in Loch Leven, but the other MacDonalds would lie for eternity in graves in the glen, often with the remains of whole families in a single spot. Uneven piles of rocks served as headstones.

By tradition, a bagpipe was to be played at the funeral, but the only bagpipe to survive the fire belonged to Callum Gillis's oldest son, Jacob. It consisted of only a small bag and a single pipe, but Laird John MacDonald played it as if it were the grandest instrument of all. He blew traditional funeral music as loudly as he could, which was intended to let those already in Heaven know that more souls were coming.

The music had barely faded in the wind when the survivors went back to the hastily put-up tents and lean-tos while waiting for what would be a slow process of rebuilding their houses. They drew lots for the order of building, and everyone worked together to see their village find its place in the valley again. Laird John insisted that everyone else have permanent shelter before any construction began on his own house.

As the weather warmed, women tilled the soil and planted whatever seed they could scrounge to start meager gardens. A few coos wandered down from the ridges, and several nearby clans, having heard of the Glencoe disaster, drove small herds of their own cattle into the glen, never expecting anything in return. It would be years before the herds would be back to their former size, but at least now there was some meat to eat.

Joneta worked until her hands were raw and blistered, and by the end of each day her back ached so much she couldn't stand up straight. Zeb worked alongside her, helping her with the heavy tasks and trying to ease her burden with his support and kind words. She barely spoke to him, and he never saw her smile.

"We'll start again," said Zeb, "ye and me. When all are sheltered, I'll start yer house. We'll be wed. Ye will accept me, winna ye? Now that there's no one else?"

She nodded, not because she agreed to be his wife but because there was no one else.

****

A small rickety carriage pulled by a swayback horse rattled to the center of the half-built structures that would be new homes for the people of Glencoe. Clyde MacDonald and his wife, Lorna, sat close together on the high seat. The horse, looking nearly as old as they were, came to a stop near a small group of people stacking stone for a cottage.

"We're looking for Laird John MacDonald and Joneta," said Clyde in his firm, strong voice.

"I'm here," came a deep voice from the back of the

152

work crew as Laird John MacDonald stepped up to the carriage. "Clyde and Lorna! I am surprised to see ye. Why did ye come here? We would come to ye. Has been on my mind to check on ye, but as ye can see, we have much to do here, and verra little to share with ye."

John reached up and lifted Lorna from the wagon seat to the ground, and then held out his hand to help Clyde. "Ian, take care of their horse. We dinna have a proper place for ye to rest, but ye can get out of the wind in this tent over here."

He led the couple to a makeshift shelter. Just outside the shelter, two women fed a fire and stirred a large pot of stew. Inside, three more women stitched together jagged pieces of cloth to make more tents, Joneta among them.

Clyde led Lorna into the tent and sat her on a bundle of straw.

Clyde said, "We came to deliver this news ourselves. Joneta, do ye have an extra blanket for Lorna? She's near frozen through from the trip, as short as it was." Joneta handed him stitched together scraps of gray and blue blankets with burned edges, which he draped over his wife's shoulders and sat beside her on the straw with his arm around her.

"We saw the smoke from the slaughter, and we regret we couldna be of any help. We watched a second regiment of king's men go by the house, but we stayed out of sight."

John said, "There was naught ye could do. They attacked at night without warning. Murder in trust."

Lorna reached out her hand and touched Joneta's cheek. "How many of ye survived?"

John spoke slowly, the anger rising in his voice.

"Thirty-eight were killed in their houses as they slept, but near one hundred more, mostly women and children, died in the caves. Some families escaped the valley, but they havena returned. Ye can see several of our wounded lying over there." He pointed to the far edge of the tent. "The weakest already died, but the strongest linger. 'Tis painful for them and for us who have to watch their suffering. We're doing the best we can, but most willna make it. We can barely keep them warm, let alone nurse their injuries. We dinna expect Callum Gillis to last the night."

Callum came up on his elbow, motioning Zeb to his side, and spoke quietly so no one else could hear. "Ye promised to take care of my four bairns." He coughed and foul pus seeped from under the bandage. Zeb knelt beside him and eased his friend's head back and spoke quietly. "Ye have my word. Yer bairns will be well cared for."

In a raspy, fading voice, Callum said, "Zeb, find a way so I can die a man worthy of my bairns. Dinna let them remember me as a dying, rotting corpse. Please! Please, Zeb, take me to the hills so I can die with some decency, no' in a corner of this tent for all to see."

"Rest easy, my friend, tonight I will carry ye to the hills, just like we planned. I will stay with ye until the end, and I will bury ye there."

Callum closed his eyes.

John went on talking to Clyde. "We came here three weeks ago to rebuild. Glencoe began with nothing, and we have nothing again."

"Ye are our clan, and we feel yer pain," said Clyde. "Lorna brought quilts, candles, and a few jars of vegetables, some jam, too. 'Tis in the back of the wagon.

We had some flour left, so she made bread. 'Tis no' much."

"'Tis more than enough. We will divide it up and feast tonight."

One of the women brought in two bowls of a thin but hot soup and handed one to Clyde and one to Lorna. "Here, these are for ye. It may no' be a fine meal, only scraps of meat, and a few root vegetables, but 'twill warm yer insides."

"'Tis delicious," said Clyde after his first spoonful.

"Nay, 'tis no', but it stops the rumbling in yer belly, at least for a while."

Lorna spoke in a quiet, tired voice. "We have news, news that had to be delivered in person."

Laird John MacDonald squatted in front of the elderly couple. "What is yer news?"

Putting his bowl down on the ground, Clyde began. "We have word from Fort William." He handed John a folded piece of paper. "Two soldiers in uniform came to our house yesterday. They asked us to deliver this. They were afraid to come farther into the valley for fear of being attacked."

"They'd be right about that!" said Zebulon.

"Let me read this first," said John. After a few minutes, he looked up. "This doesna help us much now."

"What does it say?"

"It says that because of a public outcry against the soldiers who murdered in trust, the king regrets the incident in February."

"Tell that to our dead ones! I'm certain it'll make them feel a lot better."

"Is he sending money to rebuild our homes, our stables, our lives?" asked another.

John waved his arms to silence the undercurrent of frustration. "Nay, no money will be coming, but it does say the ones responsible will be punished. He doesna name anyone, and says 'twill be done through the proper channels, whatever those are."

Alex MacDonald rested his shovel against a pile of dirt and stood next to his brother. Grabbing the paper from him and shaking it above his head, he shouted, "This is naught but a piece of worthless paper. King William thinks we should be grateful that he even recognized the error of his ways." His eyes scanned the remains of the Clan MacDonald as another stream of angry voices and sorrow raced through the crowd. The women wailed, and the men cursed.

When the sounds finally died out, Clyde said, "There is one more thing ye should ken. The king has decided there must be a public display, a sacrifice, to prove his regret at the incident. Someone must atone for the massacre." He sucked in his breath. "And that sacrifice will be Rory Campbell, who will be hanged at the fort two days from now."

After Clyde said the words "Rory Campbell" followed by "hanged," a choking fog surrounded Joneta. She couldn't breathe! Clutching her chest, she fell to her knees, gasping for air in deep braying inhales. She had tried to drain her heart of all that Rory meant to her. She had tried to believe he was a traitor, a liar, and not worth the air in his lungs, but in truth she'd only buried her overriding love and passion for him deep in her gut, covering it over with her grief. She had swallowed what she could not face, and now it burst out of her like a geyser in a hot spring, wild and furious. Zeb reached down for her, but she flung her arms out and shoved him away.

She crawled over to Lorna and grasped Lorna's hands. Burying her head in the old woman's lap, she wailed. Incoherent sounds poured out of her throat like those of a banshee on the loose. The crowd watched in horrified silence.

Finally, a strangled gasp left Joneta's throat, and she could speak again. "No' Rory! It canna be. No' Rory! Tell me 'tis no' true!"

Zebulon Keene put his hand on her shoulder and again tried to lift her to her feet, but she fought against him, slapping his hands and arms. "What are ye saying, Joneta? Ye ken he betrayed us. He helped murder ye da and mum. Ye said he means naught to ye and ne'er has."

She pushed Zeb away again, stood on shaky legs, and pressed her head against Clyde's chest, her tears soaking his shirt. "Tell me 'tis no' true!"

Tenderly, he answered, "I wish I could tell ye different, but Rory is the one chosen to be the sacrificial lamb. The captain says he betrayed the regiment by killing two soldiers. Rory claims he was trying to stop them from slaughtering more MacDonalds, but everyone believed it was his excuse to add to the savagery. Captain Campbell testified the two soldiers who lost their lives by Rory's hand while carrying out their duty were heroes, and Rory was a traitor to the crown."

"The captain only wants to justify his own actions. He gave the orders to kill at will!" wailed Joneta.

"Rory will be hanged as an example, and, in some verra strange way, as an apology."

"More death is no' an excuse! Ye canna let them!"

John grabbed Joneta by the arm and jerked her away from Clyde. "What are ye saying? He killed our mother and our father! Ye swore he meant naught to ye!"

She struggled to control her continuing tears, gagging on them. She shook off her brother's grip. "They canna kill him!"

Suddenly Alex came up behind her, twirling her around to face him. "He led the Campbells here! He was in on it from the start. If his own kind want to hang him, let them!"

"Nay! Nay!"

John shook his head. "What has happened to her? How can she care what happens to that bastard Campbell? No' after what he did!"

"There is something ye dinna ken. It may be for her alone to tell," said Lorna, "but I will say it for her. Try as she might, she canna hate him. She canna even blame him."

"The rest of us can. The rest of us will see him hang and ne'er shed a tear or even give a word of protest."

Clyde held his wife steady and nodded his head, encouraging her to continue.

"Rory and Joneta are verra much in love," Lorna said. Gripping Clyde's hand, she added, "They are married."

Laird John MacDonald took a step toward the older couple and shouted, "O'er my dead body! O'er his dead body, the bloody Campbell!" John held up his hand in the sign of the devil with his forefinger and little finger raised and the middle fingers pressed against his palm, shouting in Gaelic, "*Buitseach*!" and spit three times between his fingers. "The devil's curse on him!"

"Nay!" cried Joneta again. "John, ye think our love is wicked, but 'tis no'. Apart I was lonely and miserable, living a half-life. Together we are whole. 'Tis like the world opened up to me with Rory."

John spoke again. "Ye've been ruined by a Campbell."

A woman in the crowd shouted, "How could she? What was she thinking? She has betrayed us all! Laird, what are ye going to do?"

"It canna be true," said Zebulon. "She has promised to marry me. She canna be married to him."

"But she is. We witnessed their vows," said Clyde.

John ground out the words, "I should have killed him at the fair two years ago. I told her to stay away from him. I didna watch her carefully enough." He whirled around toward Clyde and Lorna. "Ye kenned about Rory, and ye let that bastard meet Joneta at yer house!"

Clyde slowly nodded. "They were in love. They met with our supervision. We did what we thought was right. We understand what it means to love so completely."

"Ye did it behind my back! Ye encouraged her in this reckless adventure. Ye let him make promises until he led the soldiers right to our doors!"

Joneta, pointing her finger and swinging her arm at the people of her clan, said, "We have taken vows, and none of ye can undo our pledge to each other. None of ye. Ye can say whate'er ye wish about us, but ye canna change us!" She took off running toward the hills.

"In two days, ye will no' have to worry about what anyone of us did," said Clyde. "Rory will be dead, and Joneta will grieve for as long as she lives."

"Let me go after her and talk to her," said Zeb. "She might listen to me."

The veins stood out on John's neck, but he nodded.

When Zeb caught up to Joneta, he scooped her up about the waist to stop her running. Spinning her around, he planted her on her feet. "Listen to me, Joneta. Please, talk to me."

She coughed and sputtered to clear her throat of her continuing sobs. Her shoulders shook and her hands trembled. "They canna hang him! Ye have to help me!" she begged.

Zeb rubbed his fingers across her cheeks to wipe away her stream of tears. "I want to help ye, but 'tis naught I can do about it."

"Please, I'll do anything to stop this!"

"Joneta, a few days ago ye hated Rory. Ye said so."

She grabbed his hand and squeezed it tight. "Canna ye see? After Da and Mum died, I was angry and grieving, and I needed someone to blame, but I didna mean it, no' in my heart. Ye have to help me!"

"Ye threw away yer brooch. I saw ye."

She shivered, not from the wind, but from the depths of her sorrow. "He gave it to me, and I gave him my whistle." She sucked in a deep breath. "Both are gone! I threw away the only thing I have of him." Once more she collapsed to the ground, and Zeb knelt beside her, taking her in his arms and rocking her.

"I wish I could help ye," he said. "Yer brother has no respect or caring for any Campbell, and now he thinks one has defiled his sister."

"Defiled?" she said, lifting her head. "He didna defile me. I went to him willingly."

"I can no' think of ye in a Campbell's bed, but the deed is done and canna be undone. Did ye think ye could promise to marry me, kenning full well that ye were already wed to a Campbell?"

"Dinna ye see? I thought I could hate him, but I canna."

"They'll despise ye for it. Even I willna be able to protect ye from the clan's wrath."

"Please, ye have been a good friend to me."

"I always wished there could be more between us."

Joneta looked up at his face and spoke quickly, her own cheeks drained of blood. "Canna ye understand there's naught I can do but love him? His love is my life for now, for always, forever. 'Tis more than a promise spoken in front of a priest. He's part of me. If he dies, then so do I. Even when I thought I could forget him, 'twas still true. If he loses his life, so do I."

Zeb looked skyward, trying to find the right words. "Be mine, Joneta. Ye will always have me. Please, Joneta, try to find even a small part in yer heart for me."

She brought his hands to her lips. "If ye could find a way to save Rory from the hangman, I'll do anything ye ask." She added, "I'll marry ye. I'll be yer wife. I'll reject my marriage to Rory, and I'll be yers. If he lives, I'll be yer wife! Please, help him! Help me!"

Zeb held her at arm's length away from him. "Do ye think so little of me that I'd take ye into my home, into my bed, when ye love another? Do ye think me only half a man that I'd settle for half a wife? That I'd live with another man's heart instead of one entirely my own? How could ye shame me like that?" He stood and turned his back to her.

She leapt to her feet and ran around until she faced him. She saw the glistening in his eyes and she understood. She had humiliated him.

"Ye're a good man, Zebulon, and I used ye disgracefully. I ken ye canna forgive me."

Zeb wrapped her in his arms, resting his chin on the top of her head. "Ye are the only person I will always forgive, but ye ask too much of me. Half of yer heart is no' enough for me. I see how ye love him, and every time I look into yer face, I will see another man there. Mayhap if he is dead, there will be a chance for us, a chance ye will forget, a chance I can fill his place in yer heart."

"I am begging ye to save him!" She slumped against Zeb. "I promise on his life that I will marry ye. Save him!"

"Joneta, I canna. The only way ye will honor yer word is if he is dead. I will see the deed done."

****

"I am taking Callum with me," said Zeb as he lifted his friend off the blankets in the tent. "He doesna want his bairns to see him die here. He wants to be with them to say goodbye."

"'Tis for the best," said one of the women. She gathered up the blanket where Callum had been and carried it out to the small flat cart Zeb had left outside the tent.

Once Callum was curled up on the cart, Zeb led the horse away, but instead of heading to the tent where the children slept, he headed toward the hills, climbing until he found a small cave. He carried Callum inside and laid him down.

Callum groaned, but said, "Thank ye. Ye're a friend like no other."

Zeb unloaded the other supplies, food, blankets, and started a small fire. "I willna leave ye," he said, reaching out for Callum's skeletal hand.

"It may be days afore I finally die, days of suffering," said Callum. "I dinna ken if I am brave enough to stand it."

"I made an excuse to Laird John. I told him I'd go

162

ahead to the fort and ask if the MacDonalds can come to watch the hanging of Rory Campbell. I'd only be gone for a few hours."

Callum coughed and spat up bloody phlegm.

Zeb wiped his face with the corner of the blanket. "I wish I could make this easier for ye."

"I think ye can. I've been thinking. Naught else to do while I lie here, waiting."

Chapter Twenty-Four

Two days later—July 16, 1692

Fort William loomed ahead of them as they rode, the stone walls standing dark, cold, and forbidding. Clouds obscured the landscape with ominous shadows, and Joneta absorbed every moment of it into her heart, and bit by bit, she disappeared.

"John," she said, "I beg ye, we have to stop this execution. We canna let them hang him."

"There is naught we can do," said John, "and naught we want to do. Rory Campbell led the murdering soldiers to our door. He swears to have no' killed a one of us, but 'tis only to save his own neck. Many died because of him."

"Nay," said Joneta for what seemed like the thousandth time. "Rory isna to blame."

"He *is* to blame, Joneta. Stop defending what canna be defended. The king's command has judged him guilty, and he will hang. It doesna repay for the worst of what has happened to us, but 'tis revenge, and I'll settle for that."

"Revenge is ugly."

"No' as ugly as the massacre." He leaned across the gap between their horses and put his hand on her shoulder. "I am sorry, sister, that ye will lose the man ye think ye love, but ye canna love a murderer."

She shrugged him off. "He is my husband! The king thinks with this hanging it will be done for him, but 'twill ne'er be done for us, or for our da and ma and the others. 'Twill ne'er bring them back. The hanging is worthless. How can ye let this happen? Please, John, please!"

John's chest rose with a heavy sigh. "In time yer mistake in marrying him may be forgiven but no' forgotten. Until then, ye're back where ye belong with yer clan, and we will keep ye safe. I dinna think any other man will have ye, but Zebulon Keene still might. He's a good man and will make ye forget. Ye will see."

"Where is Zeb?" she asked. "Why didna he come with us? More than anyone, he wants to see Rory hang."

"Zeb went ahead yesterday to ask permission for MacDonalds to attend the hanging, so it wouldna be thought we came to cause trouble. We are meeting him at the fort. When the hanging is done, the king hopes we will be avenged, but say another word, Joneta, and I'll send ye back home."

She straightened her back and hardened her expression and stared straight ahead. She had to get one more glimpse of her Rory, even if it was to watch him hang.

They reached the gate of the fort. The heavy doors were already open. Soldiers in their red uniforms filled the open courtyard, all standing at attention, surrounding a raised scaffold with a single noose swaying in the wind.

Joneta gagged at the stench rising from the hundreds of men and their horses forced to stand in the sun. Everyone's eyes stared straight forward, all focusing on the noose meant for her Rory. Her stomach twisted, and the small meal she'd eaten came up and splattered on the ground. Zeb, who had just come to their side, reached over to help her, but she shoved him away and wiped her sleeve across her mouth.

Zeb spoke quietly to John. "We canna cause any disturbance. To get permission to even be here, I had to swear we would be verra quiet. Why did ye bring Joneta? This will be torture for her."

"I couldna keep her away," said John. He looked straight ahead at the scaffold. "Justice at last, however meager."

"Mayhap the people who ordered the attack can call it that," said Joneta firmly, "but 'tis no' justice to hang one man for what so many others did."

"Hush, lass."

The doors leading from the main wall of the fort itself into the courtyard creaked open and out rode Captain Robert Campbell, followed by five guards marching in a tight circle around a man, his arms tied at his back and a hood over his head.

"Rory!" called out Joneta. "Rory, I'm here!" John grabbed her by the arm and pushed her back against the wall, blocking her body with his. "Hush!"

The hooded man turned his head back and forth as if trying to catch the sound of her voice, fighting his ropes until one of the guards hit him hard on his back with his stick. The prisoner stopped struggling and let himself be led to the scaffold.

Captain Campbell dismounted his horse and marched up the steps to the top of the platform. Two men in the execution group climbed the ten steps with Rory between them, their footfalls, one after the other, tramping on each tread. Rory held his sack-covered head high and made firm contact with every step while Joneta shivered with each sound of his boot against the wood.

"Look at him! He's no' a coward," said Joneta, her eyes wild. "He is a sacrifice for the cowards who did this! Cowards! Cowards!" she shouted. Zeb grabbed her from behind, locking his hand over her mouth. After motioning to John to remount his horse, Zeb lifted her into John's arms.

"Get her out of here," Zeb said. "She'll get us all arrested. I'll stay and see the deed done. Take her home. She ne'er should have come."

John urged his horse forward and carried a desperate and thrashing Joneta out through the gate, with Alex riding behind them. "Rory, Rory!" she screamed.

"We have to get away from here quickly," Alex said. "'Tis too hard for her to be here, and too much risk for the rest of us."

"Rory! Rory!" screamed Joneta over and over until they rode across the ridge and out of sight and earshot.

Zebulon Keene slowly made his way through the troops to stand directly in front of the scaffold. One of the soldiers grabbed him by the arm. "Get back!"

"I'm Clan MacDonald, and I came to see the deed done. If there is to be a reckoning for our clan, I have to see the murdering bastard hanged."

"Ye can do it from the rear," answered the soldier.

"I want to see his boots kick in the air with my own eyes. I must see the deed done for the sake of all in my clan who died."

"All right," the soldier said, "but step back so the captain doesna see ye."

Zeb took one step back to stand slightly behind and between the shoulders of the row of king's men.

Captain Campbell unrolled a parchment and began to read, but Zeb paid no attention. He focused on the boots of the man who had brought others to kill his kin, the man who had stolen the heart of the woman who was to be his. He never took his eyes off those boots for the entire hour Campbell read the proclamation from King William denouncing Dalrymple as Secretary of State, along with the Earl of Breadalbane who arranged the first meeting of the clans for the signing of the oath. He read aloud about the public outcry of the "barbarous killing of men under trust" when they were guests of the clan MacDonald. For this violation of universal Highland hospitality, those responsible would be sought out and punished, beginning with the man who instructed the soldiers in their butchery, one Rory Campbell.

Rory coughed and doubled over several times, but he always straightened up and held his sack-covered head high. Zeb watched the boots until Captain Campbell announced, "The prisoner will be hanged until dead. His murders will be avenged. Prisoner, are ye ready?"

No answer.

"Hangman, do yer duty."

The burly hangman with a black mask covering half his face tightened the noose around Rory's neck and forced him to stand on the foot-high wooden block directly under the noose. Taking three steps back, he said, "May the Lord forgive ye and me." In a quick firm motion, he kicked the block out from under Rory's feet, and Rory dropped. The only sound in the courtyard for six eerie minutes was the rushing wind and the soft moaning from the prisoner. Finally, Rory became silent, stopped kicking and hung unmoving.

Captain Campbell said, "Executioner, check the body."

"Dead," the man said.

"Dismiss the troops," ordered the captain. "Remove the body." He left the scaffold, and in well-disciplined order all the soldiers marched out of the courtyard and back to their quarters inside the fort.

Zeb never left his position in front of the scaffold. After the execution patrol released the body from the noose, they laid it on the floor with the sack still over his head, wrapped it in a heavy cloth, and stitched him in. While they worked, Zeb moved closer to the platform and asked, "May I have the body? My horse is over there, and I am willing to take him away."

"Are ye no' a MacDonald?" asked one of the soldiers.

"I am. We want to burn the body as a symbol that our clan will ne'er be vanquished. 'Twill make for an easier evening for ye and be a boon to our clan. May I have him?"

"Take him," said the older of the soldiers. "It doesna matter to us."

Zeb led his horse from the back wall to the scaffold. He hefted the body over the saddle and walked his load out through the gate.

"The deed is done," he said. "The deed is done."

****

Two days later, Laird John MacDonald of Glencoe ordered a bonfire built. The men carried stacks of peat with a few tree limbs and boards to act as kindling into a pile some distance from the few completed homes of the village. Several of them lifted Rory's body, still wrapped in the prison tarp, onto the smoldering pile and used torches to light the rest of the fire until it burned brightly.

Joneta, her eyes swollen from crying, had begged

Zeb to open the burial cloth and find the whistle she had given Rory at their wedding.

"Nay," Zeb said. "Ye dinna need a remembrance of that man."

She raised her hand to slap him, but he grabbed her wrist. "I am sorry, Joneta, but I saw the man hang. The deed is done."

"Stay away from me," she said.

No one around the fire made any sound as the body burned. The odor of the burning flesh, an acidic metallic smell, filled the air, and people covered their faces with whatever they had with them to keep the stinging smoke from their eyes. No one left the pyre until the pile had turned to a low, hot glow and any trace of the body or its burial cloth had disappeared into smoke.

Joneta could not watch. She curled up in the pile of blankets inside the tent and covered her ears. Her tears were gone, and she couldn't even cry for the man who owned her heart.

****

The next day, Zeb walked up the hillside with the four children of Callum Gillis to a small wooden cross pushed into a mound of dirt.

"Yer da died the way he wanted to, and I buried him here, where he wanted to be. 'Tis so he can look down and look out for ye. He loved ye verra much. Ye may come here any time ye want to remember him, mayhap even to talk to him. Yer da was a proud man, a fine man, my best friend, and here is where ye will find him."

Chapter Twenty-Five

Joneta's days passed more slowly than ever after Rory's hanging. His death cut her in two, and Rory took half of her with him. She trudged through her chores, never fully seeing the people beside her. She rarely spoke, and few people in Glencoe said anything to her. To them she existed as a reminder of what happened in February, which none were willing to forgive, and she couldn't forgive them for letting her Rory die. She existed as a ghost, alone and separate from the world, and she never questioned when it would end. It never would.

She tugged at the edge of her underdress, hoping that somehow, someway, the brooch she had carelessly thrown in the snow all those months ago had suddenly reappeared where it belonged, near her heart. She rubbed the two small pinholes. Those holes were all she had left of him. She didn't even have her whistle to comfort her. It had melted and burned with his body. Tears no longer released her from her endless misery, so her eyes and her heart stayed dry and empty.

New houses in the glen gradually took shape as the rocks and stones, dug up near the river or chiseled out of the stony mountains, were stacked on a base of pebbles to stabilize the double layer of walls. Between the stones, the women packed in layers of peat, topping each wall off with a layer of clay to keep it dry until a final layer of turf and grass covered the top edges. Sections of the stone in the walls were carved away to create doors and two windows.

Logs and saplings formed the peaked roof and available grass, straw, and even some hair shaved off the dead coos covered it with a thick layer of woven thatching. One small area was left open at the peak of the roof for smoke to escape from the central fire inside. Lastly, rope netting secured the roof in place with rocks weighing it down against the wind.

A chill in the air already blew across the glen, and everyone, men, women, and children knew winter would come again all too soon. Those left to rebuild needed more shelters to avoid freezing to death in the tents, while the limited food barely held off the growling in their bellies.

Zeb came every day to help Joneta with her chores. At first, she flinched when he reached to take the bucket or the hoe from her, but after a time she let him work beside her. He talked to her about simple things like the weather or how the surviving coos fared, but she rarely gave him more than one-word answers. Still, he came every day.

Joneta bent over to pick up another brick of dried peat.

"Joneta," Zeb repeated. She didn't react until he put his hand on her shoulder. Then she looked up.

"Joneta, would ye like to come for a walk with me?" asked Zeb. "Might be good for ye to move about in the fresh air. Will ye come with me?"

She turned her head in his direction and nodded, but she didn't take a step until he put his hand on her back and moved her. Eventually, she walked on her own. "Where are we going?" she asked in a listless voice.

"Nowhere special, just walking."

They reached the lower hills and started to climb. Joneta did not say a word.

"Is the climb too steep for ye?" Zeb asked.

She shook her head.

They climbed upward until Zeb turned her around to look over the Glencoe valley. "'Tis a wonderful sight, isna it?"

When she didn't answer, he kept talking. "The snows will cover it over soon enough. There's even a bite to the wind, especially at night."

She nodded.

"Do ye remember this place?" he asked.

Now she looked around. "Nay."

"Ye've been here afore. The night of the massacre. Ye lived in the cave up there for two months afore we started to rebuild. Now do ye remember?"

"I dinna want to remember this place. Take me home."

"Ye threw a brooch into the snow over there. I saw ye." He pointed to a cluster of rocks just below their feet. "The snow covered it over. 'Twas his."

"He gave it to me when we wed, and I gave him my whistle. Both are lost. Now I have nothing." Her head slumped, and her eyes closed.

Zeb sighed. By mentioning the brooch, he'd made a terrible mistake. Now she regretted even more that he stood here and Rory didn't. He had only one thing to offer her. It was all he had left. His only chance.

"I want to show ye something else. Will ye come with me?" he asked her.

He led her back into the glen to an unfinished house set back from the rest of the settlement houses. "Here it is," he said, waving his hand in the direction of the half-built walls.

"What is it?"

"'Tis yer house, or 'twill be soon."

Without a word, she started to walk away. Zeb caught up with her, saying, "'Tis yer house, the one I'm building for ye. 'Twill be done in time for ye to fix it up afore we wed, and we can move in together. Spring will be here afore we ken it. His eyes lit up. "Our house."

"Wed in the spring?" Her voice matched the dull stare on her face.

"Aye, ye promised, but we willna wed until the house is finished just the way ye like it. I'm going to put in a real chimney so the smoke willna fill up the room, and I want to add a second room on the back, a small one, for our beds, so we dinna have to sleep where we eat. What do ye think of it?"

She sucked in a noisy breath as if she'd been holding it for a long time. "Wed in the spring?"

"Aye, I gave ye time to grieve and didna mention yer promise, but the time is getting closer, and we need to plan, especially now that I'm building the house. I work on it when the rest of my work is done, but 'twill be finished in plenty of time. I promised ye a house, and here it is. What do ye think of it?"

Her eyes focused on the house for the first time. "Ye're building this for me?"

"Aye, what do ye think? Could ye live in a house like this?"

"'Twill be the finest in all Glencoe," she said quietly.

He puffed up his chest and smiled. "Aye, 'twill, and 'twill be all yers and mine, too. Do ye really like it? I want ye to like it."

For the first time in months, she looked directly into his face. "Ye have a kind face," she said. "A face a woman could trust."

Taking her hands in his, he said, "Do ye think ye could trust me? Trust me enough to be yer husband? Trust me enough to forget the brooch and forget Rory Campbell?"

As soon as he said Rory's name, he knew he'd gone too far again. How could he keep being so foolish? The mention of Rory's name jolted all the grief back into her face. Her features fell.

She left him in silence.

Chapter Twenty-Six

The first pouch arrived three months later, in November, delivered to Laird John MacDonald by a private messenger named Toby Marshall, who had ridden from Oban on horseback on the old military road.

"Ye are to sign and return this packet after ye have removed the contents. Then send the pouch back with me to be delivered the way it came, as proof. If the seal," said Toby, "has been tampered with or the contents removed, ye are to slice off my nose and send it back inside this envelope."

"Surely this is a joke," said John. "I willna slice anything off ye."

"I thank ye for that, Laird, because as ye can see the seal has no' been broken. The contents belong to ye, and my duty will be done once ye remove them."

John turned the parcel wrapped in cloth over in his hand. "'Tis the size of a cabbage, but flat. Do ye ken what is in here?"

"Nay, sir."

"Who is it from?"

"I dinna ken, sir. I am only to deliver it to the Laird of Glencoe."

"'Tis I," said John. With his knife, he cut off one corner of the package and ripped it open along the side. Reaching inside, he took out a fat change purse, filled with coins. Opening it, he spilled the coins on the table and counted them.

"'Tis near three pounds," he said. "There's a note, 'This money is for the support and benefit of the bairns of Callum Gillis. 'Tis to be used for no other purpose. Laird, ye are charged with this task to see 'tis carried out on these terms. Tell them 'tis from their brave father who loved them always and gave up everything so they could live.' 'Tis no' signed. Who gave this to ye?"

"A messenger from Inverary handed it to me along with three shillings as my payment. He said he got it from a messenger at a small inn between there and Stirling. Afore Stirling, I canna say. No names and no questions asked. Please sign the parcel, and I'll be on my way. I'm to take this signed parcel back to the town of Rannon and 'twill go back to where'er it came from on a different path."

"I dinna understand any of this, but will ye have a meal with us afore ye go?" asked John. "My wife is a fine cook."

"I thank ye kindly, but I have to be on my way. There is also a message that ye can expect another parcel to come by a different route, but no telling when."

"Are ye certain there is naught else ye can tell us?"

Toby shook his head. "Naught else." John scribbled his name on the parcel with a stick of charcoal from the fire. "Here, ye are, lad. Be on yer way, and Godspeed."

John said to Alex, "Do ye think Zeb Keene kens about this? He's built that house and taken the four bairns to live with him. I recall 'tis three lads and a lass. The lads are indentured to pay off the debt of caring for them by the Manns and the Martins for the months after the massacre. They only stay with Zeb at night, but Joneta takes care of the lass and the smallest lad all the time.

177

Somehow Zeb talked her into that.

"I ken Joneta is housekeeper for Zeb during the day, but she spends the nights here with us. He still has no' convinced her to marry him. We need to speak to him about this money. Send someone to fetch him."

Zeb stepped through the doorway a short time later. "I came as soon as I could. So sorry I'm covered in dirt and manure. The few coos we have left need to be with a herd, no' roaming around alone like they are now. They give us a verra hard time."

"No worry about the dirt. We got a package for ye today," said Laird John, "really a package for Callum Gillis's bairns, and since ye're caring for them, we need to tell ye about it."

"Who would send the bairns anything? Callum had no other relatives."

"We dinna ken, but here is what was in it." John pointed to the table with the coins scattered on it.

"Someone sent money? Who? Why?"

"The message was clear. The money is to be used for the care and support of Callum Gillis's bairns, and since they are living with ye, ye will have a say in what to do with it."

"I dinna understand."

"There was no more explanation than that I am to see ye use the money for the bairns. What do ye want to do with it?"

Zeb paced the width of the house from wall to wall. "I need to talk to Joneta. Mayhap she'd be willing to wed a man who had extra money to take care of the bairns."

"Think about it, Zeb," said John. "Mayhap she'll think ye dinna need a wife if ye have extra money."

Zeb stopped pacing. "Ye're right, but mayhap the

bairns can convince her. She takes care of them like they are her own. If she willna do it for my sake, mayhap for theirs. I will talk to them and hope that together we can convince her. I willna mention the money."

"She needs a husband," said Alex. "One that can make her forget that bassa Campbell. He's dead, and she needs to make a life for herself. Do yer best, Zeb."

****

Nearly every day for the past months, Zeb had found Joneta lifting stones to complete the walls on his house. When the walls were finally done, Joneta worked on the inside. She stomped the dirt floor with a flat paddle before Zeb carried in flat stones to be laid in a tight pattern over the dirt, packing the spaces between them with straw and dried grass. She stitched curtains from a thin quilt with burned edges to cover the two windows in the walls on either side. The two Gillis lads, Jacob and Abraham, cut firewood and kindling and stacked it next to the house before carrying some inside to stoke the fire in the shallow pit in the center of the room so Joneta could cook their meals. As the food cooked, she taught the younger ones, Moses and Ruth, to read, and with hearty meals, she made certain that Jacob and Abraham got plenty of decent food and a full night's rest before going to work the next day for their indentured families.

"Soon," she told them, "the debt of keeping ye after yer da's death will be paid and ye will work for Zeb, only for Zeb."

Three days after the pouch arrived, Zeb asked Joneta, "Will ye stay after our evening meal to spend some time with the bairns afore I walk ye home? All of us spend so much time working, we dinna have time to just be together. The bairns need to feel like a family

179

again."

Joneta nodded, and after the plates were washed, she sat down on the chair in the corner. "Would ye like me to tell ye a story?" she asked. "Me mum used to tell me stories afore I went to bed."

"I'm going to check on the animals," said Zeb. "I'll be back afore the story is over." He picked up his work gloves off the table and left by the connecting door between the house and the stable.

"Mistress Joneta," said the oldest lad, Jacob, after Zeb was gone, "we have something we want to talk to ye about first. Is that aright?"

"Of course, what is it ye want?" said Joneta.

The four orphaned children, ranging in age from twelve down to five years old, surrounded her on the floor.

"We want to ask something of ye," said Jacob. He cleared his throat. "Go ahead," said Abraham, the next in age at ten years. "Say it."

"I will!" He cleared his throat again. "Ye ken our da and mum died at the massacre, our mum in the cold and our da of his stomach wound a couple of months later."

Joneta nodded. "I am so sorry. I lost my da and mum, too, and I ken how 'tis ye still grieve. Laird John asked families to take in all the orphaned bairns as they were able, and I am so glad Zeb got his house finished so ye could all be together with him."

"But we are no' together as a family should be," said Ruth, the eight-year-old lass. "Moses and me are treated fairly by Zeb, but Abraham and Jacob are still indentured to pay for their food and lodging. That's where they go every day. They only sleep here. 'Tis no' right Abraham and Jacob to be mistreated. Hold out yer hands,

Jacob."

"I can take care of meself," said Jacob, tucking his hands under his arms. "The laird says Zeb is a man alone, so we canna stay with him like a family should."

"Jacob's hands are covered in blisters and sores that willna heal, and ye see how thin he is," said Ruth. "Lift yer shirt and let her see yer back."

Jacob repeated firmly, "I can take care of meself. 'Tis no concern of yers, Mistress Joneta. Ye are no' our mother...or Zeb's wife."

"There is little I can do, but I will do what I can. How can I help?" said Joneta.

"We want to live together. Zebulon Keene was our da's finest friend, but he is a man alone. We want to live with Zeb and no' have to work for anyone but Zeb. We can repay whatever debt is still owed."

"Laird John thinks bairns should be with a man and his wife," interrupted Abraham. "If Zeb had a wife, the laird would let us live with him all the time and no' work for anyone but him. We will promise to work hard and no' be a burden."

"If ye would marry him, we could live here with ye and him together," said Ruth. "Zeb is the only one we think would marry ye. Will ye marry him?"

Joneta's stomach clenched into a tight ball at those words. *Marry Zeb? How could she?*

"Did Zeb tell ye to ask me to wed him?" she asked.

Ruth spoke up. "He said ye dinna want him, but if ye could, please, try. He is a kind man, and we need yer help. Please." Their soulful eyes begged her.

Was this another sign she needed to put Rory aside and let Zeb into her heart?

Zeb was a good man, a man any woman would be

pleased to marry. Still, even knowing Rory was gone forever, she couldn't release herself from him, but these orphaned children might be just the ones to do it. She always wanted a family, a large family, and this one could be just what she needed. Rory had promised her a house, but Zeb would provide it with an off-the-peg family.

"I can speak to my brother."

"Will ye marry him?" asked Moses.

"He is a good man," said Joneta. "Ye bairns need me. Mayhap 'tis time I had a family."

Later, Zeb walked her back to John's house for her to spend the night, just like he did every night. He wouldn't have anyone thinking there was anything untoward between them, a man and woman who weren't married.

"The bairns talked to me tonight."

"Oh?'

"I suspect where they got their ideas, or rather who put the ideas in their heads."

Zeb didn't look at her, but said, "Were their ideas good ones?"

"Aye, they were."

Zeb turned quickly to face her. "Do ye think so?"

"I will think about everything they said."

Taking her hand in his, he said, "That's all I ask. Think about it. We can have a fine life together."

"Aye," said Joneta softly. "A fine life. Not the life I planned, but a fine life."

She paused for a long moment. "We can wed next summer."

Chapter Twenty-Seven

Months earlier—June 1692—a cell inside Fort William

Rory stepped over the puddle of dirty water on the floor and flopped back on the pallet in his cell in the lower level of Fort William. He immediately sprang up. Lice and fleas jumped all around him, and he swatted away as many as he could. Not that it mattered. He'd be hanged until dead in less than an hour, but until then he didn't want to itch any more than he already did.

Leaning against the wall and closing his eyes, he called Joneta up from his memory. The first time he'd called to her, she came to him as a shadow, her face barely visible, but now she came almost as if she stood right beside him. He reached out for her. Her lips parted as if she might speak.

"Ye're so beautiful," he whispered, and the vision smiled. "I can see the sunlight shining through yer hair. I can see the light scattering the flecks of color in yer eyes, and the sight of ye makes me strong. Ye take the darkness out of the night, and I dinna fear the death that is coming. I only fear ne'er seeing ye again, ne'er holding ye in my arms or feeling yer body against mine. I start to shake if I think about it too much."

He rubbed the heels of his hands across his eyes so he wouldn't lose sight of her in his tears.

"I've made all the plans for our house," he said aloud. "It's kept me alive since I was captured. 'Twill be of stone and two stories, like Clyde and Lorna's, except the upstairs will have two bedrooms for all our bairns. I think three lads and three lasses. The two of us will have a bedroom at the back that overlooks a huge flower garden. I ken that flowers will no' feed us, and truly serve no purpose but to please our eyes, but ye must have flowers every spring. Ye deserve them."

She smiled again.

"My time here is fading, but the joy ye gave me from the moment I set eyes on ye has sustained me. Before ye, I lived moment to moment, but ye brought forever into my life. I wish I could tell ye everything in my heart, but ken this—ye are my forever. My forever."

The door to his cell clattered open, and she vanished.

"Got a visitor, Campbell," said the jailer, a nasty man with black teeth. "Make it quick. Ye dinna want to be late for the hangman," he added with a laugh as ugly as his face.

A stranger stepped into the cell covered from head to toe in a thick black robe and hood. "Dinna fash, Rory. I'm Father Hamish," he said in a gravelly voice before he coughed up a huge glob of bloody phlegm, wiped it off his chin, and rubbed his hand on his robe. Judging from the number of stains, he'd been coughing like that for a long time.

"Make it quick, Father," said the jailer as he slammed the cell door shut and turned the key. "Work yer priestly magic on him, but he dinna have time for a sermon." He laughed again and walked away down the dank corridor.

The priest waited before he spoke. "He's right," he

said in a muffled voice, "no time for a sermon. We have to hurry. Take off yer clothes."

"What?"

Very loudly, he said, "I am here to give ye absolution," but softly added, "so take off yer clothes and get into my robe. We took it from a priest who came to Glencoe, a Father MacHarris or MacHill or something like that. He died, so he doesna need it anymore, but ye do." He stepped out of the robe and held it out. Strips of material bandaged his body across his stomach.

"I dinna understand," said Rory.

"Maybe ye will understand this." Slipping his hand into the folds of his robe, the priest took out a small item and thrust it toward Rory.

"Where did ye get this?" said Rory as he snatched the brooch out of Father Hamish's hand, the silver brooch of two intertwining hearts with a crown joining them above. "This is Joneta's. How did ye get this?" With a breathless gasp he said, "Is she still alive?"

"Aye, she is. Take off yer clothes."

Rory searched the dim hallway outside his cell to see if anyone could overhear him. "Tell me about her!" he said in a demanding hush.

"I will tell ye all ye want to ken, but take off yer shirt first. Do it while we still have time."

Rory slipped his shirt over his head, and the priest immediately grabbed it out of his hand and pulled it over his own head.

"How did you get her brooch?" asked Rory.

"Now yer breeches."

"Tell me!"

"Shout like that again, and ye'll bring the jailer, and I willna have time to tell ye."

After Rory stood naked, the priest tossed him the robe, and Rory dropped it over his head. The man put on Rory's breeches. They hung on his skeletal frame like a sack, and the man had to bunch them up at the waist, tying the loose material into a knot to keep them up. "Put the hood up so no one can see yer face."

Rory did as the man asked.

"My beard has turned gray, but I can smear the soot from the floor on my face to fool them for a while. It willna make a difference with a sack over my head. We need to trim yer beard some, so the difference willna be so noticeable when ye leave." He reached over and pulled a razor out of the folds of the robe Rory wore.

Rory rubbed his hand over the shaggy, overgrown beard on his chin. He hadn't shaved or trimmed it in four months. At the same time, he grabbed the priest's wrist, saying in a rough voice through clenched teeth, "Tell me how ye got her brooch."

The man shook his hand free. "All right. I am Callum Gillis of the MacDonald clan of Glencoe. Joneta survived the massacre and is well and safe, but my wife died in the hills, leaving me with four bairns. I took a dirk in the stomach defending them, but I made it to the mountains, trailing blood the whole way. A woman in the cave stitched it up, but the hole in my gut festered."

He lifted the shirt and part of the bandage to expose a gaping hole in his stomach, oozing globs of yellow and green pus. The stench of dying flesh quickly invaded the stale air in the cell.

"It willna heal, and I havena long to live. I couldna bear to leave my bairns homeless and penniless. They, too, would die." He let the shirt fall down and leaned against the wall for support as he coughed and held his stomach. "Give me that rag over there. I can use it to soak up the pus and blood."

Rory handed the filthy rag to him. "It isna clean."

"'Twill make no difference," Callum said as he pressed it gently to his stomach under the shirt. More bloody pus spurted out, leaving a splat on the floor.

"I am so sorry. What will happen to yer bairns?"

"They will be cared for by the clan, even though they think ye deserve to hang, that ye brought the King's men there, and that ye helped them kill."

Lurching forward, Rory said, "I didna! I tried to stop it, but there were too many soldiers. I tried to warn Joneta and MacIain, but I was too late. You have to believe me!"

"I do," said Callum. "This brooch is so that ye might believe I can give ye a chance to make amends. This brooch is to make certain my bairns ne'er forget me or their mum or the reason we died."

"'Tis Joneta's," said Rory.

"I give ye this brooch for the sake of my bairns and no one else now. If ye take it, I will take yer place, and ye will be pledged to see that my name is no' forgotten. The brooch will be yer promise. Will ye do it?"

Callum grabbed Rory by his straggly beard, jerking his chin forward, and sliced off a chunk of hair. "Stand still," he ordered as he reached for another section of beard. "If they hang me, they'll be doing me a favor." More dark beard fell on the floor. "A hanging is quick, but this…" He lifted his shirt again, exposing his foul wound. "This is beyond agony in pain and suffering. I am here to take yer place. Ye go free, and I have a quick death. A good bargain for both of us."

Callum sliced off more of Rory's beard.

"This is a gift beyond measure," said Rory. "I canna

let ye do this. 'Tis no' right."

"'Tis no' right for me to suffer. My death will be meaningless unless I can put it to good use. Dinna refuse me this last request." Callum added in a voice as cold as the death that awaited, "The brooch for yer life. A bargain for both of us."

After Rory's beard was trimmed close enough to match his own, Callum bent over a puddle of dirt, soot, and mud in the corner of the cell. Taking a handful, he smeared it on his gray beard, darkening it as best he could. "If ye dinna look too close, would ye think my beard to be yer beard?"

"Mayhap, if ye're a bawbag like my guard."

The two men stood side by side. "I'm so much thinner than ye, but I'll slump and claim to be too scared to stand up. I can also say my coughing and spitting up is fear as well. Ye keep yer face hidden and go out by the side door at the end of the corridor as quick as ye can. My horse is waiting there. 'Tis an old, tired mare, but ye can take it and go wherever ye please."

Rory rubbed the back of his hand across his mouth. "I dinna ken if I am worth this exchange."

Callum coughed again, clutching his stomach. "I have but one more day to live, and I want to give that day to ye, so ye will make certain my bairns survive. I am charging ye with the task." He groaned and closed his eyes. "Take the rest of yer days and make them worthy. Whatever ye do, make yer life worthy."

The sound of footfalls came from the corridor, and Callum fell to his knees, saying as loudly as he could, "Bless me, Father, for I have sinned."

Rory stuffed the brooch into his robe's pocket before fingering the chain and whistle around his neck.

He lifted it off and slid it over Callum's head. "The woman who gave me this may ne'er ken I am alive, but if ye wear it today, I will ken where it is forever, and I will ne'er forget the man who gave his life for mine. I pledge myself to yer bairns. I will see them grow to be proud of their da, no' a man hanged in place of a traitor. Ye will die a hero to them."

Callum clasped the necklace. "They're coming for me. Now's the time. Are ye ready?"

Rory tugged the hood of the robe over his head before muttering words he thought would pass for Latin. He spat on his thumb and smeared the spittle across Callum's forehead. "Go in peace, my brother," he said just as the jailer and five guards stopped at the cell door.

"'Tis time," said one of them. "Here's a sack for yer head so ye dinna see what's coming for ye." He laughed as he reached through the bars, holding out an old flour sack.

Rory put out his hand behind him and took it from the guard, and then handed it to Callum. Helping him put it over his head, Rory whispered, "I will ne'er forget this. I will pray for ye every day. I swear."

The jailer turned the key in the lock. "Out, priest, his soul is damned to hell, and ye canna do anything about it now. Out!"

Rory ducked his head, hiding his face under the hood of his robe as he moved out of the cell and down the corridor. He heard Callum groan as the guards lifted him to his feet and dragged him toward the courtyard.

"Please, Lord, take this man's soul quickly to paradise," Rory prayed. "And, Lord, make my life a tribute to his courage for as long as I live."

Once outside in the courtyard, he made haste

between the rows of soldiers toward the side door, keeping his head down and his face hidden. After saying "Bless ye" to the soldier standing at the door, he stepped out and took in his first deep breath of fresh air in a long time.

Chapter Twenty-Eight

Glasgow, Scotland

Robert Brown pushed the stallion's rump out of the way and dragged his rake through the fresh straw, spreading it out around the horse's feet. "There ye go," he said. "Yer stall is nice and fresh. Enjoy."

Dak Tulane, owner of Tulane's Stable and Livery, had seen the stranger from the window of his adjacent house leading a lame horse into the stable. 'Twas a young man, his boots nearly worn through.

Dak's slow footfalls sounded against the hard ground in the yard as he went to check. First came the click of his cane and then the shuffle, shuffle of his feet. "Lad, who are ye and what are ye doing here?" asked Dak as he watched the bedraggled lad use clicks and whistles to move his horses around.

"The horses will be more comfortable and easier to manage if they are in stalls better suited to their size and temperaments. See how the little roan is much calmer away from the Highland pony? I hope ye dinna mind."

"I dinna mind." Dak lifted his cane. "This stick of mine makes it harder to get around and do the best for the mounts. Have ye worked with horses much afore?"

Robert stroked the neck of a stallion in need of a good brushing. "I used to. If ye're looking for someone to help ye, I'd be grateful to give ye a hand in exchange

191

for meals and a place to sleep. That corner would do me fine."

"I take it yer no' from around Glasgow."

"Nay, sir. I've been in the Highlands for a time."

"Anywhere near that Glencoe massacre we've been hearing about?"

"Nay, sir," said Robert. "Nowhere near there."

Dak watched Robert finish settling the horses and then pick up a rake to muck out the stalls.

"I'm impressed with how ye handle the horses, so I'll take a chance on ye," said the older man. "Ye can sleep in the back room and take yer meals with me. After one month, if ye are still working out, I'll start to pay ye a penny per animal per day up to ten pennies a day."

"Thank ye, sir. Ye willna regret it."

Quickly, the two men found an easy rhythm in stabling the horses, renting them out as needed, and training the steeds belonging to the wealthy men who raced them.

The old man asked, "So how's business today?"

"Two mounts checked out and three new ones checked in for a week each," said Robert. "Owner wants this one brought ready to race. He says by February, but I ken 'twill be April at the earliest. The beast has a lot of bad habits.

"Another man came in, saying his horse balks at loud noises, that he had to be led into the city because he wouldn't let anyone ride him. I'll take him out on short walks and rides until he gets used to city life." Robert laughed. "It took me a while to get used to the noise and clatter here meself."

At the end of the first month, Dak counted out coins into Robert's hand. "Here's what ye've earned. Got any ideas what ye're going to do with yer money?"

"Aye, sir. I'm going to build a house."

****

In Glencoe—Late summer 1692

One day Joneta, exhausted from a nightmare of a man dangling from a noose, overslept and arrived to find Zeb's house empty.

"They all left to do chores," called Rumina, the woman living in the nearest house. "My hen is laying good, so I gave all of them slices of bread and an egg to break their fast. I'll let the little ones play with mine so ye can get some real work done at the house. Zeb says the wedding will be next month."

"Aye," said Joneta, "and thank ye. I could use the time to myself."

She started fluffing and straightening the quilting on all the beds. First, she shook out the pallets for each of the four children's beds. Three small rocks fell out of Moses's quilts and two pressed flowers floated down from Ruth's. Next, Joneta walked into the extra room in back where Zeb slept and where she would soon sleep with him. The blankets were rumpled in a pile at the foot of his raised bed, and after giving them a good shake, she noticed one of the stones in the wall near the floor was chipped, with bits of gravel falling out of it. She reached down and dug her fingers into the hole. She moved her fingers inside, digging out more chips of stone, until she touched something smooth. She tugged at it. Something shiny flew out and across the floor. She chased after it and picked it up.

Her whistle on the copper chain.

How did this get here? Where could Zeb have gotten it? Did he take it off Rory's neck when he brought Rory's body home? Why didn't he give it to me? But she knew why. He didn't want to remind her of her dead husband.

She slid the chain over her head and tucked the whistle into her kirtle, holding her hand over it until it felt warm against her skin. She wouldn't tell Zeb she'd found it, so that in some small way, Rory would always be with her. It might quiet her uncertainties after she married Zeb.

Chapter Twenty-Nine

September 1693

Rory leaned his ear against the bedroom door, trying to catch the sound of her voice. Her muffled words were hard to understand, but he guessed she'd come to give Lorna and Clyde something. He ached to open the door and take her in his arms, or at the very least let her see he was alive, but he couldn't. It was too dangerous. Too dangerous for anyone who might be arrested for sheltering the traitorous Rory Campbell, dead or alive, but most importantly he couldn't risk breaking Joneta's heart yet another time. First, for disappearing after they wed, then when her clan was massacred, and lastly seeing him hanged. It would be better if he carried the pain for both of them.

"I am so glad ye came," said Lorna to Joneta. "Ye look a fright. Are ye working too hard?"

"Nay," said Joneta. "I'm no' working hard enough to escape my nightmares and the memories that haunt me during the day. Ye are the only ones I can talk to."

"Come, sit here," said Clyde. "Tell us anything ye can."

Rory heard the chair slide against the floor before she sat down.

"I have prayed for relief from the constant grief in my heart, and I've worked hard to stay busy hoping to get rid of thoughts of Rory, but 'tis a ne'er-ending battle. So my only choice is to change my life, change how I live in Glencoe. I must find a way to finally bury Rory."

Rory sucked in his breath. Aye, it would be best for her to forget him, but he didn't know if he could live without that little scrap of hope he might someday hold her in his arms again. Still, better he live without it than she suffer.

"I've been putting it off as long as I can, but..." She hesitated. "I am grateful Rory canna hear me say these words."

The silence nearly stopped Rory's heart.

"I have accepted Zeb's proposal of marriage and will wed him in three days."

Rory's knees buckled, and he slid to the floor.

Lorna said, "Are ye certain?"

"I am certain of naught except that Rory is dead, and we can ne'er be together again." Her voice cracked. "He is ne'er coming back, so I must go on in a life without him. Zeb takes care of Callum Gillis's four bairns, and I have been helping him with the housekeeping and cooking and the like. After we wed, they will be mine as much as they are Zeb's, and my life will be full. Someday I may even have more bairns."

Her next words came in halting fragments. "Rory and I talked about our own bairns, some with his dark hair and quick smile, and mayhap a few with my reddish tinge to their locks. But I have to put those thoughts out of my head." She took a slow, gasping breath and composed herself, finally saying, "I will be satisfied with my life."

Rory couldn't listen anymore so he moved to the opposite wall and closed his eyes. He'd only come this close to Glencoe and Fort William to retrieve the letters Lorna held for him and Joneta. He had hoped they might comfort him, but nothing would comfort him now. She would wed another. He prayed he could bear it.

****

Three days later

Rory sat astride his horse on the ridge as the survivors of the clan MacDonald gathered around the gravesites of those killed over a year and a half ago by the king's men. At the edge of the cemetery stood an arch of twisted branches lined with strips of cloth and leaves. In front of that arch, surrounded by the rest of the clan, stood Joneta MacDonald and Zebulon Keene. Laird John MacDonald stepped up to face the assembly, his voice carrying across the glen to where Rory watched.

"This has been a long time coming, both for Joneta and Zeb, but also for our clan. Recovery from the massacre has been slow, but together we have made our land and our people strong again. In remembrance of those who died, and in celebration of those who lived, today two of our own are here to make a new beginning."

The crowd burst into applause and cheering.

When the noise settled down, John spoke again. "We have no priest, Father MacHenry was killed along with so many of our own, but as yer laird I can pronounce the marriage of my sister, Joneta MacDonald, to Zebulon Keene. As ye can see, they already come with a family, the children of Callum Gillis. Zeb and Joneta will raise them in Callum's memory, a man who died defending his own."

Ruth held Moses's hand as they stood next to Joneta, while Jacob and Abraham smiled broadly standing beside Zeb.

Even from a distance, Rory saw how beautiful Joneta was. She wore her auburn hair loose, tied back with only a blue headband that let long tendrils dangle across her shoulders and down her back. He'd never seen her dress before, a bright blue with a lace apron tacked across her breasts that draped loosely down the front, then was cinched at the waist with a dark blue ribbon.

A dull pain settled in his chest knowing another man would hold her and love her and grow old with her. She had every right and duty to marry again, believing he had been hanged in disgrace as a traitor. Those must be his substitute's children, the four belonging to Callum Gillis. Only Joneta would be kind enough to take them as her own, knowing their parents had been killed in the massacre that she blamed him for.

And there stood Zebulon Keene, the man who had finally won her heart. Zeb now would have the family he never would. Rory was a man alone in the world, a man who could never show his face to the woman he cherished. All he had left was the brooch he carried inside a slit in his belt, and two small boxes, one blue and one yellow, containing their letters. He rubbed his finger over the brooch and quietly cried for the first time since he'd been a child.

She would wed another and never know how he still loved her and would love her always, but he could not make the world stop. It went on, and he would have to do the same. He clicked his tongue and his horse moved forward across the ledges and hills until he left the glen to go into a world that he had no control over and where he didn't want to be.

In the glen beside the stone markers of the clan's dead, Laird John raised his voice again to be heard above the ever-blowing wind of Glencoe.

"First, the bairns. Do ye bairns, Jacob, Abraham, Ruth, and Moses accept as yer guardians and parents these two, Joneta and Zebulon? With all that means as adoption into a new family with all the responsibilities and duties of bairns born into it?"

Moses jumped up and down shouting, "We do! We do!" He slapped the hands of his sister and brothers shouting, "Say ye do! Say ye do!"

"I do," said each of them solemnly in order by age.

The crowd clapped politely this time.

"Joneta, afore I take yer pledges to Zeb, he has something to tell ye, and I hope it will no' make a difference, but ye must ken afore yer vows are sealed."

"What are ye talking about?" asked Joneta.

Zeb sucked in a deep breath and took both Joneta's hands in his. "I should have told ye sooner, but yer brother insists ye ken it afore we say our vows."

"What is it?"

"Well, I dinna ken what to say."

"Just tell her," growled John. "She has to ken, and I willna marry ye until she does."

Zeb sighed heavily again. "A parcel came by private messenger to John. It contained a letter and some coins. The letter directed me to use the money for the support and benefit of Callum Gillis's bairns. I dinna ken who sent it or why. 'Twas no' signed, but said that more money would be coming."

"Ye must ken where it came from," said Joneta.

"Nay. It came by some secret route, changing hands often without anyone kenning where it had been afore."

"Why didna ye tell me?"

"I worried ye might marry me only for the bairns, so

199

they'd have someone to take care of them, but now that they have money to support them, I thought, mayhap…" He took yet another shaky breath. "Ye wouldna want to marry me." He hung his head as he rubbed his thumbs over her hands. "Ye'd think I didna need ye." He lifted her hands to his lips. "But I'll always need ye, so does having this money to care for the bairns change yer mind about marrying me?"

"Have I no say in this money?" Joneta asked her brother.

"Nay," said John. "It came for Zeb, and he will decide, but how Zeb spends it will make life easier for all of ye."

"The bairns have outgrown their clothes and need new shoes. And what about books so they can be taught? Can the money be used for that?"

"Aye, shoes, books, all of that," said Zeb, his eyes brightening along with a smile. "Whate'er ye think they need. They'll be yer bairns, too. Ye tell me and I'll see it done."

"'Tis Zeb's to use as he chooses for the children," said John. "I am charged with seeing it used as the giver requested, but ye and Zeb will have the last word."

"All right," said Joneta. "All will be well."

John spoke again. "With that settled, now on to the vows to make this official. Zebulon, do ye vow to care for this woman, feed and shelter her, ne'er beat her, and keep her as yers as long as ye both will live?"

"I will. I do!"

"Now, Joneta, are ye ready to take this man as yer husband? Ye have been going to his house every morning to tend to him and the bairns during the day and then coming home to my house every night. Are ye ready now to take on yer womanly duties in the bed with Zebulon Keene as yer husband? Are ye ready to be his wife in every sense and meaning of the word?"

Joneta looked at each child as they watched, waiting, their faces beaming. She looked to Zeb, ready to accept and agree, when suddenly she felt the whistle move under her dress against her breast. Her heart began to race nearly out of her chest, and she struggled to take a breath. The air around her pressed down like the collapsing walls of a house, and she swayed on her feet. A blackness came over her eyes. John reached out to steady her. "Joneta, are ye ill?"

Struggling to stay upright, she shook her head, closed her eyes, and let the darkness pass. By the time she finally breathed normally again, she knew what she had to do. She'd known all along, but today her mind and her heart were made up.

"I love ye all and I've made ye my family." Lifting her hand to Zeb's cheek, she stroked his beard. "But I canna marry ye."

The crowd gasped.

"What do ye mean?" asked Zeb as he dragged her hand off his face. "Ye promised. Ye said ye were ready."

"I thought I was ready." She tugged on the chain around her neck and lifted the whistle free, saying, "Until I found this." She never took her fawn-colored eyes away from Zeb's light blue ones.

"Where did ye get that?" he asked.

"I found it in a hole in the wall."

"Ye were ne'er meant to find it. For yer own good, ye were ne'er meant to find it."

"I ken why ye hid it from me, but vows must be taken in honesty, and I canna do that now."

"What do ye mean?" said Zeb. A redness bloomed on his neck.

John said, "Joneta, what are ye doing?"

"I wish it were no' so, but 'tis. The whistle is the sign that my heart and my body belong to another, alive or dead. I tried to complete my life without him. I wanted it to be with ye and the wee ones, but 'twould be a lie, and 'tis no' fair or right of me. I am sorry, Zeb. I canna marry ye." She swallowed down the sobs bubbling up in her throat. "I am so sorry, Zeb. Can ye forgive me?"

Moses grabbed Joneta's hand. "Ye dinna mean it! Ye canna leave us!"

"I am sorry, wee one, but there's no other way. I will always love ye, and I hope to see ye raised, but I canna marry Zeb."

The crowd muttered in angry tones. One man shouted, "She played Zeb false from the start! Once a traitor, always a traitor!"

Joneta's eyes pleaded with Zeb to understand. She touched his hand, but he jerked it away. His anger cut through her, and she couldn't speak the words.

The crowd's taunts continued. "She's no' a MacDonald! Laird, send her away! She's no' one of us! Let her lie in the graves!"

Releasing a strangled sob, she ran. To anywhere, to nowhere, only away from the agony of betraying Zeb and knowing she could never have Rory.

She had no idea where she was going, and she didn't stop until her trembling legs collapsed under her. Wheezing, she fell to the ground and cried until her heart was dry. Tears soaked her apron. Mud stained her hands and her knees.

She looked up and saw Clyde walking toward her.

"I didna marry him," she stammered out, reaching up for the older man. She lifted the whistle on its chain. "I didna marry Zeb. I couldna. I looked at his face, and I couldna betray him with my false heart." Her tears came again. "I canna live between the two worlds of the living and the dead! Help me, Clyde, I beg ye, help me!"

He lifted her to her feet and led her toward the house.

Chapter Thirty

Once Joneta's sobs lessened to short tearful gasps, Lorna held a cup of tea to her mouth. "Here, try some of this." Joneta took a few quick swallows before Clyde said, "He was here."

With a lurch, Joneta pushed the teacup away. It dropped to the floor and shattered.

"He's alive?" cried Joneta. "Ye saw him? Tell me!" She threw herself at him, nearly knocking him down. "Tell me!"

"He wouldna tell me where he's been or where he was going. He wouldna even tell me how he came to be alive. He made me swear I wouldna tell ye for yer sake and ours, but I canna look at ye now and no' say a word."

"Tell me!" she screeched, pushing herself away from him.

Lorna's quiet voice said, "Tell her."

Clyde sighed heavily before he spoke. "He came to get the letters ye and he wrote to each other. He thought they might comfort him. 'Twas on the same day ye came with news of yer coming marriage. He heard ye from the bedroom. He said he would leave after ye were wed, but today he left afore dawn. Mayhap he couldna stay to see it done."

Joneta fell to the floor, curling into a tight ball of misery. "Rory doesna ken I didna marry Zeb!" She looked up at Lorna and Clyde. "I couldna do it! How can my Rory be alive? I saw him march up the scaffold! I saw his body thrown in the fire. How is he alive? Tell me!"

Lorna helped Joneta up and led her back to the chair. "I wish we could tell ye more, but Rory came to the door, and we both nearly fainted at the sight. He said he couldna tell us anything more, but he had to ken if ye were still alive. He wouldna tell us where he has been or where he was going. 'Tis too dangerous."

Clyde interrupted. "If the soldiers found out he was alive, we could hang for hiding a traitor, and he wouldna allow that."

"He didna want ye to ken. Said 'twould make yer heartache stronger. If ye didna ken about him, ye could marry Zeb and have the life he wanted for ye but could ne'er have himself. But ye didna marry Zeb, so there is still hope for ye and Rory."

"He made us swear on our souls to keep his secret safe, but our God will understand that we couldna keep that oath from ye, no' ye."

The anguish in her heart threatened to explode as she asked, "How did he survive a hanging?"

"We dinna ken. He said he was living the only way he could, in the shadows."

"I'm going to find him."

Chapter Thirty-One

Three months later—Chester Racecourse, St. Chester, England

"Here's your share of the prize money, Robert," said the Earl of Westcart, a tall fair-haired Englishman. "This is the largest purse of the winter racing season so far, so enjoy." The two men stood at the door of the massive stable at the Chester Racecourse while the crowd wandered around watching the stable hands get the horses ready to go home. "You trained my stallion well, and he showed himself the winner I always knew he was."

"Thank ye, sir," said Robert Brown as he sorted through the coins Westcart handed him before putting them in his own purse tied around his waist. "He's a fine animal."

"Thanks to you and the stable in Glasgow that trained him. He'll make a fine stud. I'll offer him to Dak Tulane if he has need of another sire."

"He'd be pleased of that," said Robert. "We are always looking for ways to strengthen our lines and those of the other horse owners."

"Will you be heading back to Glasgow?"

"Aye, I've been away for months. I've had three horses racing even this late in the season. Kept me busy. Our purses from the races have been verra fine this year, and we took the Carlisle Bell at the Kiplingcotes Derby. The bell is inscribed, 'The swiftest horse takes this bell,' but 'tis the owner who gets to take it home. I'm satisfied with my share of the prize money. Right now, all I want to do is head back home and sleep in me own bed."

"When King James the Sixth developed a fondness for horse racing years ago, I thought the sport would be bigger in Scotland by now so ye might stay closer to home."

With a grin, Robert said, "'Tis told that the House of Commons asked James to stop spending so much time at Newmarket racing and more time running the country!" Both men laughed. "Many didna get back into racing after Oliver Cromwell banned the sport, and taking care of the animals and getting them fit to race can be expensive. 'Tis no' for the faint of heart."

"If anyone can convince a man to invest his money in horse racing, it will be you and Dak."

"Thank ye, sir."

"Next time, will you stand with me beside the horse in the winner's circle? Get some accolades for yourself? You deserve as much credit as the jockey or even the animal who wouldn't have won if you hadn't prepared him so well."

"Nay, sir. I'd rather stay behind at the stable to greet the jockey and the horse when they come back. I get my praise when I brush the winner down and I can see how proud he is. A horse shows it by the way he stands and shakes his head or prances. I love to see that. Most horses willna do that near the crowd and noise, but they will with me."

"But people should see your face and know who you are."

"Nay, sir, they shouldna."

"The local newsbooks, and even the *London Gazette*, want to find out the secret to your success," said the earl. "You deserve the recognition."

"Nay, sir, I dinna."

The risk was too great. He was a dead man, and it had to stay that way.

****

"Master Brown, would you mind riding up top on the coach the rest of the way to Glasgow?" asked the driver in his English accent. "We're taking on a woman and an elderly couple, and I cannot ask any of them to ride up top. Do you mind very much?"

"I dinna mind," said Robert Brown. "I've been sitting on my backside for two days now, trying to get back to Glasgow, so stretching out will feel good. If I settle in between the luggage, 'twill be out of the wind. 'Tis no' too far from here. Would ye say about four hours including one stop to change horses?"

"I would. Thank you very much, sir."

Robert climbed up the side of the coach and snuggled between the bags. Exhausted from the past months at the horse races in England, he laid his head down on his arms and fell asleep.

"This way, if you please," said the driver to an auburn-haired woman, attending to the elderly man and lady with her. "The gentleman will ride up top, so there'll be plenty of room for you three."

"Thank ye verra much," she answered as she helped the woman and then the man into the coach. "Here's yer cane, sir," she said as she handed the hunched-over white-haired man a fancy walking stick.

"You are a Scot," said the coachman. "Your brogue

gives you away. The one up top is Scottish, too."

"Aye, I'm born in Scotland, lived in the Highlands all my life, but now I work for the Blossom family in Glasgow as a cook, and today I'm escorting them home from visiting their son and his wife. Sir Blossom is on a special diet, so I came with them to prepare his meals."

"Hey, mister," said the coachman, nudging the man on the carriage roof, "another Scot riding below."

"Uh," murmured Robert as he shut his eyes again.

"Come sit beside me," said the older woman, still a beauty despite a deeply wrinkled face and neck.

"Of course," said Joneta, lifting her skirt and climbing inside.

She leaned her head back against the seat. Riding on bumpy roads in swaying carriages made her sick to her stomach. On the twelve-day journey to Glasgow from the Highlands three months ago to search for Rory, she'd thrown up twice, much to the horror of the other passengers. Since then she'd learned to take slow deep breaths and shut her eyes as often as she could. Fortunately, this journey back to Glasgow was short, but as extra insurance against another regrettable incident, she hadn't eaten anything today.

Her position with the Blossoms had fortunately come soon after she arrived in Glasgow. She'd used up nearly all the coin Clyde had given her on the carriage rides and overnights at the inns—although she slept on the floor a couple of times rather than risk the flea-ridden bed. What the cooks at the stops called stew, she called slop, but at least if they offered cheese or bread she could scrape the mold off. How people could charge money for such terrible food was beyond Joneta's understanding! With the price of a room in the boarding house in

Glasgow, it left her near penniless.

She'd been in the city for three days going from place to place looking for work when she heard about a position as cook at the Blossom house from another single woman in a room down the hall. Joneta, at her first interview with the Blossoms, made griddle scones and lamb stew for the couple. They were well pleased with both dishes, and along with the letters of reference Clyde had written, which included glowing compliments and seemingly official documentation of her service in the best houses in the Highlands, the Blossoms, a well-placed family in Glasgow, hired her. The couple was more than pleasant and generous, and on her days off she was free to walk the city asking at as many liveries as she could about a bearded dark-haired man with an easy grin. So far no one knew a man like that.

Today, when the coach came to a stop in the heart of the city, Joneta helped the Blossoms out and ordered a horse-drawn hackney carriage to carry them and their luggage back to their house on the north side of the city.

"Wake up," said the coachman, shaking Robert Brown. "We're here. Off you go."

After helping to toss down the luggage, Robert picked up his own bag and climbed down from the coach. He wished he could splurge on a hackney like the woman with that couple, but he couldn't waste his money. Building his house and other expenses took every penny he had.

"'Twill feel good to walk," he said to the driver. "Only a mile or so, and I'll be asleep in me own bed."

"Best of luck to you!" said the driver.

"I dinna need luck. I make my own!"

****

The bell on the door of the Clearbridge Messenger Service shop in Glasgow jangled as Robert Brown entered. "Good morning, Shane," said Robert to the man behind the counter. "I have another purse to be sent."

Shane held the purse up by his ear, shook it, and listened to the coins jangling inside. "I heard one of yer horses won at the Chester Racecourse and another at Newmarket. Ye surely have been a busy man!"

"My nags have done well."

"I hear 'tis all because of yer training methods."

"'Tis the horse that does the running. I just encourage him."

"'Tis a modest man who gets the most done, and the one who gets the richest. Is this purse to go by the same route as the last one?"

"Nay, send the purse south first, then north, and then northwest to Glencoe. Make certain there are at least six exchanges and that each rider is sworn to secrecy about where he picked up the package."

"Aye, sir, and as always, the signed purse is to come back by an altogether different route. I will work out the routes both ways, and ye can pick up the empty signed purse after it arrives back here in Glasgow, as always. Ye have ne'er told me why ye send money that way."

"And I ne'er will. Ye and the riders are paid well to stay silent." Robert leaned over the counter until his nose nearly touched Shane's. "And I've explained what will happen to ye, if anything goes awry. Ye'll pay the price if one of the messengers is a talkative lad or if anyone hears that coin is being sent north to Glencoe from here."

Shane swallowed hard. "Aye, sir."

Robert leaned back. He handed Shane another purse filled with coins. "Here are the extra fees for the riders, which they will collect from ye after they have completed their part of the delivery, which will be easy enough for me to check. Ye're a good man, Shane. Keep it that way."

"I will, sir, I will," said Shane as he tucked the larger purse inside a heavy leather bag and wrote the final destination on it. "Ye are more than generous. Ye can count on me."

Robert smiled, creating two semicircles in his cheeks around his mouth. Back out on the street, he lifted his hood over his head, ducked his face against the driving rain, and headed back to the livery.

As he walked down the muddy street, a woman with a heavy green cloak covering her head and face walked toward him. She passed him, and he turned back to watch her climb the steps to the Clearbridge Messenger Service office. Robert had a flash of awareness from the way she walked that he might have seen her before, but the feeling quickly passed. Many women moved in similar ways.

The bell jangled again as she opened the door.

"Good morning, Shane," she said, closing the shop door behind her. "Have ye a post for me today?"

"Aye, mistress. I was wondering when ye'd come to pick it up. It came last week."

He took a small, folded letter out of one of the many letter boxes lining the wall and handed it to her. "See, 'tis addressed to Box 123, no name, and the seal is unbroken."

Joneta rubbed her finger over the wax seal. "Just as it should be. Here is payment." She slid two coins along the desktop toward the clerk.

"Will there be a reply?"

"Nay, I canna. The sender kens that, too. 'Tis for the best this way. Thank ye as always."

"My job is no' to ask questions. I just deliver them."

"I'll come back next month to see if any others have arrived."

Joneta slid the letter into the pocket of her cloak, lifted her hood, and braced herself for a walk in the rain back to the Blossom house. She turned to the right, but not before she noticed a man standing on the corner to the left, watching her. She glanced in his direction, and he quickly walked away. Many men had watched her like that since she'd lived in the city. Men in the city were different from those in Glencoe. There she trusted everyone. Here she did not. She straightened her shoulders, held her head up, and kept her eyes forward until her steady strides took her out of sight.

Once back home and safely out of the rain, Joneta dashed up to her room and closed the door. On her day off, Master Blossom permitted her all the privacy she wanted, and she took full advantage of it.

Carefully, she peeled back the wax seal and read the message written in an elegant yet unsteady hand.

Joneta,

Hope ye are well. Lorna took to her bed a few days ago. She says she'll be better soon, but I think she's in for a time of it. Eliza Prescott comes in to help with the cleaning and the cooking. Eliza asks if we've seen ye, and we say we havena. Laird John came to visit yesterday. He's leaving Glencoe to look for ye. Be careful. All else is fine. We miss ye.

Clyde

Joneta longed to write them back, but the risk was too great. She couldn't take the chance of being found by her family before she found Rory.

Chapter Thirty-Two

John MacDonald from Glencoe tied his horse at the post outside the Glasgow Westend Inn and stretched his stiff legs before entering the boarding house.

"Have ye got a room available?" John asked the man behind the desk.

"We only got one," said the barrel-chested man with bright red hair, "so ye'll have to share a bed or ye can sleep on the floor."

With a sigh, John said, "I'll take it." In Glencoe, the laird would never be expected to share a bed, but here in Glasgow he could tolerate sleeping on the floor for a few nights until he found Joneta. "Tell me where the nearest watchhouse is. I want to speak to a sheriff, someone in authority, an official authority."

"Watchmen dinna come out until night, but they patrol regular, so just look around for a man carrying a battle mace, one with a red insignia on it. Looking for anybody special?"

"I want someone to be on the lookout for a missing person."

"Who?" said the clerk as he handed John a key.

"I'm looking for my sister, a runaway bride."

"She didna take to the match ye made for her, uh? Women can be pigheaded. We got a watchhouse down the street. The city council appointed a constable just last week. Ye might check with him. They arrest a lot of people every night."

"I dinna want her arrested, just found."

The clerk shrugged and pointed to the left. "That way."

At the watchhouse, the constable, a dour-faced man with bushy eyebrows and a nose that had been on the receiving end of many a fist, led John into his office. He called it an office, but the small table in a closet was hardly that. There were no chairs for visitors, so John stood in the doorway.

"So what brings ye to Glasgow?" asked the constable. "Yer accent tells me ye're a Highlander."

"I'm John MacDonald, Laird of Glencoe, and I'm looking for my sister, Joneta MacDonald. Four months ago, she ran out on her wedding, and we havena seen her since. Her chosen husband isna here because he has four bairns to take care of."

"She left him with four bairns?" asked the constable, raising one of his shaggy eyebrows.

"They were orphaned during the massacre of Glencoe in '92, and Zebulon Keene took them in. She promised to wed him, but ran off afore the vows."

"That massacre," said the constable, shaking his head, "a terrible thing, murder under trust, a shameful business."

"Aye, a terrible thing," John said with a hint of sarcasm, "but the king claims to have made all things right by hanging one of his soldiers as a traitor. They have one dead. We have over one hundred and thirty. But I'm here about my sister."

"Finding her must be important if it brings the laird all the way here. What makes ye think she's in Glasgow?"

John shifted impatiently on his feet. "After much investigation of my own, I followed a messenger delivering funds to Glencoe back along the route through a series of private messengers heading to Glasgow. The package traded hands six times before I ended up here, but I lost the rider once we got inside the city. We dinna ken who is sending the money, all the messengers being paid and sworn to secrecy. Joneta might be following the money, too. I've got until spring to find her, when I'll be needed back at Glencoe."

"I am no' certain how I can help, but I'll do this much for ye. My watchmen patrol every evening, a different crew each night, mostly volunteers. They arrest any suspected villains, who then spend the night in the cells. In the morning, a judge decides if a crime has been committed. If there is none, they're released and sent on their way. If there is law breaking, then they stay for trial. We round up a lot of doxies who work the streets, too. Most likely, yer sister will be one of them."

"How dare ye?" said John, straightening up to his full height. "Joneta is no doxy!"

"Ye may no' like it, but 'tis verra hard for a woman alone in the city to make a living otherwise. Come back at dawn and ye can see if ye recognize anyone. Good day, sir, I have to assign the patrols for tonight."

Just then a man in a gray jacket pushed his way past John into the office. "Yer horse is out back, all shod, brushed and fed. Brown is waiting for his fee."

The constable nodded his head in John's direction. "This man is just leaving." Taking several coins out of his pocket, the constable handed them to the man in the gray jacket. "Give these to Brown. This should cover it."

"Speaking of horses, can ye give me the name of a

good livery stable? No' an expensive one, but a clean one?" asked John.

The constable didn't look up from his desk. "There are several well-established liveries in Glasgow. The closest is Dak Tulane's, about three streets south. Ye canna miss it. 'Tis on the edge of town, and Dak owns about fifteen acres for training racehorses, owned that plot for years. They just added on to the stable itself, and they're building a grand house next to it. Dak does a good business, housing and training, and doesna overcharge."

John nodded his thanks.

Robert Brown, after collecting his pay, walked from behind the watchhouse to the street and turned south toward Dak Tulane's Livery just before a stranger came out of the front door, untied his mount from the hitching post, and led the animal down the street in the same direction.

A few minutes later, Robert strode past the open doors of the Tulane stables and called out, "Dak, I'm back. I'm going into the house to finish my supper. Can ye handle everything?"

"I can," came the reply.

Robert shut the side door of the house behind him, just as a man led his horse inside the stable. "Have ye room for one more?" asked the tall man with the thick Highland accent.

"Aye, sir," answered Dak. "Put her in the empty stall over there. I'll brush her down and see she's fed. Are ye just boarding her or do ye want training?"

"Just boarding."

"Two shillings for the night and twelve for a week. Shoeing extra."

"Dinna ken how long I'll be in Glasgow, so I can give ye enough for the next few days. I'll pay more if I stay longer," said John. Under his breath he muttered, "If I can afford it."

After leading his horse into the stall, he asked, "How do ye do all the work yerself with that lame leg and cane?"

"I have help. He'll be here if I need him. Dinna ye worry. We have the best reputation in the city."

The newcomer had started out the door when he turned and asked, "I used to ken a dark-haired man who was verra good with horses, uses clicks with his tongue and whistles to train them, ne'er a whip. Quite a thing how he does it. Like a gift. Just curious if anyone in Glasgow trains like that. Ken anybody like that?"

Dak scratched his head. "Doesna sound like my man. I'll ask around for ye if ye want."

"Thank ye and good night."

Dak's first question when he went into the house and sat at the table beside Robert was "Are ye looking for extra work?"

Robert shook his head before swallowing the chunk of grainy bread in his mouth.

"Then no use bothering ye with it."

Chapter Thirty-Three

During the rainy winter of 1693, Joneta and John continued their searches through Glasgow. The Blossoms' health deteriorated, and Joneta had less days off to search the liveries, while John ran low on money and was forced to move his horse to a shed behind the inn and care for the animal himself. Robert remained oblivious to anyone looking for him at all.

In the middle of April, merchants held the annual Merchant's Fair, and shoppers swarmed the streets near the center of Glasgow on both sides of the River Clyde. On this one day, price reductions on goods brought hundreds of people into the city, all on a single-minded quest to get something for a cheaper price. The weather—especially warm for April—made the throng of potential buyers even larger than usual.

Some were shopkeepers and manufacturers looking for economically priced materials and supplies for their own businesses. Others were from the wealthy classes who either enjoyed buying things on the cheap or they were the "shabby rich" who needed to buy necessities at a lower cost to maintain a lifestyle they could barely afford. Most of the customers were working class, who mainly came just to browse and buy only a few things. The rest were thieves, pickpockets, and ruffians, who saw the shoppers as easy pickings.

Robert abandoned all thoughts of good manners and

patience as he forced his way through the crowd toward the leather factory at the end of the street. The livery needed new reins and harnesses, and he was determined to get a good price. Most people cursed him when he gave them a shove as he went by, but it didn't stop him. The horses and carriages were another matter, and he just had to wait until they passed.

He paused outside a dressmaker's shop to admire several colorful bolts of cloth and three dresses displayed in the window. He wished he had someone to buy for. He was drawn to a dark blue material with yellow specks scattered throughout, thinking it would suit Joneta, but here in Glasgow he knew no one who would use the cloth, and it would stay that way for the rest of his lonely life.

Someone, giving him a sharp jolt to his back, knocked him out of his reverie. His feet tangled, and he only stayed upright by steadying himself against the window of the dress shop, his arms splayed to the sides.

Then he saw it.

Directly across the street, a head of auburn hair moved in the opposite direction. Sunlight sparkled over the blond streaks throughout the braids.

Joneta!

He'd seen flashes of hair like hers before, and it always gave him a shock in the pit of his stomach. Each time, after he realized it wasn't her, he felt sick, lonely, and cursed to never see her again, never to hold her or say the words that stayed on his heart day and night. Even though he knew each time it couldn't be her, he always hoped it might be.

He had started toward the leather shop again when the auburn head of hair stepped up into the doorway of the ribbon shop across the road to let other people pass her. She faced toward the street now, and he got a good look at her.

Joneta!

He called her. "Joneta! Joneta!"

She looked the other way, obviously unable to hear him above the din of the passing shoppers.

He pushed himself onto the street just as the noisy wheels of a horse-drawn wagon passed in front of him, blocking his way. He pounded the side of the wagon in frustration. "Joneta!"

When he got a clear view of her again, she stepped out of the doorway and moved down the street away from him.

In a fury, he called to her again as he elbowed people out of the way, not caring if they fell into the muddy street. He screamed, "Joneta!"

Her head turned. She scanned the crowd.

He fought harder against the flow of people.

"Joneta!"

This time she caught her name on the wind. She saw him. Their eyes met. "Rory! Rory!"

She stepped into the mass of people on her side of the street, reaching for him and calling his name over and over. "Rory!" But the crowd moved her away from him. She grabbed the arm of a nearby man, who shook her off, and she stumbled into a woman with several packages under her arm. The packages fell. Joneta helped her pick them up, but by the time she got steady on her feet again, he was gone. She had to get to him. She fought harder, but it was useless. The people were too many, and she lost him.

At that same moment, near the glassmaking shop

several doors away, a young pickpocket relieved a well-dressed man of his money pouch, but not before the man grabbed him by the wrist, shouting, "Thief!" The thief shook off his grip and took off running with the man right behind him. Several others, hearing the cry of "Thief," joined the chase. "Stop him!"

People couldn't get out of the way fast enough, stepping on each other and sometimes falling. Others tried to help the young thief escape by grabbing the arms of his pursuers and shoving hard. Chaos reigned.

Rory fought to stay on his feet as the crowd closed in around him. "Joneta," he cried.

Suddenly a group of private guards hired by the shopkeepers for protection on this busy day started swinging their clubs. These men, wearing dark blue jackets and carrying clubs and sticks, shouted, "Make way! Watchmen! Stand aside!" They drove their way through the crowd, flinging people out of the way, until they surrounded the thief, the men chasing him, and several innocent bystanders, Rory among them.

The guards, locking arms and forming a tight circle, cordoned off about twenty people, pushing aside any women, but closing in on any men unlucky enough to be in their way. This circle of men and guards moved as one mass down the street in the direction of the watchhouse.

"I'm innocent!" cried several caught in the melee.

"Ye can tell the judge in the morning. Move along!"

Rory latched onto the arm of one of the guards. "I have to find that woman! Please, let me go to her. I have naught to do with any trouble."

"Tell it to the judge!" The watchman, swinging his club, hit Rory hard in the face. Rory staggered, stunned, and choked on the blood gushing out of his nose. The guard dragged him by his collar along the street and into the watchhouse.

She caught sight of him as the watchmen dragged him up the stairs. She called Rory's name over and over as she forced her way in that direction.

"I have to stop them!" she said to the guard at the watchhouse door who held out his arms to block her entry. "One of those men is innocent!"

"This is no place for a lass," said the guard. "Go home to yer family!"

She pleaded, "A man, my husband, is in there, caught up with the others, but he did nothing wrong! I can find him and take him away. Please, let me in!"

"Go home!" shouted the guard, gripping his hand around Joneta's neck and pushing her down the steps. She fell on her backside at the edge of the street.

"Oof!"

"Joneta?" She heard a voice. "Is that ye?"

Another man stepped out of the doorway of the watchhouse. Her brother, John. Yet another man she hadn't expected to see today.

"I found ye!" said John, bolting down the stairs and lifting her to her feet. "I've come to the watchhouse every day, and here ye are today!"

"Let go of me! I have to get in there," she said as she thrashed against his grip. "He's in there. I saw him. Let me go!"

"Nay, Joneta! Ye canna!"

She stopped fighting, breathless and unsteady, while John held her up out of the mud.

"She says she kens someone inside," said John to the guard.

"Tell it to the judge in the morning. No one allowed

in except prisoners until dawn tomorrow! Now be off with ye afore I arrest ye both!"

****

Rory's head pounded. The bleeding finally stopped, but his nose and cheek still throbbed. His tongue jiggled a loosened tooth.

Every memory he'd ever had of her came flooding back. He smelled the griddle scones from her booth at the fair. He felt the touch of her fingers on his when she slid the scone over to him, and he tasted its warmth and the sweetness in his mouth. He saw her eyes, and the way her hair fell out of its braids and brushed her cheeks. If he touched his lips, he could almost feel her lips on his. Nothing sweeter.

Every day since they'd been separated, he'd opened his eyes in the morning and, for a split second, could see her face next to him. Then she vanished, and he was alone. The heartache threatened to break him. Even though she thought him dead and she was wed to another, he never stopped loving her. They would never be apart in his soul.

And here she was in Glasgow, just feet away. And he couldn't get to her!

He let out a wretched cry, and the prisoner next to him gave him a shove. "Haud yer wheesht. We're all in here together, and no need to listen to ye carry on! Shut yer gob!"

Rory rolled against the wall and tucked his aching head into his shoulder.

In the morning, Robert Brown, the hard-working horse trainer from Dak Tulane's Livery, would be freed. There couldn't possibly be any charge against him, but by the time he was released, she'd be gone, lost in the city, looking for Rory Campbell, a man who didn't exist.

Chapter Thirty-Four

Inside the watchhouse the morning after Rory's arrest

John shouldered his way through the crowd of bystanders in the upstairs gallery of the watchhouse with Joneta holding tight to his belt. "Move!" said John in a voice that promised retribution if he wasn't obeyed. "Out of my way!" And the people stepped aside. Once he was at the rail of the balcony, looking down, he tugged Joneta to his side and put a protective arm around her. "Do ye see him?"

Below, jammed shoulder to shoulder on the watchhouse floor, stood all the men and women rounded up by the watchmen last night. In the corner, several jailers corralled the men who had already served their sentences, mostly ten days for public drunkenness, as they waited for release by the judge as a group.

The noxious odors of dirty, sweaty men wafted up from below and nearly choked Joneta, who covered her mouth with her apron.

"Do ye see him?" asked John again. "Ye're just imagining ye saw him. Rory Campbell is dead and burned, so if ye've brought me here on a wild goose chase, I'll be…"

"Ye'll be what?" snapped Joneta. "If ye want me to go back to Glencoe and marry Zeb without complaint, then ye'll stand there and let me look. This is my last request, and ye will honor it!"

John sighed. "All right. I did promise ye this last request, and ye better be certain 'tis yer last request. Do ye see this man ye think ye saw?"

Joneta scanned the horde of men milling around, pushing and shoving each other. Some tottered on their feet until they found a place to collapse in a hungover stupor. The watchmen barely kept the crowd contained until a man near the front shouted, "Hear ye! Hear ye! The judge will hear ye now!" When the noise continued, he added in a roar, "Quiet or 'tis all back in the cells for ye!" The prisoners nudged each other until gradually everyone quieted down to a low murmur.

A man entered, dressed in a gray wig and black robes cinched at the waist, and stood behind the desk near the wall. "Start calling the prisoners."

The watchmen dragged the men and the occasional woman forward one at a time and announced their crime. For the men it was usually public drunkenness, for the women soliciting a man for sex in a public place or a brothel. The sex itself wasn't illegal, just the soliciting, an odd distinction in the law that allowed the man to go free while it trapped the woman.

Many on the floor were repeat offenders and the judge greeted them by name, asking how they were getting along and were they taking care of their families. A few were charged with theft, and the rest denied having done any crime at all. Most received a small fine, which very few could pay so it was back to the cell for them, and the rest were released and admonished never to return.

Eventually, a dark-haired man with a black eye

stood before the judge who asked without looking up, "Name?"

"Robert Brown."

Joneta's heart flipped over. It was him! Rory! She had not been mistaken. He didn't have his beard, but his coal black hair and round eyes were the same. It was him! She latched onto John's arm to steady herself.

"Can anyone vouch for this man?" asked the judge.

She couldn't speak. If she claimed to know him as Rory Campbell, a notorious, although thought-dead traitor, he could be arrested and jailed, or worse. She watched and prayed. That was the only thing she could do for him now.

John leaned in close to Joneta. "That is Rory Campbell! Ye kenned this. Ye kenned he was alive. This time I'll make certain he is hanged until he's truly dead." John raised his arm to signal the judge and started to call out when Joneta punched him hard in the stomach.

"Nay, ye canna," she whispered. "Nay."

John coughed and gripped his gut as a voice came from the balcony across the way. "I can vouch for him. 'Tis Robert Brown."

"How do ye ken him?" asked the judge.

"I am Dak Tulane, and he is my horse trainer. He works for me. I ken him well."

"What do ye ken of the cause against him?"

The watchman holding Rory by the arm spoke up. "He was caught up in the crowd we brought in with the bag snatcher over there." He pointed toward a lad crouching in the corner awaiting his fate.

"Do ye say he had naught to do with the theft?"

"Aye."

"Then Robert Brown, ye are released. Take him out

229

on the street to Dak Tulane, who will take charge of him. Next!" said the judge.

As Rory turned to go with the watchman, his eyes glanced up and he caught Joneta's gaze. The expression on his face said it all. All they had known and all they would ever know between them had not changed in their time apart. Every misunderstanding and every heartbreaking thought vanished.

She pushed her way out through the crowd still lingering on the stairs, shoving people into the wall with a strength she didn't know she had. Rory gave her that strength. She had found him! She raced down the steps to the front door with John close behind her, still coughing and holding his stomach.

Out on the street, she dashed into the arms of the only man she would ever love.

The feel of his arms around her, his breath moving in and out, and the beating of his heart overwhelmed her senses. Barely able to stand for the relief she felt, she tugged him closer. The warmth of his body against hers eased the fear in her own chest, fear that she'd never hold him like this again, fear that she would never find him.

He's alive! He's here with me!

He snuggled his face to her neck and kissed her, over and over. "I ne'er thought I'd see ye again," he murmured.

"Ye're alive!" she said. "Clyde and Lorna said ye were, but I couldna truly believe it until now. I searched for ye. I ne'er stopped looking at every face on the street. Hold me tighter. I saw ye across the street yesterday. Ye called my name. Oh, Rory, ye're alive! I'll ne'er let ye go." Reaching up on her toes, she kissed him on the lips. It was the sweetest kiss she'd ever had, the sweetest one he'd ever given her.

John's voice dragged her out of her reverie. "Watchman! Watchman! This man is Rory Campbell, the traitor from the massacre at Glencoe!"

Every eye turned toward her brother. "'Tis Rory Campbell! The king ordered his death and he was thought to be hanged, but here he is alive."

Many had heard the name of Rory Campbell from royal proclamations, but Glencoe was far away in the barren Highlands, so his crime was no concern of theirs. No one made a move in Rory's direction until John added, "There is a reward for his capture, a king's ransom!"

All the men lingering on the street dashed forward at the same time. Rory shoved the man beside him into another released prisoner, and they fell on top of each other. Both men jumped up with furious looks, and Rory pointed to John and shrugged. The men charged at John, fists swinging. Rory repeated this trick with two other men until the melee involved nearly everyone outside the watchhouse, with John taking the worst of it. Watchmen struggled to regain control, but it was impossible in the confusion.

Rory grabbed Joneta's hand. "This way!" he shouted and ran across the street and into an alley. She lifted her skirt and ran with him.

Through alleys, backyards, and garbage-filled passageways, they eventually came to the back of Dak Tulane's livery. He led her behind the stable into the nearly completed house next door. After closing the back door behind them, he shrugged off his filthy boots and led her up the stairs to the second floor.

"Here," he said, "this will be for our bairns."

She gawked at him, still out of breath. "How are ye alive? Clyde and Lorna saw ye, but how?"

"I'm building this house for us. I've put my winnings from the horse race purses into this place and into what I send to Callum's bairns."

"So 'twas ye? Why?"

"'Tis a long story about sacrifice and escape for me to tell ye later when I'm done holding ye, making certain ye're really here, and after I've shown ye our house. Dak will live in the original rooms in the front, and the rest of the house is ours. What do ye think?"

She faced him and took his hands in hers. "We canna live here. 'Tis no' safe in Glasgow for ye. John will see ye arrested. The king used yer death as atonement for the massacre, a feeble gesture at best, but he willna forget ye need to die so he can save face. Ye will always be a wanted man." She paused. "Dead or alive. Rory, we canna stay here."

His face fell. He wrapped his arms around her and rested his chin on the top of her head. "Living here with ye is all I've thought about for the past year. It got me out of bed every morn to work on yer house."

"My house," she answered slowly. "And 'tis a verra fine house. Just what I always wanted."

He stroked her hair. "'Tis ye I've always wanted. Remembering ye kept me alive through the worst of it, the hiding who I was, the struggling to find my place in a world I ne'er wanted to be, and somedays I couldna bear the torture of missing ye so much. When it got really bad, Dak would hand me the reins of a horse, and say, 'Do yer best, lad. This animal needs ye.' And I'd do my best to make it through the day."

She spoke in a muffled voice. "I wish the world were

a different place." She reached up and ran her finger down the faint but lingering scar on his cheek. "No Campbells, no MacDonalds. I wish we'd had more time for just us. I've relived our days together at Clyde and Lorna's, and our night when we wed. But the world came between us. Even so, naught ever got in the way of how I feel about ye or stopped how much I needed ye. I may have tried to forget, but 'twas impossible. Naught changed my remembering of yer shining eyes and yer smile that warmed me in my darkest hours."

"Do ye think we'll ever be together like that again?"

"In our hearts we are always together."

The tension of wanting each other completely began between them. It drew them close, arms locked around each other, his at her waist and hers around his neck. Their lips met and the memory and the sensations of their lovemaking on their wedding night surged.

He stepped back. "I see ye now differently than I did afore we wed."

"Have I changed that much?"

"Nay, ye havena changed a bit. 'Tis me. At first, I loved ye like a fire burning hot and fast, but now I love ye like the coals that warm every part of me. I canna love ye enough."

She ran her thumb over his chin and cheek, tracing every curve and mark, saving his scar for last. Her thumb slid down the scar and across his lips. Then into his mouth.

He sucked it in.

He knelt before her, keeping her thumb in his mouth, and she followed him to her knees. He slid his hand under her skirt and up her thigh, slowly and by design, while she leaned into him and whispered, "With ye I am who I was meant to be."

"I want to make ye mine," he growled from deep in his throat.

She leaned to one side and lay on the unfinished wooden floor, tugging him on top of her. "I am always yers."

"Ye ken this time will be only release for how long we've been apart," he said as he adjusted his breeches for her. "Later, I will love ye as ye deserve to be loved, slowly, completely."

"Enough talking." She put her arms around his neck, slipping her fingers into his hair and pressing him on top of her.

He slid inside her and they became one. The power and strength of their joining shuddered through both of them as they moved in unison. The waves of emotion and the physical sensations rocked them, first one, then the other, then together. He covered her mouth to stop her crying out. She scraped his hand with her teeth. He latched his mouth onto hers.

As the throbbing sped through their bodies, she arched, panting, "Rory Campbell, ye…" She couldn't finish her words as he gave his last thrust inside her and she quickly followed with a release of her own.

When they both breathed normally again, he rolled off her and saw a tear slide down her cheek. He wiped it off with his finger. "Did I hurt ye?"

"Nay, nay, ye loved me, and I've been waiting so long." She softly touched his bruised face. "Again ye've been hurt for my sake."

"'Tis naught, since I found ye."

Both rested limply together until they heard the door slam downstairs.

"Robert, are ye here?" called out Dak Tulane.

Rory quickly fastened his breeches and tugged his shirt down. He put his finger to his mouth for Joneta to stay silent.

"I'm alone," called out Dak.

"We're up here," said Rory.

Halfway up the stairs, Dak said, "Ye have to get out of Glasgow."

"What happened?" asked Rory as he helped Dak up the last two stairs, his cane thumping against each tread.

"Ye started quite a melee when ye set that mob in action. The watchmen swung their clubs all around, knocking many to the ground, all except the one who said he came from Glencoe to find ye. Called himself John."

"He is my brother," said Joneta. "He came looking for me to take me home."

"Somehow he stayed on his feet, shouting the whole time about the traitor, Rory Campbell, how there was a reward for his capture, how King William would favor the man who finally brought Campbell to justice. He started in how we kenned him as Robert Brown. That's when a few of them started for me."

"Are ye all right? They didna hurt ye, did they?"

"Nay, lad. I'm fine. Swung my cane and set them back until they started after each other again, more interested in the reward than an old man. The watchmen dragged most of them inside, including the man, John. That makes both of ye fugitives now. Ye canna stay here, but I have a plan."

"Do ye want to hear the truth of the story of how I came to be Robert Brown?" asked Rory.

"Ye can tell me on the way. Now listen carefully."

Chapter Thirty-Five

The next morning, the Justice of the Peace reluctantly released John MacDonald from custody. "Ye began this brawl, and I should hold ye for ten days." When John started to protest, the judge lifted his hand. "The cells are too crowded, and it would be a waste of my time to search for a supposed dead man, so ye are released. I dinna want to ever see yer Highland face in here again, or I'll leave ye to rot." He pounded his hand on the desk. "Next!"

"Afore I go," said John, "may I have a set of shackles to take with me?"

The judge's face turned red. "I dismissed ye. Now get out!"

"I want to arrest an escaped traitor wanted by the crown. I saw Rory Campbell in this room yesterday."

The judge leaned over his desk and bellowed, "First, ye canna arrest anyone! Second, if the king wants Rory Campbell, let him find him. Get out of my courtroom afore I arrest ye and put ye in chains!"

One of the jailers tapped John on the shoulder and spoke quietly. "Leave now afore he does what he says. I'll give ye some shackles. We got enough for an army. We could chain up the whole district if we had enough men to do it."

John nodded and followed the man to a room down the hall cluttered with chains, shackles, clubs, and a broken pistol or two. "Take yer pick. I canna guarantee its worth, but ye can have one."

"Why are ye doing this for me?" asked John as he pushed aside one pile of shackles to choose a pair that looked sturdy and still had the key in one of the locks.

"We need all the men we can to keep the lowlifes in line," said the guard. "And ye're big enough to do the job yerself. Now get out of Glasgow and dinna come back."

John strode out of the watchhouse and down the road to get his horse from the shed behind the inn. He also wanted to question Dak Tulane about why he vouched for Robert Brown, or Rory Campbell, or whatever name he went by. Tulane would surely know where the man was.

Chapter Thirty-Six

On the road south

An old man and a young lad rode on the seat of the horse wagon as two mares pulled the cart carrying a stallion in the back. Horse wagons like this one were becoming a common sight as more wealthy breeders transported their horses to the racecourses in England instead of riding them there. The horses arrived much more rested and ready to run and thus produced more winners. This wagon, however, was not headed to any racecourse.

Joneta wiggled her bottom against the seat, trying to ease the itch from the woolen breeks she wore. The oversized linen shirt wasn't much softer, and the cap she'd tucked her hair into made her head sweat.

"Stop wiggling," said Dak, sitting beside her and holding the reins of the two horses in front. "Ye're making me nervous."

"Sorry, Dak."

"Robert has it worse in the back, buried under the hay and riding with the horse so no one can see him. At least ye get a breeze out here."

"I ken. I'm sorry to complain." She twisted back and spoke through the slats of the wagon. "Rory, are ye all right?"

Rory's face appeared in the opening. "I'll be more

238

than glad to be out of this hay. This horse in here keeps trying to step on me. He doesna like me underfoot. We've been on the road for three days. How much longer until we get to yer relatives in Wales?"

"Mayhap two or three more days for ye," said Dak. "Ye can go faster on horseback without this wagon, so I'm leaving ye at the border. Joneta, have ye still got the letter I wrote?"

"Aye. 'Tis addressed to yer cousin, Ambodd, in the town of Tregaron, Wales, and it introduces us as friends of yers who need shelter and protection. Ye said he's an outlaw. We've already been stopped twice by men from Glasgow trying to find Rory for the reward. Will yer uncle want to turn him in for the reward, too? Are we going from one danger into another?"

"Tregaron is the only place ye may be safe."

"So ye believe Rory's story about the massacre?"

"I believe Robert Brown. He's talked of ye every day since he got to Glasgow. I would have recognized ye easily from what he said, and a man who loves like that couldna kill innocents. He didna tell me the whole story, and I dinna want to ken. The less I ken, the less I can tell anybody who asks."

Joneta patted his arm. "Thank ye."

They rode in silence for a time until Dak slapped the reins on the horses' rumps, saying, "Ambodd's grandfather was my father's brother, making us cousins, second or third, something like that. I've gone back to Wales for family gatherings every year since I was born. They're good people, and we have a grand time, good food, lots of laughter, and I get to practice speaking Welsh again. 'Tis a hard language to learn, let me tell ye."

"What about him being an outlaw?"

"Ambodd is one of the Plant Mat gang, just about all our family claim some relation to them, but how dangerous they are is almost entirely made up."

"Made up?"

"Aye, some folk tales get started and those tales take on a life of their own. The storytelling is more exciting than the truth. Ambodd and the extended family around Tregaron do live on the wrong side of the law sometimes, but they are no' as dangerous as the tales told about them. The sheriff would like to make his bones by hanging some of them, but they've outsmarted him every time. Still, their reputation will protect ye and Rory from anyone coming around to look for ye."

"What if yer cousin believes Rory is a traitor and a killer?"

"Dinna fash, lass—I mean 'lad.' The letter explains it all. Ye and he got caught up in something beyond yer control, and I want to give ye a chance to live a life together. Ambodd will do the same. He understands about being falsely accused. Ye'll have to become different people in Wales, but Ambodd will help ye with that, too."

"My brother vowed to hunt Rory down even afore the soldiers at Fort William hanged him, and now that he kens Rory is alive, John willna stop until he finishes the job. The massacre at Glencoe was a horrible betrayal, and I lost me mum and da to the killing along with so many other kin and friends. The pain lingers, but Rory didna cause it."

"I believe ye, I truly do. Now hush up. Some riders are coming up on us from behind."

Three men on horseback slowed down to a trot

behind the horse wagon. Joneta held her breath, praying it was no one from Glasgow looking for them. She didn't relax even after one shouted out, "*Allwch chi dynnu draw i ochr y ffordd?*"

"He speaks Welsh," Joneta whispered.

Dak said, "Aye, he wants us to pull to the side of the road so they can pass."

Dak leaned out over the side of the wagon and looked back at the riders. "*Dyw fy Nghymraeg i ddim yn Saesneg da, os gwelwch yn dda.*" To Joneta he said, "I told them my Welsh isna good and could they speak English."

One of the riders shouted back, "English? Ye're heading to Wales. Ye better learn to speak the language!"

"I will," said Dak as he reined the horses and the wagon close to the side of the road. "I canna go much farther or I'll be in the ditch. Ye'll have to squeeze by. Dinna let yer horses stir up mine in the wagon."

The riders trotted past in single file and waved their thanks. "Ye'll be in Wales in just a few more miles," one of them shouted back. "*Rydym yn eich croesawu!*"

"They welcome us," translated Dak. "Wave back. Mayhap ye'll see a familiar face later and it might turn out to be a good thing for ye."

Joneta waved.

"No' much farther," said Dak. "There's been no sign of anyone following us for a day now. I think ye dinna need to worry that anyone will find ye this far south. Ye'll be safe."

"'Twill be a relief to get across into Wales," said Rory through the slats. "We canna thank ye enough for everything ye've done for us. Mayhap someday this will all be forgotten, and we can come back to Scotland to thank ye proper."

"Until then," said Dak, "I'll keep sending the money from yer last two horse race purses to the man in Glencoe. The bairns should be grown by the time I run out of money, and I've got yer letter introducing me to the man at the message service."

"I thank ye for that."

"Robert, if ye dinna mind, I might send a note or two without giving ye away. I'll write it myself. It would make sending the money more personal, more like from one person to another, no' like a business transaction. If ye think I should."

Rory hesitated. "I'm keeping a promise to a man who gave up his life for me. 'Tis a debt I can ne'er repay, and the truth can ne'er be told, but I hope someday, somehow, they can forgive me."

Dak went on. "I've grown quite fond of ye, more than just yer knack with the horses and how ye've built up the name of Tulane Livery for all to see. Ye're a fine man, and I'll miss ye badly. I'll do my best to keep up our reputation, and mayhap find another young lad with yer talent to help me. I'm trusting this fine lass to yer care, and I'll finish building yer house. Someday mayhap the two of ye can live in it."

Rory reached his arm out and patted Dak Tulane on the back. "I may ne'er see ye again, but ye gave me a new life, and I'll be forever grateful. Ye gave me hope and a future, and ye're doing it again by bringing us here. Rabbie and Jane Gwadd thank ye for our new names and our introduction to yer kin."

"Look ahead," said Joneta. "I see a sign. I canna read the words so we must be in Wales."

"Aye, lass, ye are," said Dak.

Chapter Thirty-Seven

Two days' ride later, deep into Wales, Joneta dragged her leather saddle off her horse and let it fall beside Rory's on the ground near their makeshift campsite. Rory staked the horses in a patch beside a small stream and made his way back to her. Both of them stretched out their tired backs and legs, but even more they looked forward to spending another night beside each other, in each other's arms.

"The ground is cold and lumpy," she said, "but I'd rather be here with ye than anywhere else in the world. If ye'll start the fire, I'll heat the last of the meat. How much farther do ye think it is to Tregaron?"

"From Dak's map, mayhap only a half day's ride, down that hill, then follow the road the rest of the way. If we leave early tomorrow, we'll get there in the daylight and have time to find Dak's cousin. But afore ye cook, I have something else I want to do first." He tugged her close.

"Are ye too sore from riding?"

She grinned. "If I was to be sore, it'd no' be from riding, but from what we've done every time we stop. Ye claim 'tis to get a rest, but the horses are the only ones resting." She leaned into him and rubbed her hand between his legs. "Are ye sore?" she purred.

He responded by lifting her up. "I canna get enough of ye," he said before sitting her against one of the saddles and tugging down her breeks. For safety reasons, she continued to masquerade as a lad. "Ye are no' wearing yer rope belt," he said.

"Takes too much time."

Neither of them said another word until their fingers and their mouths had stroked every part of the other. Tender lips and hands eased any aches and knots from riding, and the final joining made them one. Each trembled until the physical sensations passed, and they rested in each other's arms, satisfied, warm, and safe. A hoot owl reminded them that the cooler air of night was coming.

"I'll get twigs and branches for the fire as soon as I get dressed," Rory said, slipping his shirt over his head and pulling his breeks up. "Have I told ye that I love ye yet today?"

"Ye can ne'er say it enough."

"Then so be it. I love ye."

He finished dressing and tugged on his boots.

Rory heard the click of the pistol behind him as it cocked.

"Dinna make a move," said the man.

Joneta jumped to her feet. "John, dinna do it," she cried. "Dinna kill him!"

"I'm taking him back to Glasgow so he can be hanged properly this time," John said. "I want him alive until then so I can see his feet swing. I want to hear his last gurgling breath. Dinna move, ye sorry bassa Campbell." He tossed heavy iron shackles on the ground beside Rory. "Joneta, put these on his ankles."

"Nay!" she said. "Ye canna do this. I willna let ye."

"Do as I say or I'll shoot him right here, right now, and save the soldiers the trouble. I can carry him back dead a lot easier."

She snarled at her brother, "If ye murder him, I'll see ye dead any way I can, if 'tis the last thing in this life I do!"

"I'm taking him back, Joneta. I'll make certain he dies in a public hanging this time. Believe me, I will."

John moved to Rory's side, keeping the gun pointed at his head, and hissed, "Step aside, sister." He lowered his pistol toward Rory's foot. "Or I can shoot him in the leg. I promise he willna run away then."

"Nay, John!" shouted Joneta as she charged at him. John raised his gun in her direction as Rory grabbed her by the wrist and held her behind him, saying, "I'll do it meself." He sat down on the saddle and closed the iron circle around each ankle with his free hand.

John squatted down in front of him and locked each restraint before slipping the key into his vest pocket.

"I'll hate ye forever, John," said Joneta, pulling herself out of Rory's grip.

"He's a traitor, a criminal," said John. "How did ye escape the scaffold, ye Campbell traitor?"

Rory didn't speak.

"When I got released and went back to Dak Tulane's livery, ye were already gone, but a neighbor told me ye'd headed this way in a horse wagon, and I tracked ye here. It matters no' how ye got away, but ye'll go back for yer just punishment." He raised his voice and added, "And ye, Joneta, will go back to Glencoe with me, and ye will marry Zeb. If I have to chain ye, too, I'll do it, but ye are going back with me. Do ye understand?"

"Do ye understand that Rory is my husband, and ye willna keep us apart?"

"He deserted ye—a marriage easily annulled. And

once he is dead, it will be a marriage easily forgotten."

"'Twill ne'er be forgotten! He didna desert me. The army jailed him until he was forced to come to Glencoe with the soldiers. Then, after he tried to help us, he was unjustly hanged to make up for other people's mistakes, and I thought him dead. I didna ken he was alive until Clyde and Lorna saw him. He risked his life to make certain I was aright. He thought I had married Zeb, and he was determined to live without me, but neither of us could forget. I've been looking for him ever since. I promise ye this, if Rory hangs, I'll hang meself and join him in death."

"Nay!" cried Rory and John in unison.

John lowered his pistol and tucked it into his belt. "Dinna be a fool, Joneta. Ye're making me choose between my sister and the man who betrayed our clan, a man who caused the death of our parents."

Rory said, "I didna betray ye. I tried to warn ye, to warn everyone. I went from house to house, but I got to yers too late. I didna kill any MacDonalds."

"He brought the supplies we found outside the cave," said Joneta. "The soldiers could have killed him on the spot if anyone had seen him, but he risked it for us. He tried to help, but then the soldiers caught up with him and locked him up again."

John didn't speak for a long moment. "I dinna believe any of this, but I'm listening. Tell me something I can believe."

As she cooked, Rory and Joneta told John everything that had happened since they met at the Highland Fair, how they met in secret at Clyde and Lorna's and then were wed by a traveling priest.

John interrupted, "Father MacHenry made it to

Glencoe, but he was also killed by the troops. Can ye live with that on yer heads?"

"'Tis no' on our heads but on the king's."

They told him how Rory escaped to Glasgow and how Joneta searched for him, taking the job as a cook. "Joneta, ye're burning the rabbit meat," said John. "Turn it afore it catches fire."

A few minutes later he asked, "Who stood in for ye at the hanging?"

"I honor the man who took my place, but I willna tell ye his name," said Rory. "He died a hero, and I want it to stay that way."

"I suspect 'tis ye who sends the money for Callum Gillis's bairns."

Rory didn't answer.

John said, "'Tis of no matter. What is done is done and there's no changing it. As the tale is told in Glencoe, Callum wandered off to the hills alone to die as a hero, trying to save his bairns the horror of watching him die as a shell of a man. 'Tis easier on them to let them keep believing that."

Joneta speared another chunk of meat from the spit on the fire. "I love Rory and he loves me. That is the one thing I have been certain of ever since I met him. Ye may drag him back, but no one can take him from me."

John patted the gun in his belt. "This pistol and those chains say I can."

"I'm begging ye no' to do this."

The rest of the meal, such as it was, passed in silence.

Joneta, after wiping out the tin plates and bedding down the horses, pulled two blankets out of her pack, spread one on the ground next to Rory who scooted over onto it while she laid the other one on top of him. She crawled under the blanket and snuggled under his arm.

"'Tis no good there," said John. "Move over next to that tree."

"Why?" demanded Joneta.

"He's going to chain my legs on either side of it," said Rory. "It'll keep me from running off."

After Rory was seated, John checked the shackles to make certain they were locked and held his prisoner's feet securely on either side of the tree.

"Ye are cruel," said Joneta as she moved the blankets and settled them around Rory. "I'll hate ye forever."

"I am no' the one ye should hate. I saw the truth of him at the fair, but his smile and glib tongue betrayed ye. Ye'll get over it."

"Ne'er," said Joneta.

"The key will be in my pocket, little lass, so dinna let him give ye ideas about getting away. I can always chain ye to him, his leg to yer leg, so dinna give me cause. I'll sleep over by that big tree with my hand on my pistol, and we'll leave at first light."

"I hate ye," said Joneta. "If Da were alive, he'd be ashamed of ye."

"Da isna alive," said John. "I love ye, sister, and I am no' the hard master ye think me to be. No more talking."

Joneta burrowed under Rory's arm, hoping to find comfort, but she didn't close her eyes. Instead, she watched the smattering of stars above her head, her mind empty except for the thought she could lose Rory again.

"John loves me," she whispered. "I canna believe he is so cruel."

"He thinks he kens what is best for ye."

"He is wrong."

Neither of them slept, but suddenly Joneta tossed back the blanket.

"Where are ye going?" whispered Rory.

She didn't answer, but tiptoed slowly over to John. She stopped moving with each of his snores and held her own breath until his breathing became slow and steady again. Squatting beside him, she eased her fingers toward his vest pocket. He stirred and rolled over on his side.

She crept around his outstretched legs until she could reach the pocket again. When John relaxed, she slipped her fingers into the opening. He snorted. Again she didn't move. Her legs cramped. Taking a deep breath, she touched the key and started to ease it out.

John's hand clamped over hers, but he did not open his eyes. Soon his hand dropped to his side, and he eased into sleep again. She took the key.

After making her way back to Rory, she pushed the key into one of the leg irons. It opened with a loud click. Both of them held their breath. John didn't move. She unlocked the second shackle, but as it opened, it fell. Rory caught it with his hand just before it clattered to the ground. He eased it off his ankle.

Hand in hand, they ran toward the horses, tethered at a nearby tree. He turned back and mouthed to her, "Ye bring the saddle bags." Picking up the empty shackles, he carried them over to John, locking one of them around John's ankle until John stirred and rolled over again. Not willing to take the risk with the other shackle, Rory tossed the key into the grass and dashed back to Joneta and the horses.

He lifted Joneta bareback on the horse and, using

only clicks with his tongue, guided it away from the campsite and down the hill. Once out of sight, he leaped on the horse behind Joneta, and they rode toward the road and freedom.

Neither of them looked back to see John standing against the tree with one shackle around his ankle, watching. They didn't hear him whisper, "Lead a good life, sister. If Campbell treats ye wrong, come back to the family that loves ye like I do."

****

Ambodd barely glanced at his cousin's letter of introduction and greeted the newcomers with open arms. Until Joneta and Rory, now Jane and Rabbie Gwadd, learned to speak Welsh, communication was with hand signals, gestures, and facial expressions, but they felt safe together for the first time in a long time.

Chapter Thirty-Eight

Six years later—1699

Laird John MacDonald gestured to Zebulon Keene to sit at the table and enjoy the stew and biscuits laid out before each of them.

"How are the bairns doing?" asked John once they were seated.

"Jacob willna be home from university in Glasgow for a month or so, but his letters say he is pleased with his classes. Now that his fees are paid, he can devote his time to his studies instead of working."

"What about the other three?" John slathered his biscuit with butter.

"Ruth is talking often about a young man, Angus MacDonald. Seems to be a fine lad, but I willna let her wed until she's sixteen. As for Moses and Abraham, they are growing up straight and tall, and the operation on Moses' feet after they were frostbit has done verra well for him."

"Speaking of the money we use for the bairns, another pouch came yesterday. This time there was a note in it, printed in a hand I dinna recognize. 'Tis no signed."

Zeb's spoon clattered to the table. "A note? What did it say? Who was it from?"

"Here 'tis," said John, sliding a single piece of paper

over to Zeb.

Only two words were written on the note. "Forgive me."

Zeb pushed his chair back and paced the room.

"He sends the money and now he wants me to forgive him? Ne'er! I'll hate him for the rest of my life. I do all I can to keep Callum's memory alive, and I'd do it with or without the money. I ne'er wanted his money. I didna do it for him, only for her. I did it for Joneta. She deserves better than a Campbell, but 'tis him she chose, so I accepted her wishes and now the guilt money he sends."

"I always suspected that Callum was the man hanged in his place."

"His bairns can ne'er ken. They think him a hero and can ne'er find out he died in the place of a traitor at the end of a noose. Please, John!"

"They will ne'er hear it from me. How did ye manage it?"

Zeb sat back down at the table. "Callum chose to do it of his own free will. The plan was his, no' mine. I only promised to see the deed done and for none to be the wiser. I had found Joneta's brooch in the snow outside the cave, and I gave it to Callum as proof. Later, when I cut open the burial sack for one last look at my best friend, I saw Joneta's whistle around his neck. I took it, but I didna hide it verra well, and she found it, which is why she didna marry me. Still, no one kenned it was Callum we burned.

"The grave in the hills is empty, but it is a place his bairns can go and be proud of him when he saved them from the slaughter. That Campbell is alive in his place will haunt me all my days."

"So the money is Rory's way of repaying Callum's sacrifice. He must struggle with that, the guilt that another died for him. Why did ye agree to help Callum do it?"

Tears formed in Zeb's eyes. "Every time a pouch comes, I have to remember I did it for her. I take his money, but I do it for her. I loved her long afore she ever heard of Rory Campbell, and for the rest of my life, I will do whate'er she asks." He wiped his palms over his moist eyes. "She wanted Campbell, so I gave him to her. She begged me to save him, and I couldna refuse her."

John folded his hands on the table. "Do ye think the note might be from Joneta? She kens she hurt ye."

"I can forgive her anything. I always will." He picked up the note and tossed it into the fire before walking to the door. "We can ne'er speak of this again. The Gillis bairns must always ken their da died a hero, no' at the end of a king's noose." He swallowed hard. "And we canna speak of it because I canna bear thinking of how she isna mine. I can forgive, but I can ne'er forget."

He walked out and softly closed the door behind him.

Chapter Thirty-Nine

Forty years later—1732—Glencoe, Scotland

Her oldest son, Dair, helped Joneta ease her stiff legs
out of the wagon until she stood resting on her cane in
front of the stone house she'd left so many years ago.
'Twould always be Clyde and Lorna's house, but now
she would live in it.

"We're here, Rory," she said, patting the plain
wooden coffin in the back of the wagon. "It looks the
same, only worn a bit. The roof needs repair, but
Struan—ye remember our youngest—and our daughter-
in-law, Isla, will take care of it. I'm going to live here
with them. Ye remember that, dinna ye?"

"Who are ye talking to, Mam?" said Struan, calling
her by the Welsh name for mother when he stepped out
the front door and held it open for her. Struan was their
youngest child and a dark-haired near-twin to his father.
She and Rory had struggled to learn Welsh, but her seven
children learned it from birth. Still, inside the house, she
always spoke English with a proper Scottish accent.
They all spoke both languages with ease, and that would
be a tremendous help now that they'd be living in
Glencoe.

"Yer tad—I mean, yer da. Ye ken how many times
I had to tell him things these past few years."

Five years ago he had begun forgetting things like

where to hang his coat, or how to put the reins around a horse's mouth, and several times he got lost in town and passersby had to bring him home. It had been nearly two years since he'd remembered the names of their seven children. He sometimes recognized them by face or voice, but he was never certain how he knew them. For the last month he hadn't even known her name. He could only repeat it after her, "Joneta."

She read to him from their letters, the ones saved in the yellow and blue boxes, and for a time it made him smile, but two weeks ago, he couldn't even dredge up his own true name, Rory Campbell. That broke her heart worst of all. Her husband had always been a strong, spirited, passionate man, and his illness had taken him from her long before it took him from this earth.

"Aye, Mam, but he ne'er forgot he loved ye, and I'm certain he remembers everything now. Heaven fixes all in its time. He kens ye brought him back to Clyde and Lorna's. He ne'er felt like he belonged in Wales, but here he'll be at peace. He loved this place, talked of it all the time."

Joneta said, "I've missed this valley. We lived in Wales longer than we lived here, but this is the place I will always think of as home."

After escaping Glasgow, she and Rory had lived in Tregaron, in the Credigon region of Wales across the River Brenig, changing their second name to Gwadd, chosen from the Welsh word meaning "guest." Tregaron was safe for them because of the reputation of a gang of thieves called Plant Mat that terrorized the region and discouraged strangers from searching for the outlaw formerly called Rory Campbell and now named Rabbie Gwadd.

Rory/Rabbie made a good living trading horses in the already established market in Tregaron for cattle, sheep, and geese being driven from Wales into England to sell. Although he couldn't risk leaving the region and being recognized at the big racecourses in England, he did introduce smaller horse races in this part of Wales.

"Mam," asked Struan, "do ye want to come in and see how Isla has cleaned everything up? 'Tis fit for more than the birds now. How was the trip, Dair?"

His oldest brother, Dair, a tall, auburn-haired man, tossed down two carpetbags full of clothes and treasures from their home in Wales. "All went well, no delays, but I can only stay for a day afore I have to start back. I canna leave the livery for too long. Our tad wouldna approve of leaving his horses in the care of Joseph. Our stable man takes direction well, but he hasna the knack with the beasts the way Tad did. He taught me well, and I'll run the livery the way he would want it."

The sight inside the house both heartened and saddened Joneta. The walls and the floor in Clyde and Lorna's main room looked the same as she remembered them, but the furniture had all been changed. An iron stove stood in front of the fireplace. The curtains were a bright green and the door to the bedroom had been sanded and re-stained to a shiny tan color. Numerous books had been added to the shelves, and on the back wall, the ladder to the loft was now a black iron one, far sturdier than the wooden ladder had ever been.

A few of Clyde's wooden carvings still hung on the walls. The one of a young Lorna hung beside one she hadn't seen before, a carving of a young, bearded man and a woman with braids across her head. Memories flooded her, and she had to look away. There would be time to study it later.

Joneta smiled. "This looks beautiful, Isla. Ye've done an excellent job of fixing it up."

"The bedroom will be yers until we can get the extra room for ye built on the back. Struan and I and the wee babe will sleep in the loft."

Joneta peeked into the bedroom. The only thing missing was the thistle-patterned quilt on the bed, the quilt the Cameron sisters had made so long ago. She had taken it with her when she went to search for Rory, and now it would keep Rory warm for eternity.

"Mam," said Struan, "I've been to the village in Glencoe, and yer nephew, Laird Alexander MacIain MacDonald, son of yer brother John, is in ill health, but along with his own son, John MacIain MacDonald, who will soon be the new laird, they agree ye are free to live in this house. They will visit when they can. We didna mention Tad's name or the massacre, only that ye are the daughter of their grandfather, Laird MacIain MacDonald, and ye left Glencoe long ago."

"The massacre will ne'er be forgotten, although I think most who lived through it are gone now," said Joneta. "But this is where yer father wanted to be laid to rest, back home, the place where we wed. I want to see where yer father's grave will be, and where I'll lay beside him some day. Ye do promise me that?"

"Aye, Mum. We promise."

The small cemetery nestled up against the ridges held only two headstones, one with "Clyde MacDonald - age 91" carved on it, and another one reading "Lorna Cameron MacDonald - age 88." Between the graves sat a small stone carving of two hands clasped together, one large and one smaller, linking the two loves buried there.

"This is just as Clyde and Lorna wanted it. Ne'er apart, together eternally," said Joneta. "We will place Rory beside Clyde, and I will rest next to him when the time comes." She lifted the silver whistle on the chain around her neck. "I want a whistle carved on yer tad's stone and his true name. No more Rabbie Gwadd, but Rory Campbell. And I want the Luckenbach brooch carved on mine with the name Joneta MacDonald Campbell, no more Jane Gwadd." Lifting the edge of her jacket, she revealed the brooch pinned to her dress. "The actual whistle will be placed in the coffin with yer father on the day we bury him here, and the brooch is to go with me."

"We promise, Mam. We willna forget. Ye've told us often enough."

"Should we go inside?" asked Isla. "I have a stew on the stove. Ye must be hungry from yer trip."

Joneta leaned on Struan's arm and made her way over the rocky ground back to the house. "Yer father and I loved each other from the first moment at the Highland Fair, and even when we were separated, that love ne'er changed. Make certain that yers and Isla's love is like that. Naught can change it."

"We will, Mum. We promise."

That evening, Struan and Dair raised a tattered yellow flag on the pole for all in Glencoe to see that love lived in this house again.

Historical Information

The causes of the Massacre of Glencoe in Scotland on February 13, 1692, were rooted in politics—the rise of the Jacobite cause—and religion—Catholic versus Protestant—but a sizable portion of the blame was a bid by John Dalrymple, Master of the Stair and Secretary of State for Scotland, to ingratiate himself with the new King William and his wife, Queen Mary. Dalrymple, an ambitious man who served under the deposed Catholic King James II, needed to raise his status with the new Protestant King William, and he chose the backs of the Highland clans to do it. Several other clans also did not sign the loyalty oath, and exactly why Dalrymple singled out the MacDonalds for the murderous punishment is unknown.

About three years later, a public outcry grew up over "murder under trust." This ancient Highland code required anyone to provide food and shelter to another when asked. It obliged the host and the guest to defend each other against all comers, regardless of the circumstances, and it served as a means of survival in the rugged Highlands.

The people who protested the massacre did not speak up so much about the slaughter of innocents but about a blatant violation of the Highland hospitality custom. Such a show of "bad manners" by the soldiers after staying for two weeks in Glencoe would not be condoned. King William, needing to unite the Scots under his rule, offered a meager apology, claiming

Dalrymple "misunderstood" his instructions. However, the consequences he proposed for the persons responsible for the massacre were minor at best.

Dalrymple, although dismissed from his position as Secretary of State, was soon back in government, playing a key role in the unification of Scotland and England. The earl of Breadalbane, who met with the Highland lairds, was charged with high treason for sending a secret letter to King James in France. He spent some time in prison, but no trial was ever held and he continued to serve a minor role in government. Captain Robert Campbell of Glenlyon from Fort William was ordered to stand trial, but he never did, and he later died of alcoholism. The leaders of the two other regiments also ordered to Glencoe to aid in the destruction were late in arriving, many believe intentionally, and were simply reprimanded for failure to follow orders. The Clan Campbell withstood the worst of the public censure for the attack, even though there may have been only a dozen or so Campbells in the one hundred twenty-eight murdering troops.

A survey taken between 1747 and 1755 showed the clan MacDonald had rebuilt their houses and their lives, indicated by seven separate clusters of houses along the glen, each with six to eleven buildings. However, the glen is uninhabited today.

For my purposes, I softened the character and reputation of the Plant Mat gang (Children of the Mat) in Wales because I needed a place where a wanted outlaw like Rory could be assured safety and protection from arrest. In truth, these outlaws were a vicious, much-feared gang. People were so terrorized, they often put scythes, point end up, in their chimneys to prevent the bandits from getting into their houses.

A fun fact: The third Harry Potter film, *Harry Potter and the Prisoner of Azkaban*, was filmed on location in Glencoe, using the rugged mountains as a backdrop.

A word about the author...

Susan Leigh Furlong knew she had a special connection with words since she was a child. When she was nine years old, she wrote and directed her first play for the neighborhood children.

Susan's love for history fuels her resilience against the sneezes and coughs that old books give her as she delves into research for unique historical events to inspire her historical fiction romance novels. Susan captures her readers' imagination with a highly enthralling style, chronological events, and smoothly flowing narratives that keep one's eyes glued on her novels from the first page to the last.

Susan has written two non-fiction books and three novels set in sixteenth century Scotland, and her most recent book is set during the American Revolution. When Susan is not researching and creating her stories, she writes, directs, and performs with a music and drama group.

Thank you for purchasing
this publication of The Wild Rose Press, Inc.

For questions or more information
contact us at
info@thewildrosepress.com.

The Wild Rose Press, Inc.